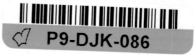

Distant Judgments

By

Bruce Netland

5/3/04
Thanks for your interest
in this book.
Bruce Netland

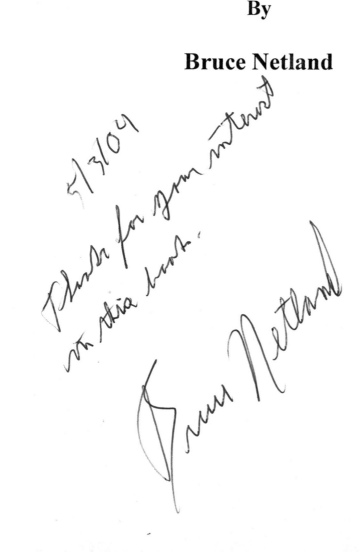

ISBN: 1-4033-3039-5 (e-book)
ISBN: 1-4033-3040-9 (Paperback)

Library of Congress Control Number: 2002106666

This book is printed on acid free paper.

Printed in the United States of America
Bloomington, IN

1stBooks - rev. 9/19/02

To Mom, Dan, Dwayne and Joanne, Peter, Kris, Corey and Abby, my loved ones and faithful fans. To Kat, my writers' group partner and hard-working editor.

Chapter One

Peter Hoffler stood wearily, stretched his angular frame and sighed, placed his long, bony hands on the back of the chair and once again looked at the silent group. This had gone on for an hour. Too damn long! He beat back a thunderous urge to just grab them by their shoulders and shake them like a dog with a rag doll and rattle their bones in his frustration, for God's sake! For eight years he'd provided all manner of legal services to the citizens of Nuevo Del Rio, charging nominal fees. He had a thing for widows; they seldom saw a bill. But all of that time and effort, all the untold hours he spent on their behalf, it all paled before what faced them on this cold January evening.

One more time, he sighed, summoning the fire he was known for displaying. He leaned forward, arching over the back of the chair as he glared at the one hundred-some residents, all staring back at him. "People," he shouted, "we are not talking about the problems your parents faced: when some employer stiffed them out of a few hours' wage, or a grower set the scales too light for the crop they picked. Those are little things. They happen, but life goes on." He grabbed a bundle of stapled papers and shook them, waving them in their faces. "But this!" he shouted, "this plan will destroy the homes you have built, the community you have here, and the jobs many of you have with Lloyd Dahlenberg!"

Dahlenberg was sole owner of the local cabinet shop, which employed ninety-seven workers, fifty-three of whom resided in this village. Ten years ago he began the business and opened a facility to train those whom he hired. So long as one had a good grasp of basic mathematics, and a willingness to study hard and learn, he would take them through the principles of fractions, ratios, percentages, basic algebra, and into the rules of geometry, all the skills needed to produce quality kitchen cabinets. He had one additional requirement, which he pointedly told all who applied. "This is year around work, not something you do when you aren't working the fields. If you accept this job, you leave the migrant stream forever. If you go back there, don't ever come here asking for another job. Make your decision now." He offered a competitive wage and benefit package and, despite all the dire predictions by those of great experience, he had negligible turnover.

"If this plan is approved," Peter went on, "the freeway will be widened by two more lanes in each direction, from here all the way to Minneapolis. You will be bulldozed to the ground!

"Many years ago your parents and grandparents drove here from Texas and Mexico to work the fields at rock-bottom wages, not even knowing if they'd find work at all. When they got here, where did they live?" A few nodded. "They lived in filthy coups that housed turkeys and maggots the rest of the year! When they arrived in the spring, as early as March, they had to sweep out the turkey shit and maggots so they could sleep on the floor. Then they opened the windows, if they could, to get rid of the smell of shit and maggots!

And they lived there, whether the temperature was zero or a hundred above!"

Peter glanced to Manuel Cardenas, the village mayor, a man grown wise by a lifetime toiling in the fields under suffocating heat or soul-chilling cold. To his left was Raul Montero, a young attorney Peter partnered with on many issues. A quiet man, skilled in legal research, he was the feet behind Peter's ringing voice. "Each year there was less work for them and they left the migrant stream, settled here, and began building what you now have. Years later many of you built better houses, two churches, this community center, other businesses, everything! This is your home!" he shouted, his fist crashing down onto the table, sending a pencil pirouetting to the floor.

He took a drink of water to cool his searing chords and noticed a slender young woman in the back row. He hadn't seen her before. What in this little village would interest a young white woman? He pointed to the east. "Many of those pushing hard for the freeway expansion live just one mile from here, in that new development called Bellwood Hills, where the average price of a house is eight hundred thousand dollars! That's just for an average house. Many of them cost much more. That same plan also calls for a turn-off into Bellwood that would cut right through this village, and there goes your clinic and your school. There will be nothing left for you!"

"Then we demonstrate!" shouted a young man who now stood and faced Peter and Cardenas. It was Rolando Torres, the one known as the loose cannon. "I say we all go to those fancy houses, stand in their yards and demand they back off this idea! We get nowhere sitting here and talking!"

"And what law have they broken by merely advocating for what they want?" Peter answered. "Isn't that what—"

"They want to tear down our homes and our community! Destroy all our industry! And you say they've done nothing wrong?" Torres rose and strutted slowly toward the front of the room, his lips curled, eyes ablaze with fury. "Are we to just sit back and let them have their way, like we've always done?" he shouted. "Chase us out of here because they are the rich ones and we're the poor ones? We should give up our homes and move because one day a few rich folks decide they want to drive over the ground where we live? I say we all go over to Bellwood and make them hear us, right on their front lawns!"

"You'd be stopped at their security gate," said Cardenas.

"Then drive right through it!" Torres shouted, glaring at him, his fist raised high. Now a few of the others who had sat quietly joined in the commotion. "There are five hundred people living in this village. How can they stop five hundred people?" That brought nods of agreement and again murmurs rumbled through the crowd, side to side, front to back, like a rogue wave. Most were now standing and turning to the others, talking briskly, as if ready to storm the stone gates of Bellwood.

Cardenas held up a hand, grunted and slowly rose to his feet, six decades of working in fields eroding his stiff joints. The crowd quieted for him. He glared at Torres. "Rolando Miguel," he said, using the Hispanic custom of addressing by first and middle names, "you listen to this man," he pointed to Peter. "He speaks the truth. Peter is a good man—"

"And you are a foolish old man!" Torres snarled.

Cardenas's voice was soft. "He cares about us. Many years he has taken care of our problems with the laws in this country. These are laws we don't understand."

"What you don't understand, old man, is action! We need action and we need it now! We can't just sit back and—"

"Many have traveled that route before," Peter interrupted. "We can't just do a frontal attack on the system, Mr. Torres. It's too well defended for that to work. I learned that a long—"

"They control the law because they control those who make the laws!" Torres shouted, sweeping his arm wide, then glared down hard at someone who cautiously rose to speak, then sat again. "Everything they want they get, because they have money to pay the right people. They have all the money and they have all the politicians in their pocket! So the poor have to be heard, and if that means interrupting their nice, quiet little world, then by the love of God we must do so! I say we act, and we act now!"

Peter shook his head. "No, Mr.Torres, it doesn't have to be that way. They are few in number over there and we are many in number here."

"Yes, many in number here but few in dollars! What else can we do? Bribe every county commissioner, every city council member and everyone on the Metropolitan Council?"

"We will find our voice," Peter answered "The voice of the people is powerful when it speaks as one. That, too, I learned the hard way, through long years of activism."

"No, not when they speak! Only when they act are they powerful! You and that old man, you think everything will go our way if we just sit back and be quiet, like we've always been. I say we must demonstrate! Far too long we have been a silent people! Now we must act with a loud and united voice or we will be knocked down again, like it's always been!" Murmurs rumbled through the crowd as more of them now stood, talking earnestly with others, heads nodding, some looking to Torres, others still watching Peter.

Again Cardenas rose slowly and held up his hands. The crowd quieted. "Rolando Miguel, the people lose when they do not speak and act together. As one voice we will keep our homes. Listen to this man and follow him. He is our best hope."

"Our best hope? Hah! Words! Nothing but empty words, you crazy old fool! Sit down and stay—"

"How dare you talk to Mr.Cardenas that way!" came a razor-like voice from the back of the room that suddenly went utterly silent. The woman Peter noticed earlier now stood and strode slowly, swaggering, to the front, her eyes blazing with anger as she glared at Torres who stood stunned by the sudden outburst. "This man is your mayor, your leader! A man who has grown wise through his many years, unlike you Miguel Rolando, or whatever your name is! You insult him and bring shame to the community all these people have built!" Even Peter cringed; her rapier voice slashed like a whip and he could almost see deadly, shimmering rays emanating from her fiery eyes, stabbing the confused man as he stood before her. She was slender and fairly tall and stepped right up to Torres, eye to eye. Cardenas looked sideways at Peter who returned the dazzled look. "You want to save this community?" she demanded, her eyes boring straight at Torres. "Well, there is a way, but it's not through some foolish nineteen-sixty-style demonstration. If you don't believe me you can ask Mr. Hoffler, who knows all about demonstrations and other direct clashes. He's a veteran of many of them."

What? How does she know this? Peter wondered. He never saw her before. Who is she? She still held Torres skewered by her laser-beam eyes. "You say words aren't enough, that we need action. Well, for once you're right, Mr.Torres! Words aren't enough. But words represent ideas, beliefs, and it is these ideas, the faith and the beliefs behind all the words that move people to action. It's been that way since the beginning of time. Not the words, but what those words stand for. People have died for that, Mr. Torres, so wake up, now, if you want to save your community! If that's what you want to do, then listen to these men. You're a teacher, Mr. Torres, and we could use you, too, so please put aside your impulses. You can do that, can't you?"

She turned to go back to her seat, then suddenly turned on him again, her eyes still blazing hot, stepping again in front of Torres as she pointed to Cardenas. "And you treat that man, your elected mayor, with the respect he deserves!" She turned sharply and returned to her seat, a sea of heads turned silently toward her, then slowly back to the front toward Peter and Cardenas. The room went still. Most of those who had been standing now sat again. Torres forgot he was still standing.

Holy Christ, Peter thought. She breathes fire! In and out! Whoever she was, she'd done her homework. What was left to say after that? There still would be many meetings of the county commissioners, the city councils and the Metropolitan Council in St. Paul, which had authority over large-scale public works that crossed jurisdictional boundaries. The state Legislature was involved, for any project of this magnitude required the state to match federal funds.

The evening was drawing late and many of those here started the morning shift at Dahlenberg Cabinet at seven. He saw their attention was wavering. *Bring it to a close*. "People, we do have choices rather than just construction of more and wider freeways. We can beat this and save our community." He always referred to Nuevo Del Rio as "our community" even though he and his wife lived in St. Paul, about twenty-five miles away. "We will win if we all think and act together. I wish you all a good evening." Peter sat heavily, hoping he sounded more confident than he felt.

They all rose and began moving toward the exits. Torres among them, one part angry, two parts stunned by the sharp confrontation, still wearing that stricken look. Light rail, referred to as LR, had the governor's support, as well as many others, for environmental reasons as much as traffic congestion. Every three-car rail unit takes three hundred would-be drivers off the road. LR projects were already operating in many U.S. cities, but it was a new concept in Minnesota.

The forces aligned against it were powerful, well-funded and politically connected, particularly with the state's Republican party.

It was nine-thirty and Peter's wife, Mary, was waiting, growing less patient with his evening work in the village, but Cardenas did what he always did after one of their meetings. He insisted Peter share a glass of home-made wine with him. How do you turn down a wise and kind old man? You don't. "I really should be on my way," Peter would tell him.

Cardenas held up a hand, as he always did, and Peter stayed, as he always did. "Let us sit at this table," he told Peter. "There is a great legend."

"Manuel Emilio, you've said that for years, and still I don't know what it is. You must tell me some day soon."

Again the old man's hand went up. "Yes, yes, some day you must know, but maybe we don't talk about that tonight, no?"

"No, Senor Cardenas," Peter sighed, "not tonight." As Cardenas opened a cabinet, Peter glanced back into the meeting room. "Who is that woman who bowled over Torres? She must have left with the others."

"I think we should find out. We could use someone like her, don't you think?"

"Oh, yes, I do. She'd be a big help to Raul."

Cardenas returned with two glasses, cigars and a bottle of his red wine and emitted a short, throaty laugh. "If she doesn't eat the poor man first."

Peter grinned. "Raul is quiet in a group but he'll hold his own in a debate with anyone, her included...I think."

For a half hour they participated in their ritual of the last seven years. The small room grew smoky and the wine settled gently in Peter's stomach, the steady buzz starting. "Manuel, I have miles to drive and your wine and your company are very good." He rose and Cardenas shook his hand. "We shall meet again soon, but please try to find out about our guest."

Peter glanced at his watch as he drove into the garage. It was nearly eleven. Another late evening and he'd hear about that in a couple minutes. He knew the script: *Have you seen your daughter since early this morning? And then for only ten minutes?* No, he hadn't. *Your involvement out there is really becoming a burden, you know.* Yes, he knew. More than a year into fatherhood and it was still a scary, alien entity. He wasn't one of those who just took to the role naturally. He concluded that parenthood wasn't some natural human state every new father or mother easily slid into, as if by some primordial instinct.

This was a career marriage. That was the original arrangement, anyway, then Emmy came along sixteen months ago. *It would have been nice if you had watched Emmy tonight*, she told him. She was in her last year of law school; three years that dragged painfully into four, and dreading the upcoming state bar exam. For Mary Hoffler, law school had been one long nightmare of a struggle, far more than Peter ever imagined it would be for her.

The bar exam was still six months away but even now Peter knew Mary would graduate in the lower half of her class. Well into the lower half. Not everyone passed the first time. Some never did.

He entered the living room and saw the slot of light beneath the door of their spare room. She heard him arrive but the door stayed closed.

Peter went into the bedroom and looked at the small figure sleeping quietly. Then it hit him; it always did in the privacy of these few moments with her. A beautiful child, an energetic, brown-eyed bundle of noise and whirling activity. She was his own, his little girl, and he had barely seen her for three days. He reached down and lightly stroked her blond hair, then ran his finger gently across her tiny shoulder and she lay there, her favorite teddy bear snuggled against her cheek.

An anguish welled up from deep below. His lips quivered and he closed his eyes to stop the tears while something rose in his throat. His employer, Advocate Services, known AS, Inc., didn't require him to spend ten hours a week in the village-he did that on his own. What compulsion drove him when the pressure from Mary was so palpable? Why? He knew her duties as mother and law student were weighing her down. He needed to be there for her. For their little one, too.

Because he chose to do it this way.

Because, once away from home, he felt a powerful compulsion for his work. It pulled him, like some giant towrope. Mary would learn all about this once she began practice. He hoped she could find a better way to balance life. He hoped that would happen some day.

He was weary. Peter turned quietly, walking back to the empty living room. He wanted nothing as much as several hours of sleep, but that wouldn't come tonight, not with that door closed. She would continue her silent, desperate struggle for another two or three hours.

He hated this stilted silence. He wished she'd kick open the door, scream, and fling a book at him. But all he could hear was an agonized, unspoken wail from behind the closed door, like a sailor washed to the sea by a cold, black wave.

Chapter Two

These nasty morning skirmishes had become routine for the Martinsons, the kind that began the day on a sour note. They usually started while Ann was using the bathroom mirror, or in the kitchen where coffee and a blueberry muffin made up the daily breakfast. Today was another episode in the running squabble that started about four years ago when the pace of technology streaked past Lakes Electric, of which her husband, Vince, was twenty per cent owner, the firm's estimator, writer, researcher of codes and regulations and managing partner with the two Belland brothers, John and Albert. He was not, to his bitter regret, a licensed electrician. That was another lost opportunity that zipped past him, only to wish he had taken an apprenticeship when it was available thirty years ago.

Time marched onward, steadily and swiftly, and now at fifty-one that was out of his reach. Scary, he often thought, how decisions that seem so workable, even sensible at the time, turn around and haunt you decades later. There must be a river called Time, he thought. It would be a raging torrent of white water with big rocks just beneath the surface, its shores littered with the ruins of many boats and their occupants. For the past ten years Ann had served as director of curriculum for a large suburban school district that was facing a budget deficit: one million six months ago, closer to three million today.

This morning she was seated before the large mirror finishing her hair, a complex task requiring an hour at best, and more than that on a bad hair day when tensions were palpable. Vince was standing out in the hallway, having finished his morning routine before Ann started hers. The bathroom had two sinks, but he learned long ago to finish his business before she arrived.

"Bellwood would be an excellent investment, Vince," she again told him. "We wouldn't live there forever but the realtor tells me that property has tremendous potential for value enhancement."

"They say that about all their listings. It's their business. But while it's value is enhancing we're paying at least twenty-five hundred a month in mortgage payments."

"The bank will pre-approve the loan," she said with emphasis. "You remember we have a hundred and forty thousand income."

He emitted a barely audible sigh as his shoulders slumped. "Against a loan of a half million or more. It's not going to leave us with any flexibility, even with the equity we have in this house." He was aware his voice was becoming squeaky. Calm down.

"You must look to the future. You can't go by what we now pay." She recently heard a TV real estate promoter explain how those with their level of income could finance loans to the tune of four hundred thousand to six hundred thousand. The best investment anyone could make! Look to the future, they said. Future earnings. It didn't occur to her that their intended audience was younger executives or others expecting large increases in income.

As part of their promotional scheme, several young, very attractive couples had given their testimony about how wonderful it was; how this plan enabled them to live the life they always thought they deserved, whatever that meant, always while seated together on a comfortable patio with palm trees waving gently in the background. They were young, beautiful, and evidently successful couples. Ann tended to endorse without question what these ads suggested; Vince was skeptical about promoters of every kind. "Peddlers," he told her. "The updated version of the old snake oil salesman."

"Ann, I don't know if the business will be there in a year. It's directly in the path of that freeway project."

"Yes," she replied quickly, "that has been my point: you and the brothers stood and watched the computer installation business fly right by. Let the city or the state buy the property and build their freeway. With the proceeds you can start a modern business, information systems, free of that millstone the brothers have become. I have told you this before: you have to disengage from them and position yourself in the modern age. You have a long way to go before retirement."

Do I ever, he thought, wondering how he was going to get there at all. "Ann, I'd love to part with them but I can't sell my share if no one will buy. Who wants one-fifth interest with two aging brothers controlling the operation? Someone would need to buy them out as well, but in two years no one has made an offer the Bellands would accept. So where does that leave me?" There would be no answer for this, unless she'd recently watched another developer solve that problem.

Ann sighed heavily. "I just think it would be so nice to move into a new house, not something as outdated as this place."

That made his eyebrows arch. "When did a custom-made house with workmanship not seen anywhere now, four bedrooms, a big family room, a den and ultra modern kitchen and dining room suddenly become obsolete?"

She was finally finishing with her hair and her patience was running thin. "Have you looked at the plans I showed you for those four homes at Bellwood?"

"I have—"

"A casual glance. A quick once-over?"

He nodded. "I haven't sat down to really study them. You only gave them to me last week."

"That's what I thought! You don't care how important this is to me, do you?" She gave him that petulant, abandoned look, her lips pressed tight.

It always took this turn. In his own way he loved her, all the slings and arrows aside. For him, caring was something global; very broad, arching over all lesser things, floor plans included. For her, care meant all those little items: floor plans, new cabinets, formal dinnerware. Yes, he liked them all. Thought they were just great. His accounting mind told him the cost was horrendous.

"I have worked hard, put in the extra time and effort, because I want to be noticed and given serious consideration for a superintendent position somewhere. When that happens it will be necessary for us to leave this neighborhood and take our place among those who are in our league. You do know what I mean, don't you?"

Vince thought for a moment. "Most of those around here are professionals. We have four or five attorneys, lots of business owners and an architect up the street."

She sighed again and her patience, never abundant, was draining away. "That is not what I mean!" she snapped. "I want my neighbors to be corporate CEOs, the best doctors, top professionals in every field, not just a few who happen to own some small business or some quasi-professionals like…whomever that is up the street."

"Ann, the people out there have yearly incomes of a half million or more. We're at a fourth of that. We wouldn't fit into their little world and we'd end up like outcasts. These people know how much superintendents are paid and they could take a good guess at what I'm pulling in. We would be among them but not a part of them. Is that what you want?" That last sentence came out a bit louder than he intended and now he felt his own patience slipping away. "All right, let's say you land a superintendent's job somewhere. First, are you willing to commute fifty to sixty miles or more each way, every day? And if you do, what's the salary? A hundred and ten thousand to maybe a hundred and twenty-five thousand a year? Even if I hold my own, and I can't hope for more, we would still be under two hundred thousand, a fraction of what our Bellwood neighbors are paid."

"Vince, I said we have to look to future earnings. You're too wrapped up in the present to see the possibilities! We belong in

Bellwood!" she declared, her voice thin and strained, face flushing. "That is the kind of house and neighborhood I want us to live in. Those are the people I want as our associates." She sighed loudly and glared into the mirror.

Vince shook his head. "Associates? Ann, you haven't associated with neighbors in any place we've ever lived. Why would you suddenly start doing that? Do you think they throw block parties out there? They're so busy, busy, busy with their business and careers they don't talk with their neighbors."

She dropped the hairbrush on the vanity, suddenly rose with another sigh and brushed past him. "This conversation is going nowhere and I have to leave. I have meetings all day and another this evening. I don't know when I'll be home but please don't call the school. We don't answer phones after hours." There was that steely quality in her voice that signaled closure. He understood what she wanted: status and recognition, however little that meant to him.

Ten years ago he made the effort to know his neighbors, which was an easier task than today. Now people kept to themselves more than before. A few of those he met still talked with him; the others drove on by and closed their garage doors, seldom to be seen outside. He knew it would be that way in Bellwood.

For Ann, the house was a symbol. It announced your tastes, your level of income, aspirations and attainments as well as your preferences for neighborhoods. It proclaimed that you were among the elite. That the monthly mortgage payment would be a heavy burden wasn't important to her.

Ann glanced at her watch as she drove out of the school parking lot: seven thirty-five pm. She left the school board meeting early. It had been a long day and she had no desire to be at home. She dialed a number on her cell phone, one not programmed for automatic dial, and he answered. For the first time today she smiled, then told him of her latest dispute with Vince.

Carter Newman epitomized everything she valued and sought to attain. He was wealthy, having owned and sold several businesses as well as stock and real estate holdings. It was rumored he had access to the Mayor's office in Minneapolis and a conduit into the Governor's office as well. In the higher strata of business and political society, Carter Newman cut a wide swath.

His wife died several years ago. He also owned a very elegant trend-setter in Bellwood Hills.

Chapter Three

The ancient organ wheezed out the final strains of "Amazing Grace" as the Reverend Aaron Young looked out over his small congregation, the same ones who gathered every Sunday morning at the Waters of Life Church on Third Avenue. Mostly skins of color, the balding heads of men like islands amid a sea of gray and white hair. No tailored suits here; mostly pension widows struggling along through their waning years, eking out a Social Security living. On any Sunday the collection plate held only what they could sacrifice from their meager resources. A good week of collections paid the month's utility bill.

Not that they were all elderly and poor. A few younger families with small children joined the fold in the past year. New blood brought willing hands needed for the work of the church and added precious dollars to the collection plate. He knew every member by name, including the recent arrivals, which was not difficult. It was a congregation of one hundred and twenty-five souls in a church that had stood for eighty-three years in a neighborhood deep into decline, crunched up against the Interstate 35W right-of-way and drowned by the constant dirge of freeway traffic.

The organ stopped and he noticed it was out of tune again, as did others who still had their hearing. The old bellows were worn and dried, like their organist, a widow who lived across the street. He raised his arms. "May the Lord bless you and keep you. May His face shine upon you and give you peace. Thank you for coming today. Go forth to love and serve the Lord and all His people." Then he delicately stepped down from the altar, walked ponderously to the doorway and turned toward his flock trailing him out the door. For ten minutes he shook hands, felt frail bones through thin skin, gripped tiny shoulders and spoke the platitudes expected of him by the faithful.

When they had scattered he went back inside, checking to make sure it was empty, lest some homeless soul find refuge within. Seeing none, he turned off the lights and locked the door, which was a sacrilege. The House of God should stay open, its arms spread out toward the turbulent sea of humanity, awaiting those who needed a place where they could feel the presence of their Lord and master. But for the past twenty years locks became a necessity imposed by the strictures of their insurance policy and the realities of an area cursed by crime, homelessness and drug abuse.

He slowly turned and walked a half block to another decrepit building that served as the church's parsonage. He stepped carefully on the narrow sidewalk, glancing down to avoid tripping on cement heaved up by emerging tree roots decades older than his church. He looked up, across Interstate 94 as it passed downtown Minneapolis, up to the towers of glass and steel. Do the people occupying those mighty fortresses ever glance down here and see where my people live and work? he wondered. This world of crumbling apartments, boarded buildings and streets lined with the rusting hulks of older cars. Who are they? Do they care, or are they so damn busy building data bases they haven't the time to care? Too busy chasing Mammon to see or care what went on around them?

He unlocked the front door with a loud, rusty squeak and entered the small house. It was as quiet as…as a tomb, always the first thought that came to his mind. His wife died twelve years ago and he still felt the void every day, and Sunday afternoons were the worst, when his flock dispersed, the roar of freeway traffic and the rumble and hiss of the buses at a minimum. They had a daughter, now thirty-one, who rebelled against them years ago, joined some commune and hadn't been heard from since. That was his family. He threw his suit coat across a worn couch, went to the tiny kitchen, stared at the cabinet door, feeling the same struggle as always. But today he felt his own weight, and that of the world. He would not fight. He sighed, opened the doors and took out a glass and the half empty bottle of gin. He mixed it with tonic and dropped wearily into a threadbare recliner and sighed heavily, sitting back and feeling the relief of weight taken off his swollen ankles.

Aaron Young was old for sixty-four, staring at the dark prospect of retirement, only briefly assuaged by the solace of these quiet afternoons, aided by the sedative effects of gin, whiskey, or whatever was on hand. Waters of Life was the district's way of pasturing him; a quiet exile where his outspoken ways would be swallowed in the urban abyss of poverty and silence.

He was a thorn in the saddle of the synod office. While serving at another parish he had the audacity to question why that office even existed. "You sit around your nice offices out in the new suburbs and talk endlessly," he told them, "but you produce nothing for the people you represent." With great efficiency they produced his present assignment and here he would remain till he trudged off into the oblivion of retirement. But then what? And where? This cramped little house, in bad repair though it be, had been his home for sixteen years. His salary had skidded downward, along with collections and membership, and the insurance death benefit was all that kept him going.

The tangy bitterness of the gin felt good as it slid down his throat and he pondered how he could maintain what little was here. He hardly knew where to begin, but it would have to be with the church. Its roof was rotting, so shingles and sheeting were a top priority. Every window and door let in a cascade of cold air. The water taps all leaked. He couldn't remember the last time the exterior was painted and the interior was covered by a layer of greenish mold. A wide ring of rust ominously surrounded the base of the water heater and one day it would all spill out across the floor. The carpet was worn down to the threads and you couldn't tell what color it had once been.

Two years ago he requested assistance from the synod, and as he expected, they sat on their thumbs and did nothing. Several months later they said no resources remained in that particular fund. Why wasn't he notified when there had been money in that particular fund? Did his colleagues out in the suburbs know more about that particular fund? Some of his younger members would donate their labor, but materials had to be bought. He shifted heavily. What we really need is a very friendly and sympathetic banker. But what banker, even in the name of God, would take a risk with a church on the brink of collapse? It was a matter of faith and credit. Plenty of the former; damn little of the latter.

Selling or moving wasn't an alternative. He knew of other inner city churches relocating to the suburbs. If his members owned autos that might work. But few could afford that luxury, and getting to the suburbs on Sundays would be impossible when the MTC bus system was at minimal service. People should worship where they lived.

There was the slimmest possibility of a merger, but who would have them? He talked about this with some of his counterparts but nothing came of it. After all, what did Waters of Life have to offer a merger partner? These weren't serious options, so here they were and here they would remain. Either repair it or it would fall apart, and it would have to be done soon.

He once wrote the Minneapolis city council inquiring about possible assistance from urban development, or from whatever other source the city might provide. Apart from interest shown by his own friend and council member, Forrest Turley, his response from the city was to express thanks for his interest, but you know how it is when you mix church with state. Really explosive. Besides, the council was overwhelmed by the welter of competing demands, most coming from quarters better connected then he. Turley was only one of thirteen members of the council.

How unfortunate that Aaron Young studied only theology and philosophy at the seminary. Courses in networking and marketing in the real world were still decades in the future. How could one aging black minister, from a decaying corner of a forgotten part of a big city, ever network a wave against the well-heeled interests of the polished set in those glitzy towers?

He relaxed in the quiet of this small home. His swollen ankles pleasantly at ease, his ponderous weight taken by the recliner, and in these private moments gin made the world turn easier.

Before coming to the fourth drink of the afternoon he picked up the Metro/State Section of the Minneapolis Star Tribune, Sunday edition, and scanned the articles. There were the usual write-ups about city council meetings; dealings of the Hennepin County commissioners; a budget crisis out in one of the south suburban school districts; features detailing the fortunes, upward and downward, of various businesses in the city. More articles about safety in the schools and how to stop the flow of guns into the classroom. He was happy in some perverse way that those years were behind him.

Near the bottom of page three was a small article about a group out in…where…? Nuevo Del Rio? Where was that? He had spent the last ten years entirely within Minneapolis and St. Paul. The article described it as a small village south of Burnsville, where a noisy confrontation occurred at an exclusive housing development between the property owners and a small group of twenty others from the nearby village. It was about the rail plan. They were led by someone named Torres. The article reported some minor damage to the security gate but the sheriff's deputies dispersed the mob. Torres was being held pending charges in the Dakota County jail.

He read the article, then reread it, more slowly this time. It must be age, he thought. How could he have forgotten? There hadn't been anything about this for a few months and it slipped from his memory. Waters of Life was set to fall to the wrecking ball and become a very minor piece of history. He remembered the plan calling for a light rail track built either in the freeway median or above the road where no median existed. There was no median where I-35W passed his church and met Interstate 94 south of the downtown loop. Councilman Turley attended an earlier meeting in that village, he noted, and spoke about a network of bus lines connecting the rail with inner city neighborhoods to the east and west of the route.

He pondered this for several moments. That demonstration must've been some rag-tag, misdirected effort. You don't bring down the big boys throwing stones. Well, good for Turley, staying right in the thick of things. It was time to call his good friend for an update.

Chapter Four

The Transportation Committee was gathering in the spacious two-story chamber of the Metropolitan Council in downtown St. Paul. The nine other committee members were taking their seats as the chairperson rapped the gavel to begin the proceedings. He glanced at the agenda, then noted several small children watched by parents at the back of the large room. Some of the parents were here to offer their testimony concerning the only item on tonight's agenda: freeway versus light rail for Minneapolis and its southern suburbs.

He rapped his gavel again and the big room went silent, even the children stopped when they heard the loud THWACK! and looked to the front of the room at the U-shaped bench and the intimidating man holding the big hammer.

The chairman explained the purpose of the meeting. At issue was the one and a half billion dollars needed to widen I-35W by two additional lanes each way and an alternative calling for an initial city and county expenditure of four hundred and seventy-five million to construct a light rail line to the southern suburbs. On a large easel were drawings and maps outlining the route and other details. There was a small table and two chairs positioned directly in front of the council bench where those giving testimony were seated. "We shall call our first witness to the stand." A young black woman with a small child approached the table, radiating uneasiness looking at ten rather serious-looking members of a committee whose purpose she only vaguely understood.

As instructed, she gave her name, then took a deep breath and began. "I, ah, I haven't done this before, and, uh, well, I'll just tell the things that are bothering me about the thing with the freeway. I live on Third Avenue in Minneapolis, just north of Lake Street, in an apartment building that faces the freeway. I, ah, well, what I hear is that me and my daughter gonna have to move. It ain't much of a place…I mean, it's real old and run down, but it's our home, me and my daughter, and, well, we can't afford to move, sir," she said, looking straight at the chairman. "There's a lot of others just like me in that building, single parents and holdin' down a job somewhere, some have two jobs'n none of 'em can move. I mean, we can't afford to move if that freeway gets wider."

She kept staring at him in an almost pleading way and he felt compelled to say something. "Ma'am, the final decision is not going to be made here tonight. Our purpose is to take testimony from you and the others, to learn your views, then to pass on our recommendations to the state Legislature where the final vote will be taken." He smiled at her as she leaned over to whisper to her little daughter who was getting restless.

"Thank you, sir," she said. "I work in a laundromat on Lake Street, about a mile from my apartment. There's a bus that goes right by there so I take it. I make, ah, about eight dollars an hour and after payin' for the rent, my groceries and the child care, well, there ain't nothin' left. If I got to move I've been checkin' around and I know the rent's gonna be higher and I can't afford that. I heard the city would help me pay for the move, that's what a social worker told me. But that don't help pay the higher rent. I go to school two nights a week. English and computers, so I can get a better job."

As she continued, Dave Behlen, who was seated near the back, arms folded across his chest, turned to his attorney. "Didn't you tell them to put us on first?" he demanded.

The man nodded. "The council's scheduling protocol doesn't allow for preference."

Behlen snorted, half out loud, and a few seated nearby heard the noise and turned toward him. He glared back at them. "This is a farce! Those jokers get up there and think the whole world's supposed to cry fat tears on their behalf!" Behlen turned back to him again. "What's the deal with that babe? She babbled something about a social worker, so what have we got here, another welfare mom who thinks the world stops for her benefit?"

"She hasn't said she was on welfare. The social worker could be from another agency. Earnings from her job may entitle her to a reduced welfare payment, if she has a grant at all."

"Wait a minute! If she's working what the hell is she doing on welfare? Tom, what's the bottom line here?"

He shrugged his shoulders. "It's possible she may have started a grant, then found that job and had her grant reduced because of the earnings."

"I can't believe this!"

"The dollar-for-dollar reduction was tried several years ago and the number employed actually dropped. The grant reduction formula was brought back and the number employed increased. As I understand it, the increased income helps to pay for child care."

Behlen snorted. "Then find the daddys and make them pay the freight or lock 'em all up!" He sighed heavily. "The sad thing is if that rail plan passes, guys like me will have to keep looking at all those shacks by the road every damn time we drive by! Tear 'em all down!"

Tom read the anger on Behlen's face. End the discussion now. He was retained as Behlen's general counsel, not as an adviser to explosive issues.

Behlen grunted and muttered something. So what have I got here? he thought. I keep this guy on retainer and he's got all these excuses for those slugs staying on welfare? Is this guy some kind of wild-ass liberal masquerading as a business lawyer?

The first woman at the table was followed by two others from the same neighborhood and who gave similar testimony. All three worked full time at wages less than ten dollars an hour; two having more than one job, and still rent, child care and food ate up most of their earnings. Throughout all of this Behlen squirmed in his chair, sighing, glaring at anyone who looked at him. His eyes swept the figure of each of the three as they walked back to their seats.

Peter Hoffler and Raul Montero approached the table. Behlen sneered. "We're on next, aren't we? Get that bushy-haired weirdo and his Mexican sidekick out of the way. Then we can end this farce and get out of here. Listen, there's only one question that needs to be asked and all this crap would be eliminated: 'Who is paying the tab?' You answer that and everything's taken care of. Bottom line!" A woman sitting ahead of them turned to him. He glared back.

Peter started. "It has been said by its opponents that a light rail system will not solve the traffic congestion problem. They are right. No single mode of transportation, by itself, will solve the congestion problems every urban center faces. But it is a part of the solution, along with continuation of regular city bus service and freeways. Consider this: Each rail car carries about a hundred passengers, each train has three such cars—three hundred passengers riding on each train. Even if just four such units make a daily round trip from the southern suburbs into Minneapolis, that's twelve hundred commuters who are not using the freeway, and that's on just a single route. Multiply that by the number of rail routes we should have in the Twin Cities, now home to 2.8 million citizens, and the total rises to the tens of thousands of commuters freed from the tension and frustration of using our overcrowded freeways.

"It is said by the freeway supporters that the overwhelming preference of commuters is to use their own auto, so therefore we must build new freeways and add more lanes on our existing arteries. So we expand our roads and what happens? With more lanes open, more commuters will switch from bus or train back to their auto, and in a very short time the gains from this new construction are offset by the greater number of autos clogging the routes and slowing the pace of traffic. Are we to repeat this yet one more time at a cost of over a billion dollars?

"Rail commuting may be a new experience in the Twin Cities, but it operates successfully in other cities throughout our nation, including Boston, San Francisco, Portland and San Diego. The city of Portland built a light rail route and a billion dollars of private business development resulted along the rail route within the city itself. Small business centers, called transit villages, sprung up along the rail line and these included day care centers, laundromats, coffee shops and newsstands, food stores and other outlets serving the needs of commuters. This is private sector development within the city itself. I know this sounds a bit nostalgic, from the time of the street cars and passenger trains, but this is bona fide, private inner-city development that translates directly into business profits and new sources of revenue for our city and county governments.

"Let's take this from another perspective." He knew Behlen was behind him—he could almost feel his eyes bore into him. *Fry in hell*, Peter thought. "Welfare reform. How does that tie in with light rail? Welfare reform is all about jobs, not training, not education. We know most of the growth in employment has been in the suburban areas, but the majority of welfare recipients still reside in the inner city areas and only a few have reliable transportation."

He glanced at a table to his right where Turley and several other officials sat. He seemed to have their attention but Turley was looking toward the back of the room. Then he continued. "Permanent reduction of the welfare rolls requires that recipients have access to jobs paying wages leading to economic self-sufficiency. Most of those jobs are in the suburbs and because the unemployment rates have been low for several years, many of these remain unfilled. These are jobs that could and should be filled by our inner city workforce, if only transportation was coordinated with their work schedules. Freeways, no matter how many lanes you add, will never resolve that problem, and inner city residents will continue unemployed and without transportation while our suburban jobs continue unfilled. Production is lost and profits dwindle.

"We can't allow that to continue. Light rail, when coordinated with bus routes, has the flexibility to set schedules so that residents may commute from the inner city to the suburbs, fill the vital needs of businesses and leave welfare forever. Think of that as reverse commuting, and only rail aligned with the bus system can meet his need for our business community.

"I leave you with just one thought: Progress has always been defined as moving forward, and in the cities that has always meant an ever outward movement and greater sprawl. We must offer workable alternatives; to look back to where this all started; rebuild that from which we all came and in the process create new and more efficient means of moving people where they both need and want to go.

"With your recommendation there will be a bill introduced in the Legislature calling for one hundred million that will be needed to obtain the one hundred and fifty million from the Federal Transit Administration. The Governor has announced his support for the bill, but we must act now, for the federal funding is rapidly being committed." Peter paused for a few seconds. "Mr. Chairman and members of the Metropolitan Council, this concludes my part of the hearing this evening. I am grateful for the opportunity to address this group and now my associate, Mr. Montero, has a few words for you. Thank you and good night."

Behlen squirmed again and leaned toward his attorney. "Honest to God! Have you ever heard such drippy sentiment? All we need to do is clear out this rabble and get right down to the bottom line! We could have it all done in a year. That's the way we do it in business and I see absolutely no reason for doing it any different here!" He shook his head and noticed the black city councilman who kept looking to the back of the room.

Raul Montero looked to the council members, then briefly to Turley and the others to his right. "It is very hard for me to match the eloquence of my associate, so I will leave you with a few numbers which will add to what Mr. Hoffler has said, much of which was obtained from the council's website. First, the council now knows that by the year 2020, the number of daily commuter trips within the seven county metro area will increase by 2.2 million, for a total of thirteen million trips daily. If the outward growth continues, parts of five additional counties will be in the metro area within ten years. How many daily trips will these twelve counties have then? Fourteen million? Fifteen million? We all know that our roadways are at capacity during rush hours, and nearly so at other times of the day as well. We do not have sufficient land to work our way out of this congestion by building more roads and pushing people out of their neighborhoods. That is what brought us the congestion we now live with. Our region's economic health depends in large part on efficient use of transportation to move people and goods in a quick and reasonable fashion. Bus transitways, acting as feeder lines, will make our rail system flexible, and Mr. Turley from the Minneapolis city council will address that point. I thank the council for your attention."

Behlen straightened himself, buttoned his suit coat and strode confidently to the witness table, attorney in tow, looking straight ahead as eyes followed this lordly man whose tailored suit shouted "*Two thousand!*" He looked at the council members, then to the others seated to his right. Turley was looking off to his left, toward the back of the room. Behlen turned back to the council bench. "Good evening," he began. "My name is David Behlen and the gentleman on my left is Mr. Tom Wilson, my legal advisor. For the past eight years I have owned a small business consulting firm in downtown Minneapolis. I wanted to be here tonight to talk about one side of this transportation issue that has been ignored in all of the rhetoric we've heard.

"Some have said that we should build railroads out from our central cities. That somehow small businesses will spring up to serve commuters in some way or another. We have heard that it's not feasible to build new roads or to even expand our existing network as this will cut through neighborhoods and somehow divide people off from each other. These objections are largely emotional and rooted in a way of life that existed fifty years ago—the era of railroad passenger trains and trolleys, when urban dwellers resided only in what is now called the inner city area. What are now growing and bustling suburbs were remote fields of corn and wheat.

"But the fifties gave way to the sixties, then came the seventies and the rapid growth began, and continues today. The idea was put forth that this outward growth is somehow not a good thing; that it increases dependency on personal autos. All of this growth came about because people exercised their right of free choice and they choose to find homes in the outlying areas. Builders, working within the free market, responded to these wishes and built homes for them. As this process of free choice continued, others chose to set up businesses there to serve these new residents. No one from any central government told those families they must go there. No one from those same organs of government told businesses they must build in those suburbs whether or not they wanted to do it. This growth occurred because millions of people exercised their right of choice granted them in a democracy and choose to live with their families in the outlying area.

"They chose to do this because we have a society that grants every citizen the right to make free choices. We should thank our Maker that we do not live in a nation where these freedoms are a mere illusion. Do we want the heavy hand of government to tell us '*No, you cannot do this because I said so*.'? Is that the kind of society we want to live in?" Again Behlen looked at every member of the council sitting in front of him, and also to the four seated to his right.

"Two people meet, decide freely that it is in their self interests to do business with each other, free of the ponderous power of distant bureaucracies. That is the reason we have survived in comparative peace for more than two hundred years.

"The cost of building any rail system, which of necessity lacks the flexibility needed to keep pace with private growth and development, would be prohibitive beyond any reasonable calculation. The bottom line, members of this council, is that rail is a singular, one-dimensional system that cannot grow and adjust as free citizens exercise rights available only in our system. This issue has far less to do with piles of conflicting statistics than it has with citizens living, working and trading in a society that was made open and free only by the supreme sacrifices of millions of our own people.

"I thank you for giving me the time to be heard on this matter. I hope I have given you a perspective in which to make the choices that have been put before you. Good night to you all." He abruptly rose and left the room, his attorney again in tow. He stole another quick glance back at Forrest Turley.

For at least fifteen seconds no sound could be heard in the large room, save for a few small voices of the children in the back. Then the chairman turned toward the table at the side of the room. "We have one more who wishes to come before the council. Minneapolis Councilman Forrest Turley…Mr. Turley?"

Turley turned toward him with a jerk. "Oh, I'm sorry, Mr. Chairman." He rose and walked to the table in front of the council and took his seat. "By now we have by now examined nearly every aspect of this problem before us and you have a mountain of data to digest, much of it very conflicting and confusing. There are so many items to consider whenever you must make such distant judgments on public policy. You have heard tonight from Mr. Hoffler who has described a vision for the rail system as it would be built and operated to serve our central cities and our outlying area. Peter Hoffler spoke the truth when he said that economic development occurs whenever and wherever commuter rail systems have been built. His vision of small businesses springing up along the routes is no mere sentimental memory of a bygone era. I have seen these in Portland and in Boston.

"You have also heard from three young, single parents working to support their families, studying to improve themselves, who have told you how their lives will be impacted should Interstate 35W be widened. Those three women speak eloquently for thousands of others whose lives would be disrupted when forced to commit an even greater share of their limited earnings to housing."

He walked to the flip chart clamped to an easel and turned a few pages, stopping on what looked to be a street map of Minneapolis. A thick dark line ran from the downtown area southeast, then it turned southwest toward Interstate 35W. On this map were several other lines, most running in an east-west direction.

"As you know, the current proposal calls for using the present Hiawatha Corridor tracks from the Target Center southeast to the Franklyn Avenue station, then turning southwest, across the Phillips Neighborhood, meeting 35W at Fortieth Street. From there it follows the freeway median south across the Minnesota River, through Burnsville, ending either in Lakeville or continuing further south to the village of Nuevo Del Rio, some twenty-five miles south of Minneapolis. Part of the line from the Franklyn Avenue station to the freeway passes through my ward, which is the poorest in Minneapolis and the most heavily dependent on public transportation.

"The gentleman who testified before me might be a great spokesman for the free market, but I sense he has no feeling for life as it is lived in the poorer neighborhoods. He was correct about one thing: light rail is not particularly flexible…in the very same manner as a freeway, once laid down, is not flexible. So how do we add flexibility to such a system?" He turned back to the street map and pointed at the east-west lines. "Light rail is fast, it is economical and it is also environmentally friendly. It requires very little space and does not permanently sever neighborhoods. Earlier you were provided convincing information about the impact on the environment of rail versus the damage that will be done if we further increase our reliance on the auto. But to obtain the flexibility needed to reach neighborhoods that are not close to the rail lines, we use the city bus system on east-west routes bringing commuters from the more remote neighborhoods to the rail terminals.

"At these points they board for their trips north into Minneapolis or south into the suburbs. Peter Hoffler told you about the needs to transport inner city workers to the unfilled jobs in the suburbs. This is how we do this: The bus system reaches out, away from the rail lines, and brings the commuters to the stations along the route in the mornings and brings them back home at the end of the work day.

"I will end by saying this: We cannot pave our way out of the terrible problem of urban congestion, no matter how many miles of new freeway, or new lanes we may build. Many of the newly created jobs are in the service sector and do not pay a wage sufficient to maintain both a private home and personal transportation. This is why public transportation has become a major issue in every urban area of this country."

Then he turned back to the street map. "This plan represents the needs of the great majority of citizens in our cities. I urge you all to give this plan serious thought, for this is both wise and just public policy. I want to thank all of you, my colleagues on the county boards, the Legislature and all others who came here tonight."

A half hour later the meeting was adjourned, Behlen and his legal hawk having long since departed. "Stick around," Peter said to Montero as he steered him over to a corner where Turley and Aaron Young were conversing. "Gentlemen," Peter said, "I think we have a common cause." He introduced himself and Raul. Fifteen minutes later all four were at a coffee shop across the street.

An hour later Forrest Turley walked into his modest home, turned on the lights, threw his necktie and suit jacket on a couch and stared out the dark window. Did I overstate my case? he wondered. He hoped they saw him as a straight-shooter from the inner city, as one talking about the lives of his constituents as these were lived out each and every day.

He was horrified that the chairman had to call his name twice. Did it show? He thought for long moments and shook his head. It all started four years ago, didn't it? Or…did it? He walked slowly into his bedroom and once again picked up the photo by the bed. Conflicting emotions ripped at him and he wondered if they would ever leave him alone. She was only thirty-three and the little boy just turned seven, a second grader, as he was proud to say. Then in one jarring, screeching moment it was all taken from him, when the eighteen-wheeler spun out of control on that rainy day. The pain was normal; would be there for a long time, but still it hurt so badly, each and every day. It would never go away, they told him, but in time the pain would lessen, lose its sharp, ripping edge and become manageable. But that other one. The one that got started just a little later, a few months after they died. That one he didn't understand and it scared the hell out of him.

There was so much of that he didn't grasp; how something like that got its hooks into you. He had seen others struggle with obsessions and wondered why they were so unable to rid themselves of whatever was haunting them. Now he knew. Three months ago he started therapy at that clinic. It was painful, but he had to do it if he had any hope of driving off those demons dancing their pagan ritual in his head. Tonight would be no different. He would lay there alone, shadowy images flowing through his mind, one scene after another, all the questions, the whys. If this was what he feared it might be…what then? What if this ever gets out?

An hour after the meeting ended Dave Behlen brought his attorney back to his car in a downtown Minneapolis lot. "Tom, send me the bill for your time. You're done as my attorney."

Chapter Five

It was a wet, gloomy spring day common to Minnesota when raggy clouds scudded low and dirty gray, the April rain hammering a staccato beat on the roof of the aged building housing Advocate Services Inc. The old structure shuddered as wind splattered the rain against the windows and the water distorted the outside images like mirrors in a circus fun house. In a perverse way, Peter Hoffler hoped the deluge would continue for a while longer. He wondered if people like the two gentlemen sitting in his office were ever exposed to the same hassles and buffeting ordinary mortals endured daily. Today just might be the first time in their sheltered lives they experienced the indignity of being rained on. *If only the sky will hang low and dirty for just a little while. It would be good for them,* he thought. Even board members should experience first hand a few of the inconviencies and discomforts their clients faced every day of their lives.

They were insulated New Yorkers who rode elevators down from their townhouses to the building's garage where a warm limo would bring them to warm garages in the buildings where they did whatever they did while serving on a board of directors, then back at the end of the day, never once catching a drop of rain or a puff of wind in their face. It surprised Peter that they would even consider flying here rather than remaining in the sanctuary of the national headquarters and sending some underling to pontificate the current line to their warriors in the trenches. Of course they flew first class, as they did everywhere, but they were fair about that. They paid the difference from coach class out of their own deep pockets; then took it as a tax write-off for charity.

Peter paid scant attention to the constant turnover on their national board, all of their infighting, maneuvering and changes of emphasis that seemed to occur weekly. He had grown indifferent to their politics and petty concerns of the moment, believing these were directed more by transient whims of trend than any line of rational thought. The two well-dressed gentlemen seated across the desk from him, Whitman and Pollard, held seats on the boards of four or five other organizations where they dealt only with the broadest formulation of policy and were, by Peter's thinking, useless for all other purposes. What knowledge had they of the daily travails and worries of their clients?

Today Whitman and Pollard were expounding on the latest change in policy creations. "It is the board's wish," Pollard was saying, as sober and serious as one could get, "that we adopt a more cooperative and collaborative approach with our partners in the private sector." By partners he meant the business world, where Peter often clashed for the benefit of their clients.

Peter looked across his desk at Pollard, as if expecting more elaboration. Don't these people ever smile? he wondered. "Is there the belief that we have adopted an adversarial posture toward business?"

Whitman leaned forward slightly. "The board feels that we need more collaborative approaches to business that are consistent with an era in which union influence is declining and issues of productivity are paramount. Our policy must be oriented toward collaboration within an environment of the stresses brought by global markets. Our emphasis is on merging the interests of our traditional customers with those of the private sector."

Peter had to ponder that prospect for a few moments. "Is there the perception that we have taken positions inconsistent with its direction?"

"We are not suggesting that you have taken such approaches," Pollard said. A howling gust of wind rattled the old windows and the rain renewed its attack, the building seeming to tremble before the onslaught.

"The element of adversity is built into the fabric of our legal system. Are you suggesting that we no longer advocate for our customers?" Peter knew that neither of them had any legal training and somewhere down deeper he resented these two ornaments, for lack of a better word, telling him how to practice law. Both had been businessmen at one time, which was what brought them to the board. Another recent policy change required a majority of its members to be from the private sector, which reduced the number of seats held by client representatives, thus assuring their own clientele remained a voting minority on the board. They were also considering a change in organization name; one that would drop any mention of advocacy and thereby ease into this new era of good feeling; partnership and brotherhood all around.

Pollard wrinkled his brow just a little. "We have made no changes in eligibility, Mr. Hoffler. We continue to be an agency providing legal services to those who meet our requirements."

"I'm sure we are, Mr.Pollard. You are aware that well over ninety per cent of our cases are settled out of court, saving both parties substantial time and expense? It would seem this would be consistent with our new mission." Whatever the hell the mission was today, he wanted to say. "If you have the time I would invite you to review a few of our case files. I believe you would see that our current orientation is, in fact, quite collaborational." Neither had never examined a case file nor had any intention of doing so. Their concerns were very broad.

"The board has not expressed any concerns that this center is operating in a manner inconsistent with the new mission," Whitman said.

The discussion went on in this circular fashion for another half hour while the heavy rain continued drumming on the roof. It was a cheaply constructed, low rent building, noisy and not well ventilated, typical of ASI offices across the country. But the roof did hold out the rain. They were near the end of their visit and Peter was feeling optimistic: the rain continued its onslaught, flailing away at the tired old structure. For a fleeting moment he felt the barest twinge of guilt. It quickly disappeared. Because of wide sidewalks, no vehicle could come within fifteen feet of the building. Then Pollard glanced at his watch and looked first to Whitman, then to Peter. "Could you call a taxi for us, Please?"

"Certainly." Come on, rain, hang in there just a bit longer. He called the firm they used for their clients, then felt his heart drop: Oh no! The rain was subsiding.

Ten minutes later the taxi arrived—just as the skies cleared—and Peter accompanied the two out to the curb, glancing ruefully upward. They all shook hands in a gesture of good will, wished each other the best—of whatever—then he watched as they pulled away from the curb. No doubt about it: some people just lead a protected life. The seas part just for them, where 'er they go.

It had been a slow afternoon and only two other attorneys were in their offices. Peter returned two phone calls then sat back and folded his arms behind his head. However obliquely they had put it, their message was clear: support business in its dealings with Advocate Services while the board seeks a new name, one more in keeping with market trends. Or else get out. Eight years he had put in here, the last two of which were spent as a lead attorney; they had no local director. ASI thought of their national network of twenty-five offices as self-directed work groups. On a good day when all egos were in harmony that theory worked fairly well. At other times they needed someone with enough authority to keep the associates from throttling each other.

Now that Pollard and Whitman were sent off in a cab, all warm and dry, Peter reviewed his options. He could stay here, try fusing together the interests of employee and employer, renter and landlord, creditor and borrower, all in this new spirit of collaboration, everyone moving forward in happy lockstep fashion. Sure. And wrestlers all collaborate in the ring. He could go into private practice, though certainly not in the legal division of some corporation or as an associate in one of the blue ribbon law firms downtown. Not with his bushy hair, steel-rimmed glasses, casual dress and an outlook not in keeping with today's proper business attitude. There were government agencies in need of legal talent. He might fit in there.

Over the past few months he had talked several times with two attorneys who had a small practice down the street. Both were approaching retirement and seeking a replacement. They offered good terms, knew what Peter could do with his talents and weren't put off by his somewhat anti-establishment attitude and appearance. He could moderate his wardrobe if need be. Somewhat, anyway. He could be accommodating. He looked at his watch: three forty-five. He could leave; it was Friday and he had his forty hours in late yesterday afternoon. He should go home and spend some quality time with the family. Mary was trying to watch Emmy and study for upcoming tests on tax law, something she loathed. At the moment he was needed there far more than here.. He stood in the lobby thinking about that for a few moments. Then he went back to his office, opened another file and began reviewing its content.

Three minutes later he quietly slid the folder into a file cabinet, turned off the light and walked the six blocks to his home.

Chapter Six

They gathered in the small, cramped room that served as office for Lakes Electric-Vince and his two partners: the Belland brothers, John, who just turned sixty-four, and Albert, sixty-six. It was their final meeting after eighteen years in partnership. Their electrical contracting firm was being dissolved and for Vince Martinson it was like watching a corpse being embalmed. Or was it him on the stainless steel table? The brothers had finally run out of steam and wished only to cash out their shares and spend the remaining years settling for double-bogeys on the pleasant fairways of Florida. Vince had watched their diminishing drive for five or six years, but they both clung to their shares and now it came down to this.

"Yes, we understand your situation, Vince," Albert said. "We will take the blame for letting the technology business get past us. You made your wishes known and we weren't fast enough. Before we knew what had happened the market roared on by. Maybe if we'd been ten years younger when that market opened, well..." he shrugged, "I don't know."

"That's all in the past now," Vince said. He could have said much more; such as why didn't you take my word that this was a new market with no boundaries, get off your asses and become players rather than watching the profits flow to our competitors' bank accounts? "I hear you found a buyer."

John nodded. "For the building, yes. To continue the business, no."

"It's that damned freeway matter," Albert said. "Most people think the Legislature's going to ask for the federal highway funds, and if they do, this building gets the wrecking ball. We know that rail thing's a dead issue."

"You can't convince a buyer it would be a good investment at this point," his brother added, as if this wasn't painfully obvious.

"What's our buyer offering?" he asked, fearing the answer.

"Not what we want but it's close," Albert told him. "Four hundred and eighty thousand for the property and vehicles and we sell off the equipment and supplies. The Realtor recommends we accept."

Vince thought for several moments, then snorted. Close? he wanted to ask. "We've had it on the market for eighteen months. They probably want to get it off their listings and go on to something better. What does our attorney say?"

John nodded. "He recommends we accept."

The property was worth more than that, but the prospect of being bulldozed to the ground would devalue it to any buyer, and everyone knew about the freeway issue. They'd be at the mercy of the city, the state, or whomever if the bill passed the Legislature and federal funding was obtained. It had been and still was, a long, tortuous path through the federal and state bureaucratic maze, and no guarantee of the outcome. Still, condemnation loomed over them like a rolling thunder cloud. Shit! Eighteen years of work, planning, taking the risks, and a few lumps with it, the seventy hour weeks and it finally comes down to this.

A year ago he envisioned buying out the brothers, updating the firm with the markets, then selling a solid, profitable business when his time came. Two years ago they talked about the brothers financing his buyout but that frittered away in the winds of time and was never discussed again. So, here it was, and a whole lot sooner then he planned, and for a lot less than he hoped. "Then we'd better take the offer," he finally said. "I've talked with the banks and I can't finance a buyout of your shares." Ann was going to throw a fit when he told her what his take would be. She'd never worked in the commercial world and was unaware how fluid business can be; that closing meant clearing off outstanding bills when a business ceased to exist.

Albert nodded quietly. "We estimate your gain, after settling all accounts, at about sixty-five thousand. Not a lot, Vince, but at least we're all getting out with cash in hand. That's better than Marty did." Marty was one of their smaller competitors who also missed the emerging technology markets, with far more horrid consequences, including an IRS workover with a nasty outcome.

Sixty-five thousand wasn't very much, but he knew that wouldn't deter Ann from her singular quest to reach Bellwood Hills. She would add this to their equity on the Bruce Avenue house, sputter about him getting another bad deal, but still declare it a start on their Bellwood career. Always that goddamned Bellwood. The fact that their income was now down to her seventy-nine thousand dollars a year, his future being unclear at best, didn't enter the equation as it worked out in her mind. “So it comes down to this: either we take the offer and get out, or refuse and run the risk of condemnation. Is that how you see it?”

The brothers nodded. “That’s how we see it,” Albert said. Easy for them, Vince thought. They’re each pulling out a hundred and thirty thousand and setting up their tee times. I’m headed for the black hole with half that much.

“Then take the offer.’

He wasn’t looking forward to the evening, but if Ann had another marathon board meeting, or whatever, their time together would be short. Their evenings together meant occupying the house at the same time. He busied himself with the firm’s paperwork, all their estimating, researching electrical codes and keeping their manuals and other records up to date. It was his job to rewrite the business procedure manual whenever electrical codes changed—a task without end. That required him to read law, the rules that stemmed from the law, and also to maintain contact with the State Board of Electrical Examiners.

Being a hard-driving career-oriented person, Ann immersed herself in the details of curriculum development. They each had a room they used as an office and over time those evolved into a kind of demilitarized zone. During the evenings she hunched over her computer writing and compiling data for her thesis leading to a doctoral degree in education, which she expected to attain within a year.

Her thesis addressed diversity issues relating to educational curriculum development in a multicultural environment, which struck Vince as rather odd, considering her district was ninety-eight per cent white and she had virtually no experience with minority students. It seemed little more than a pile of disconnected facts and statistics gained through isolated study and research and not tempered by on-line experience.

This dormitory-like arrangement was not an encouraging response to the empty nest syndrome, as some couples enjoyed, but this was the pattern that developed between them. It had been years since they had taken a vacation together. She used her spare time visiting friends and relatives in Ohio or in other places; he usually went fishing with his own friends—after first arguing with her—the ones Ann thought were below him in the hierarchy of things.

Their son and daughter graduated from college and went their own ways; him to a computer firm in Denver, her to a clothing designer in Chicago. Their visits home were rare and usually limited to a couple days at Christmas. Vince was an old line disciplinarian; her ideas of parenthood stemmed from readings in educational psychology, which tends to be faddish. Both viewpoints had their merits but when applied concurrently it made for confusion and encouraged the siblings to play off one parent against the other.

He envied those couples who always seemed to be on the same wave-length with each other, always knowing what the other was thinking and who were in agreement as to how life should be lived together. Vince noticed that even their differences seemed somehow to bring them together, as if each found value in their diversity. What was their secret? How had these people succeeded where he and Ann clearly failed to find common ground?

The warning signs were there: their sex life had gone into the tank, and tension pervaded their household. He wondered if she missed the joy of earlier sex as much as he did. Well, he couldn't keep this a secret forever. She was in the bathroom doing her hair again. "We have to accept the offer," he told her in his succinct fashion. Let her carry the argument, if that it be.

"How much does that leave you with?"

"...Sixty-five grand."

"...Sixty-five thousand?" Her voice rose sharply. "I thought you stood to gain at least a hundred and fifty thousand or more. What happened?"

"The prospect of a freeway happened and that made the business itself worthless. The only value is in the land."

She sighed and threw the brush down on the counter. It bounced off the wall and landed on the floor "Why do you let them do this to you! This is an outrage! Vince, we need that money if we have any hope at all for moving—"

"When your partners hold eighty per cent, you're influenced, like it or not. Look, Ann, let's not get into how it was run, okay? We had some bad luck, made mistakes and ended up paying for them."

"I didn't say we should argue about it, did I?"

"Then let's not. We'll just, ah, drop the matter."

"Fine," she snapped, finishing her hair with another brush. "I have another board meeting tonight, as I told you last week. It will be late, so don't bother to wait for me."

"They haven't solved that crisis yet? That deficit must be growing bigger by the hour."

"It's manageable and we will handle it."

"Your job isn't going under the knife, is it?"

"Of course not! I have an assistant and he'll go first."

"That's the guy who's also the computer system wonk, isn't he?"

She grunted. "A small part of his job. Someone else can do that."

"The system technician is only a minor duty in a school district?"

Again she slammed the brush down. "I'm running short of time and I have no desire to pursue this discussion any further! You can fix whatever you want for dinner or go out if you wish."

Thanks for the choices. A few minutes later the garage door closed and she was down the street. Well, hell! He couldn't blame her for being upset. It wasn't much for all the years but a something far different than he ever thought possible overtook them. Ann had no experience working outside of education, and she had a distinct blind spot when it came to business and the short time frames often allowed for decision-making. She never understood what competition meant, nor the hard decisions that were often reached in the hot crucible of competition. In her field, issues first appeared on the horizon well before decisions needed to be made, and that left time to take a look at what was coming at them.

"Jesus Christ!" he muttered to the silent room. "Is it that hard to understand?" He sat in the kitchen and thought. There were other contractors, his former competitors, and with all the construction in the Twin Cities it shouldn't be too difficult to hook up with one of them. Pick up where he left off. Maybe not quite where he left off, but close.

He'd start in on that soon enough. Right now he had to deal with disposing of the company equipment and the inventory, an unpleasant task left behind by the brothers. He would soon need to advertise a going out of business sale. By then Albert and John would be roaming the golf courses in Florida while he stayed here trying to figure out what in hell to do with it all.

Carter Newman was an accomplished entrepreneur, having bought and sold many businesses, and always counted his profits afterward. He knew what could happen and wasn't surprised when Ann called on her cell phone as she drove to his house in following the short board meeting. "I just can't believe he'd settle for that: sixty-five thousand! There had to be more potential than that."

Carter sat on his sofa, the fireplace aglow, the soft heat of burning logs blown into the room from the heatilator, candles burning softly. "I've seen too many businesses sold for less than they were worth. It's all in the circumstances. But that's history now. I have your favorite Chardonnay chilled and ready." He glanced to the tall bottle sticking out of the bucket of crushed ice.

Ann smiled at the thought. "I need it, Carter. I also need to talk with you. It's…it's important. I don't know how much more of this I am willing to accept. I have a fear he is about to backslide…and I don't want to go there with him."

Carter Newman flinched at these words. She had vented about that the last time she was with him. What was it she really wanted? He knew she craved a house in Bellwood, that such a move was seen as important for her career. Still, he was puzzled. She talked about her relationship with Vince, then later she spoke of vacancies for superintendents or curriculum directors in distant cities. Puzzling. Carter knew Vince had few options, given the partnership structure. That was the flaw: allowing himself to be a minority owner and the control passing to the brothers. In all the ventures Carter Newman ever owned he operated with one cardinal rule: be the sole owner, or if that is not possible, then hold a majority of the stock. Partners are fine as long as you have the majority vote. Keep the control in the hands of the one you trust the most.

That's how he had been with Ann, too. Keep control; always know where it's going. His number one rule. He'd hear much more when she arrived in a few minutes. His own marriage had been a bitter-sweet experience but any doubts he held ended when the big C claimed his wife. Though he missed her in many ways, he was enjoying life as it came to him now, and he valued what Ann brought to him over the past several months. She was bright, articulate, even if a bit eccentric and intense. For a minute he stared into the flickering fire, then saw the two headlights turn into his driveway.

Chapter Seven

Peter Hoffler sat at the table between Manuel Cardenas and Raul Montero and looked at the group that now numbered close to two hundred. In the audience he saw Rolando Torres glowering in the far corner, arms folded across his chest. Peter wondered, if by some natal accident, he'd been born pissed off. For all his belligerence and boisterousness, he questioned whether the man really cared if the community was plowed into the dirt.

A few more people entered the room, then he saw her—the slender, blond woman who bowled over Torres during the last session. Peter watched her as she took a seat across the room from Torres, in the fashion of boxers and wrestlers in opposite corners. A shadow seemed to cross Torres's face as he eyed her for a moment.

This wasn't going to be easy, but they had to know that his time here was coming to an end, and despite the lofty words of Pollard and Whitman, he had no wish to cast his employer in a bad light. He took a deep breath. "I have come here tonight to tell you that I will be ending my work in the freeway issue. I have worked with all of you on this for more than a year, but I will be leaving my position with Advocate Services in another week." He expected the reaction: subdued, the downward cast of their eyes, the tightened lips and a few sighs from somewhere in the silent room.

For fourteen months he had been their spokesman and leader in fending off the threat posed to the small village by the plan drafted in that big city up the road. "This was not an easy decision, but my employer has decided to, ah, change the way they do business and I could no longer serve you as I have for several years. While I will be ending my service as your attorney, I still hope we can continue the many friendships we have formed in the time spent together." He smiled thinly. "Please be assured that you will have the legal help you will need, for Raul Montero has agreed to stay on here. As you know, he is not an employee of Advocate Services and can therefor work with you at his choice. A choice I no longer have."

He didn't tell them about the letter from the national board asking, in their convoluted style, for his resignation. "So, it is now time for me to move on to another part of my career in law. I want to thank you for the memories and for your willingness to let me serve you on this and on many other important matters. You people deserve the very best and I wish no less for you as—"

"So this board you work for can drop the matter, just like that?" Torres demanded as he quickly rose to his feet, a challenging glare in his dark eyes. "Right in the middle of the whole issue?"

Peter nodded grimly. "Yes, Mr. Torres, they can do exactly that."

"This is absolutely insane! This outfit you work for, isn't it set up to provide legal services to people just like these? If so, how can they merely drop the matter and walk away from it?"

"Advocate Services is a private-non-profit organization controlled by its own board of directors. It receives its revenue from a wide variety of private sources. It's not a unit of government controlled by politicians."

"But you can do nothing to change this?"

"I am only one of about two hundred attorneys on staff nation-wide. My opinion was neither requested nor given. The board answers to the parties and organizations that contribute money. If they want to head off in another direction, and their contributors are okay with that, well, that's their choice."

Torres glared at Peter for a second. "So that means we're down to using Montero?" he snapped.

"You're not down to anybody. Mr. Montero is an experienced attorney and knowledgeable about the issue. He can represent your interests."

Torres shook his head. "Hah! He's a technician, that's what he is!"

Peter started a response but Montero held up a hand, then rose slowly. "Try to see it this way, Mr.Torres: I will soon be the only attorney you have in your corner. If you're not happy with that, then find someone else equally familiar with the issues and willing to do this for nothing. If you can do that, then I will leave. Is that what you want?"

"We need a leader!" he snorted.

"In another week I will be the only leader you have, unless you'd like to step up and direct this effort. Would you like to do that, Mr. Torres?"

"Oh, for God's sake," Peter whispered, "don't encourage him!" Torres was recently released after a week in jail for his role in the fracas at the Bellwood Hills gate.

"Maybe I will!" he snapped. "If that's what we need then—"

"Then go right ahead and take the lead!" Every head in the room jerked toward her as she rose quickly, then slowly swaggered toward Torres, her chin up, shoulders squared, staring him in the eyes. She pointed to the table where Peter, Montero and Cardenas sat and her voice suddenly dropped to that low, slashing quality she used on him before. "Go on!" she snapped, pointing to the front table. "Walk up there and be the leader you seem to think you are. Go ahead! Mr. Montero just extended you the invitation. Don't you want to be the savior of Nuevo Del Rio, Mr. Torres?"

Torres glared at her and she approached. "Mother of Mary!" Cardenas whispered to Peter. "She's going to beat him up again!"

"You don't live here," Torres answered, his own voice shifting between hard and soft. "What do you have to do with this? What do you know about this?"

"Mr. Torres, don't you live about two miles west of here? That's beyond the village limits, isn't it?"

"Yes, but—"

"Well, I live even closer than that." She pointed toward the east. "Over there, about a mile away, in that fancy new development."

"Bellwood?" Montero whispered. "What is her interest in all of this?"

Peter shrugged. "I don't know, but she's sure fired up."

"You live in Bellwood?" Torres asked.

"That's not the point." she snapped as she turned from him, walked to the table and stood behind Peter and Montero, placing one hand on each of their shoulders. It caught Peter by surprise. A sharp tingling shot through him. He hoped his face didn't betray what he felt.

"Raul Montero is Peter's successor, whether you like it or not. He has been to all the meetings at the Metropolitan Council, the Minneapolis City Council and the Hennepin County Commissioners. He has followed this from the very beginning. I haven't seen you at any of the meetings, Mr. Torres. Raul was there. And he will have help, because tonight I am making myself available to this community. We face great opposition, and while I'm white, and female to boot, I know the opposition very well."

"How would you, a white girl, from that enclave open only to the white and rich, know what we're up against?"

"Because I know the opposition."

Torres snorted. "The opposition? And how would you know who that is?"

"Because our opposition comes mainly from Dave Behlen."

"So you know this man?"

"Indeed I do."

"And how would you know this man?"

"He is my father."

A hush descended as everyone stared at this young woman who came from that exclusive development and had already challenged Torres once before. Eyes went wide and murmurs rolled and coursed their way around the room. Cardenas wiggled his finger and Peter leaned over toward him. "Maybe we should invite her tonight. You think so?" Peter nodded so. It had been a rather exclusive club: Peter, cardenas and occasionally Montero. But tonight, Cardenas was feeling the need to open up the membership a bit more. "We should listen to her, don't you think?" Cardenas whispered. Peter nodded quite definitely. "Maybe she'd drink a glass of wine?"

"Oh, yes," Peter nodded. "She might even want a cigar."

Cardenas thought for a moment. "Really? You think I should have an extra one on hand?"

"I sure would."

Melissa looked at the others. She still kept her hands where they were and Peter's pulse was racing. "My father is a successful businessman. He owns a consulting firm in downtown Minneapolis. About a year ago, we moved into a large, very expensive home in Bellwood Hills. I don't see the world the way he does, so I'm a thorn in his side. My father is leading the opposition to the light rail project. He formed a group that supports widening Interstate 35 and eliminating this village. They have raised money which they'll use to get what they want, no matter how this effects you.

"My father thinks that since you're all Hispanic you pay no taxes and that you're all getting some kind of payments from the government. He also believes that he, and others of his kind, pay all the taxes and therefor, they should have whatever they want, even if that means you give up your homes, your jobs with Mr. Dahlenberg, and your entire community. There are many others living close to the freeway in south Minneapolis who also would be forced out of their homes. He simply doesn't care about anyone who is different from him and his upper middle class business associates. He sees all of you, together with thousands who live in the poorer sections of Minneapolis, as very different. This is what we are up against. I will work with Raul and the others in your struggle. Thank you." She smiled to them as she returned to her seat.

A half hour later they sat around the same table as was their custom. The three men lit cigars, Cardenas eyeing Melissa. She took the wine but passed on the cigars. The old man looked at Peter who was idly staring at the glass. "You have done very well for us, Peter. We all thank you."

Peter sighed. "I regret having to do this. We are coming up to a major fork in the road with this issue."

"Yes," he said, "but you must do what you must do. That is the way of things. It is what my people have always believed. It will be as it will be, Peter. There is someone stronger than us who decides these things."

Peter puffed thoughtfully, then took a deep swallow of wine "Yes, Manuel, we can't fight the big guy up there, but there is one down here on Earth whom we must fight. What can you tell us about your father's plan, Melissa?"

“I don’t know his strategy, but I have overheard him on the phone, one of those few nights when he’s home before 10pm. He and a few others are getting signatures for a petition supporting their position, which they plan to bring to the city council. They hired an attorney but I don’t think he will let the finer points of law stand in his way.”

“In other words,” Peter said, “he’s ruthless. Why does he feel so strongly about this matter?”

“His attitude is fairly typical of a few of those in his class. To him, all forms of public transportation carry a stigma. Using a common conveyance says you’re too poor to have your own auto. It tells everybody that you’re in the lower half and inadequate. To him, an expensive auto says you’re independent, upscale, and you have the means to support a car. If you have money for that, then you also pay taxes and are thereby a worthy person. Poorer folks should step out of your way.”

Raul grunted. “Primitive.”

Melissa was seated beside Peter and she laid a hand on his arm. The rhythm of his breathing was broken again. “He does have a couple weaknesses. First, he is not too discreet about what he says or to whom it is said. Second, though he is well financed, he is not politically connected. He despises government at every level, though he won’t hesitate to use it for his own purposes. He doesn’t understand how it works and he has no patience with its deliberate pace. He feels it should work for him and others like him, with great efficiency, but for no one else. I hope you can use this in your dealings with him.”

They talked for a while longer, a second round of wine was served, then soon after Melissa and Raul left. A sudden, strange sense of disappointment came over Peter. Cardenas filled his and Peter's glass a third time. "Peter, tell me what you think of her."

Peter paused for a moment, sending up another puff of cigar smoke to the ceiling. "My first impression was that of an unguided missile carrying a very big warhead. But she seems intelligent, articulate and focused. God knows she's outspoken, and I gather she's very energetic. We could use that."

"Peter, I think maybe she likes you," Cardenas laughed, imitating Melissa placing her hand on Peter's shoulder.

Peter's face flushed. "Oh no, no; that's just, ah, her way of doing things."

Cardenas thought for a moment. "Well, I think we should keep her. She can be our connection with Bellwood. Not to change the subject, but tell me, where do you live? I know you live in St. Paul, but where?"

"On Virginia Street. A little over a mile west of downtown."

"It would be in an older house, yes?"

Peter looked a bit surprised. "Yes, actually, how did you know?"

Cardenas smiled and laughed in his low, husky way. "You don't belong in some new, fancy house, like our girl told us about. A big, old house with lots of rooms, yes?"

"Yes, it's big, three-bedrooms, in the Carriage Hill area, just off Summit Avenue. Lots of old mansions; many have been divided up into apartments. A very mixed area racially, and otherwise. I can walk the streets and see Blacks, Latinos, Orientals, many from the African nations. I like to watch them interact and hear them talk."

"I hear your wife will finish her school soon."

Peter nodded. "Yes," he said softly as he took a swallow of wine and puffed slowly. "It was a very hard time for her but she made it." He didn't say she finished in the bottom quartile of her class. "Manuel, that is part of the reason I must turn things over to Raul. There are family issues that I need to deal with."

Cardenas nodded quietly. "Yes, we must take care of our families first. That is our way, too."

"Thank you, Senor Cardenas. Now she has to deal with the bar exam."

"What is that?"

"A test all law school graduates must pass in order to become licensed to practice law."

"She is worried?"

"Oh, yes."

Cardenas sighed and shook his head. "I don't understand your ways." The "your" referring to the white culture. "You work so hard and you worry so much, to get through your law school. Pass all those tests you take. When you get done with all of that you have to take another big test? Isn't it okay that the school gives you the diploma that says 'Now you can practice law.'? Agh! The white man, he makes too many things to worry about. It's no wonder you all get gray hair and then go bald. You'll be that way some day, too. Ah, well, I was raised in the old ways. So much less to worry about, just money, food and work. Now I am sixty-eight and still I don't know very much about you white people. I never will. You are so hard to figure out. Anyway, you tell your wife she must sue only the bad people. People like us should be left alone. That is best."

Peter nodded again. "Yes, Manuel, that is best." The glasses weren't large but this was his third fill and he had twenty-some miles mile to drive with a good buzz already setting in. "I will tell her, but she knows that already. Manuel, my time as your lawyer has ended, so now you must tell me. What is the story of this table?"

Cardenas let out a throaty, rolling laugh. "Peter, if I tell you now you might not come back. No, I think it is best I tell you later. When we are together and have our wine and smoke another cigar, then I will tell you." He emptied the bottle in their glasses. I have a twenty-two mile drive, Peter thought as Cardenas drained the bottle. He has a hundred foot walk.

But Peter merely smiled and looked at him, at the deep wrinkles beneath his eyes, the skin leathered by a lifetime laboring in the fields. His ways are the old ways, his values are those of another generation. He left behind the grinding poverty and oppression of Mexico and came to a nation that still seems incredibly complex to him.

In their earlier sessions Cardenas questioned him about many things; about the violence that seemed to be spreading; the naked vulgarity in what passed for entertainment; the confusion and divisiveness that permeates public policy and the shrillness that characterizes public debate. He saw the old man's anger when lawyers popped out of the woodwork to defend the perpetrator of the latest outrage, then grab the attention of the media. He was a man of no formal education but a shrewd observer with a sharp sense of justice. He deeply despised those whom he saw working to blur the lines between right and wrong, then collected fees for doing it. More than once Peter saw him throw a newspaper across the room in rage.

"Manuel, I must be on my way. It is late and there are many miles to drive and many patrol cars to avoid. Raul will do well, and perhaps I can help him. I will return, for you have promised to tell me about this table."

Cardenas stood in the doorway of the community center and watched the tail lights as they turned the corner and headed toward the freeway. For a moment, he scanned the empty street, from the looming, brooding bulk of the Dahlenberg building at the north end to the Head Start school at the south end of the street. Yes, it was a lot. For my people who lived here it was a lot. Our homes, built by our own hands, from the filthy, drafty chicken coops into livable homes, businesses and service centers.

He looked to his left, past the Dahlenberg building, toward the glow of city lights that moved ever closer, rising higher in the sky, becoming brighter with each passing year. He stood there for a minute or more, as if transfixed, and then he shuddered. A terrible image: an enormous, towering machine came rumbling, plowing its way down the street, destroying everything in its path as buildings and homes were crushed beneath its mighty steel wheels, people fleeing, screaming in terror. He shook his head, trembled, then went back inside, switched off the lights, locked the door and walked down the street, a little unsteadily, to the small home built with his own hands.

Chapter Eight

They often arranged their schedules to meet at Kelly's. For Dave Behlen it was ideal: large enough for them to blend in, small enough to retain the intimate atmosphere he preferred. The working day was ending, the big tap room was filling with its regular customers, the business and professional types, and the rising hum of mixed conversations filled the room.

He looked at her across the small table situated in a dark corner. "Lynn, I'm convinced the majority of business people see this issue for what it is: the rail project will be the biggest financial boondoggle his city has ever seen, or ever will see. I'm just amazed that any of the city council members would be so dense as to even think of backing this, but that's government for you. They've never been known for foresight or intelligent thought. I hope you can see fit to sign this along with many of our colleagues."

He handed her the petition, an eight page document beginning with all the usual Whereas, Whereas, Whereas..., Therefor Let it be Known That...Lynn Alveson studied the document while he studied her with greater intent. She was tall, slender with long honey brown hair. She owned a data processing firm down the hall from his office. Lynn was divorced several years ago, and it seemed to him she preferred keeping it that way. That was fine with him. His plans for her were not long-range. They had been seeing each other off and on for two years, having met at a building tenant meeting. After that they kept finding reasons to do more business together.

She glanced at the articles for a minute, then looked back at him and smiled. “Dave, I’ve worked downtown for twelve years but I only recognize a few names. These are all downtown business people?” She had a vague suspicion that a few of these names might have been entered either in absentia or post mortem. She knew he valued ends far more than means.

Behlen shrugged. “Sure, they’re guys I’ve known for a while,” he answered vaguely.

Lynn nodded, looking down the list of names. “Thurgood Miller? He owned that copying service down the street, didn’t he?”

“Yes. We’ve used his people for a lot of our bulk copying. A good man.”

“Was a good man. He died two years ago. How many others here have gone on to the next life?”

He looked at her for a moment, worshipping those dark brown eyes, then shrugged. “All right, the list’s maybe a year old, but we’ve got to come together and put a stop to this insanity.”

“Right, the living and the dead as well.”

“Lynn, there are only a few fuzzy-brained radicals like that…what’s his name…Hoff…Hoffman character and a bunch of his liberal buddies backing that rail scheme. Well, him, that black guy on the council and some minister from a run-down church in Minneapolis. That’s not much opposition and I’m sure we can show strong support for our position just by pure logic and common sense.”

"What do your staff think about the issue?"

"Mine?" He shrugged again. "I'm sure they'll stand behind it. They all signed the petition."

"I'm sure they did. Every one of them."

"Sure. Why wouldn't they?"

She laughed lightly, as she did during his tirades, flashing her broad smile and oh, God, so appealing to Behlen. Just like the first time he met her. "Were they given a choice? Your consulting staff probably lean toward the wider freeway, but do you think your support staff might feel differently about it?"

He stared at her for a moment. "I don't know why they would. No, I'm sure they feel the same way. why wouldn't they? That other plan is—"

"How do they get to work? Do they all drive their own cars?"

He shrugged. "I don't know, but they all signed it—"

"Sure they did. Who pays their salary?" She looked at him, smiling again, and when she did that there was no background, no tap room full of customers, no other sound than her voice. The borders of his world shrunk down, leaving only her face, and that same strangely attractive look she wore in his company. Then a tiny shadow seemed to flow over the soft lines of her face, and its angled planes seemed to change in some subtle way. "I have twenty-one support staff who do data entry. Not one of them drives their own car into downtown."

"Really? They all use the bus?"

"A few car pool; the rest depend on the bus system."

"I wasn't aware of that."

"I could double their wages and they still couldn't afford the monthly parking rates. Most of them are second wage earners and their spouses work in factories, the trades, or in other industries around here. If that's true for my workers, then it's just as true for others. How many thousand workers would that be, Dave? They can't afford to drive, which is, as you like to say, 'the bottom line.'"

He pondered that for a moment, then sat upright. "Okay, we widen the freeways, add a few buses and the problem's solved," he declared, raising his hands. "It's as simple as that!"

"Look at it this way: one commuter train can carry as many passengers as four buses. The MTC can be used as a feeder, bringing people to the rail stations where they board for the longer trips into or out of the city. Most of my workers live either in the inner city or in the first ring of suburbs. Every time we have a bad storm they're either late or don't get to work at all because of road conditions. Light rail operates in just about any weather conditions. I want my people to be here, on time. Don't you? It makes sense to have at least one form of transportation that doesn't all but shut down every time the weather turns ugly. Multiply it all out: workers stalled on ice-bound roads aren't productive."

"Are you going to sign this petition?"

She laughed softly. "Along with the dearly departed? No. So what do you think about that?"

She could say anything and he'd just have to smile. "Lynn, it's such an extremely expensive proposition and whatever the cost, it won't make a dent on the traffic problem."

"Workers caught in gridlocked traffic are also expensive. It may cost three quarters of a billion to build this rail line, including demolition and condemnation, but additional lanes will cost equally as much. Consider this: both cost money to maintain, but a rail line brings in dollars from user fares. You don't have a return from any freeway unless you build toll booths. Are you ready to do that? I don't know how long rail tracks last, I'd think at least thirty years, but freeways require new surfacing every five or six years, and as traffic increases that time span shortens. From the experience of my own workers, I can't support the cost of more highway construction, which only adds more drivers till the problem rises to another critical level. The gains of the lanes are gut by the glut…I just thought of that now."

Behlen sat back and smiled. "I'm impressed! We could use that talent to promote—"

"Sorry, poetic skills are not for sale. Nice try, though."

"Lynn, have you been listening to that city council member, ah, Harley, Tur…whatever? Okay," he said, stuffing the paper in his jacket pocket, "forget about the petition. Let's go somewhere else." Then he leaned toward her and his voice dropped. "I'm going to a conference in Denver in a couple weeks. Come along with me."

"Tell me, Dave, does your wife know about this? About us?"

"I've always discouraged her from calling the office. She knows I do a lot of client contact away from there, anyway. She can leave a message."

"And you'll call her back later. Whenever."

"Cheryl has a business at home, sort of. She really doesn't work at developing it and that drives me crazy."

"Why?"

"She does desktop publishing and that's an exploding market she could penetrate if she would just develop a business plan and upgrade her technology. She doesn't do that. Instead, she just takes whatever comes her way, usually advertising circulars, then sends the rest of her time fluttering around the house or jabbering with the daughter. She doesn't seem to realize if she doesn't grab a part of that market someone else will take it away and bring it up to the next level."

"Maybe doing all of that isn't a priority for her."

"But why? Why would anyone not want to develop the huge potential that's out there? It's an emerging market waiting for someone to break into it big time. She's just nibbling around the edges. I've told her this but she just keeps doing what she's doing." He shook his head sadly and sighed. "She doesn't listen"

"Maybe she's trying to balance business and family. Most women I know strive for that balance if they have a family. Maybe she sees the need to spend time with Melissa. Do you?"

"Do I what?"

"Spend time with your daughter?"

His shoulders seemed to drop. "It's true my daughter and I occupy the same house. I mean, we live under the same shingles, but for all other purposes we're on separate planets. Every time I open my mouth around her she takes the opposite view, then we get into some crazy argument. I think she does this just to aggravate me. Now she's racking on me about this rail thing. Of course she's siding with that weirdo Hoffman, Hoff…God, I can't remember his name!"

"So you just avoid each other?"

"Oh, she never avoids me, In fact, she goes out of her way to find something to fight about."

"Why do you think she opposes you in this way?"

"I don't have a clue. Maybe that crazy lawyer friend of hers fills her head with bizarre ideas and she's falling for it all. She's twenty-two, managed somehow to get two to three years of college behind her with no major in mind. She hasn't a clue what she wants to do, so what can I do to change her?" Now his shoulders squared again, bright eyes beaming, his voice swinging up. "On the other hand, my son is finishing law school and will make a fine corporate lawyer."

"Which is what you want him to be, right?"

"As a matter of fact, yes, it is," he said, his voice filling with pride.

"And he always does what you want him to do?"

"Sure…I mean, he thinks like I do."

"Melissa's behavior might be her way of getting the attention she needs from you. She may not be as radical as she appears to be. Maybe this is her way of saying, 'Hey, Dad, I'm here. Listen to me.'"

"Then why doesn't she just say that?"

"Probably because it hasn't worked, so taking the opposing viewpoint gets you communicating with her. Arguments are better than silence. Associating with certain people and their causes gets your attention, even if it's in a negative way. Your way of dealing with that it to avoid her." She paused and looked at him, the big smile making its return, her softer lines again more evident. "I'm sorry, I'm not the one who should be telling you about those things. I don't have children of my own."

"How much time do you invest in your business?"

"About fifty hours a week. I want time for volunteer work with the charities and some private time for reading and travel."

"Fifty hours isn't that much any more. How do you keep your foothold in the market with anything less than seventy hours a week? Every other businessman I know puts in at least that much, usually more."

"I'll run my operation and let it grow to a certain level. When it's grown to where it begins to own me I'll sell and move on to something else. I want to control my life as well as my business." She flashed that wide smile that so captivated him. "Maybe you should try that approach."

He mulled that over in his mind for a moment, then quickly dismissed it. Lynn drained the last of her martini, then looked at Behlen. "Okay, Mr. seventy per week, let's leave here."

Behlen rose and they walked out of the tap room. "Any ideas where we should go?" He had an idea and was hoping it matched her own thoughts.

Kelly's Bar contained several other dark corners, one of which was positioned opposite the entrance where someone could sit unnoticed, but watch everyone coming or going. Partially hidden by a thick potted palm sat a tall, slender man, bald except for a rim of chestnut hair, who watched the two as they left. He scribbled a quick note, rose and discreetly followed them out the door and down the sidewalk, merging into the crowd, forty or fifty feet behind them. After two blocks he stepped inside a bus kiosk and watched through the Plexiglas as they entered a building which, except for the shops on the ground floor, was a well-known private residence.

Chapter Nine

It was ten minutes past the scheduled time of the hearing and still the employee, the one who filed the appeal, was nowhere in sight. At the table sat the employer with an expression that went from frustration two minutes after the time of the hearing to one of hopeful anticipation ten minutes later when it appeared his ex-worker would be a no-show. That meant the original decision on the unemployment insurance claim denying benefits to the worker would be upheld. It was worth the hassle to see the little asshole get stiffed, thought the employer.

This was a new experience for him, but Peter wasn't surprised. "Lots of folks get in a boil about something, then file an appeal," he told the man. "When the day comes they've forgotten all about it," Peter thanked him for coming and assured him the original decision would be upheld.

For the past ninety days he had been employed as appeals judge for the state unemployment insurance board. He had no further role to play in what was now called National Legal Consultants, the politically correct moniker of his former employer. Their new logo had impressive lettering in gold relief over a background of hunter green with gold bordering. How solid, conservative, all in keeping with the new wave of collaboration.

All in all, this wasn't bad work. The board issued him a car to use for those long drives to rural communities, but he disliked the overnight stays. He was city born and bred. "After a couple overnights you can't tell a porterhouse from a hamburger," he told Mary. These inconveniences aside, the benefits were good, far better than what Advocate Services provided. The hours were regular, which Mary appreciated, his salary was ten per cent above that of his previous life and he had another ten thousand before reaching the top of his salary range. Something told him he would never stay here long enough for that to happen. Appeal hearings are fine for now; they wouldn't be his meat and potatoes for the next twenty years.

Throughout his years with Advocate Services he heard complaints from clients about unemployment claims being denied when, as they told it, they had every right to the benefits. "I was the best worker they ever had!" he often heard when the person was fired. "I was doing everyone else's work for them."

Therein was the problem. "The next time you're hired, just do your own job, okay?" he would tell them. Then he'd advise them to file an appeal and while a few went in their favor, nine of every ten decisions were affirmed.

At his orientation he was told the decision turns on what was referred to as the moving party, that is, the burden of proof rested with whomever took the final action ending the employment relationship—employer or employee. On the surface, it seemed fairly straightforward. Which party ended the lash-up? But often the decision turned on those messy "I quit- you're fired" issues where the working relationship had already gone in the tank and both parties seemed to play the role. These were the cases that brought the most appeals. The claim adjudicators needed to make their decision and given the short time constraints, it was usually done with conflicting and often incomplete evidence. The issues Peter struggled with the most were where the employer fired the employee, complaining vaguely about their behavior. "He just had a bad attitude."

"How was this attitude expressed?" Peter would ask. Their answers were varied and vague. "Were tardiness or absenteeism the problems?" Well, yes, sometimes. "Was there a problem with insubordination?" Occasionally, but not all that often. "Was there an issue with theft or damage to property?" Less often. "You did hire this employee?" he would ask. Well, yes, they did. "Can you tell me what is the issue with this employee?" Peter would finally ask when all other probing attempts failed.

What he learned in three months was that firings were often subjective decisions, based on gut feelings. "He just didn't fit in, somehow." A bad cultural fit. The new employee didn't fish or hunt in a workplace where this was the customary week-end activity and the subject of the Monday morning chatter. And every other morning, noon and afternoon. A half dozen women worked together for fifteen years and would freeze out every newcomer, first from the office social circle, then eventually from the communication pattern. Not one could say exactly why this happened; She just...wasn't part of the office sorority.

A man was fired for drinking on the job. When Peter first questioned him he denied doing so, but later in the hearing he admitted that yes, he did imbibe just a bit. "But I was their best worker, drunk or sober! Why, just ask any of my past employers."

"How many employers would that be? One? Two?"

"Nnnnooo…six, I think…No…seven. I don't remember exactly."

There was this bizarre case where the employer fired an assembly line worker the first day because, as he put it, the worker "just couldn't work on the line without all kinds of adjustments to the bench." The worker came to the hearing in a wheelchair.

"Was he in the wheelchair when you hired him?" Peter asked.

"Yeah, sure," said the employer. "But hell, I can't go around raising up his own work bench. What would all the others think about that?"

"Have you made any sort of accommodations to this employee?"

"God, no! I'm not about to get everybody all stirred up, makin' 'em think I'm being partial."

"If he could reach the work station, would he be otherwise qualified?"

The man shrugged. "I guess so."

"Did you ever hear of the ADA, Americans With Disabilities Act?" Peter asked.

"Yeah, somewhere, but so what?"

Peter thought for a moment, turned off the recorder, then asked politely if the employee would mind leaving the room for a couple minutes. Peter turned to the employer. "Off the record, how many employees do you have?"

"Twenty-eight," said the man.

"Then you'd better acquaint yourself with this law because you're covered under it, so let's make a little arrangement between us. You bring this man back and you raise his work station so the wheelchair fits beneath it. Then you keep that man employed, because if you don't, I'll see that a certain lawyer friend of mine hauls you into court and sues you for so much in punitive damages it will make this unemployment claim look like pennies. And I don't care what your other workers think! If they're not smart enough to see why you're doing this I don't have much hope for them."

The man stared at Peter, his eyes gone wide, mouth dropping. "You can't be serious!"

"Want to try me?"

A minute later the employee wheeled himself back into the room. "Mr. Wilson," Peter said to him, "your employer has thought the matter through and has decided he wants you back on the job. Can you arrange to be there Monday morning?" Yes, he nodded. "Good, your employer has already determined what accommodations are necessary and these will made available to you at that time."

There was one hearing, thank God the only one, when he expected the employer to pull out a gun and shoot someone, or else go to pieces, right in front of everyone. He owned a small store and hired a twenty year-old boy to run it for him when he was gone, which was quite often. They didn't do a great business so there were a lot of down times. During one of those the owner returned after several hours absence, saw no one at the counter and went back to the stockroom. There they were, oh Lord, the boy atop the man's wife, pumping, working their way up to that joyous ecstasy, unaware of the intrusion. The man told the story in a rising, breaking voice, all the while thumping the table, harder and harder as his rage rose ever more in the telling. "They were…they were…on that narrow counter!" he hollered, his face turning beet red, one eye twitching furiously, his voice trembling while his wife sat stone-faced beside him.

'You mean, they were…?" Peter was searching for the right words. This was all being recorded.

"Yes!" he shouted. "They were…" he was gesticulating wildly, hands thrashing through the air, groping desperately for the words. "They were…you know!" Then he crashed into his chair and buried his face in his hands, shoulders heaving like waves, sobs pouring from him. Then he suddenly wiped his eyes and glanced at his watch. Peter didn't know if he should call 911, end the hearing, or whatever.

The man's wife sighed heavily and looked at Peter. "He has an appointment with a psychiatrist in ten minutes," she said. "I'm sorry." Then her own voice broke into a keening wail and the tears tumbled down her flushed face. "But at least the boy paid some attention to me!" Now he had two people weeping at the table, with the recorder catching every sound.

"Are there any other questions?" No, said the young man. He asked the same of the distraught employer and as best Peter could discern, between the man's heaving sobs, his response was no.

Neither did the man's wife, who glanced mournfully at the young man. Peter nodded, then ended the hearing. He'd have to deny payment on this one.

An hour later Peter stepped through the door of his home and heard muffled sobs coming from their bedroom. For a moment he was seized by panic. Was she ill? Then he saw it: an opened envelope on a small table. The letter was from the State of Minnesota Office of the Law Examiner. Panic gave way to a monstrous ball of disappointment that settled hard in his stomach. A glance at the text confirmed four years of dreaded anticipation.

Should he go in there or wait for her to come out? Mary's emotional behavior was complex, oblique and highly subjective. It was like grappling with a fleeting phantom in a dark room. He opened the door to Emmy's room and looked in. She lay in her small bed, so peaceful, so untroubled and oblivious to her mother's anguish, and to the world that swirled in mad fashion around her. He leaned down and stroked her hair gently, then turned and left the room.

He sat for a few moments on the living room couch, then walked to her door and opened it slightly. Mary lay face down on the bed, her long brown hair splayed out on the pillow. He sat beside her and gently rubbed her shoulder, his voice soft and low. He knew the fear and disappointment. He had classmates in law school who also struggled, passing the bar exam only on their third or fourth try, paying the full fee each time. Retaking the exam meant weeks of study in areas he knew she hated: business and tax law. At this point in her life, with a small child to care for, studying law would be light years away from her concerns. He groped for the right words, always a challenge for him in times like this. "What you're feeling is okay, really. I'll be here," he said softly. "If you want anything just let me know. I'll take care of Emmy."

She slowly rolled over and he saw her flushed face and looked at eyes that hadn't been that swollen and reddened since the death of her mother three years ago. He brushed back the tussled hair."

"Please go away," she said, a timbre of will rising through the soft, broken voice. Then she turned away from him again and buried her face in the pillow.

Peter stood where he was for several moments, then with a tiny sigh, walked out of the room and closed the door.

Night descended on the village of Nuevo Del Rio. Melissa and Raul walked slowly along the main street now deserted but for a few customers coming and going from the small cantina a block away from which came small bursts of laughter mixed with the Mexican music. "I can't understand how Peter could be so involved in this," Melissa said, "then one day turn and walk away from it all."

Raul was quiet for a moment. "All things change, Melissa. Advocate Services was the basis for his involvement, even though he went well beyond what was required. He spent a lot of his own time here. Then one day their executive board gets swept up by another trend. It happens all the time. I don't know what he has told you but he hinted something about problems with his wife, but he didn't elaborate. We all must make our own decisions. That's the way of things and we must not hold that against him."

"And your decision was to stay here."

"Yes...It has passed now to me. I will do what I can, but—"

"But you can't do it alone, and not just with my help, either. Raul, there are many people living in south Minneapolis who will have their homes destroyed by this. We need to partner with them."

"Who are they? There are so many organizations located there, all with a different focus. I've only dealt with a few of them."

"Yes, and they all deal with one aspect or another of inner city life. It's only a matter of teaming up with the right people. Then we have more voices."

"More voices but no more money. We're outgunned politically and financially, Melissa. This village is not the row of chicken shacks it once was, but it's far from being well off. The governor favors the rail project but the Legislature is split and there are powerful voices there who want wider freeways. I don't think they'd let this village stand in their way."

Melissa thought for several moments. "Raul, we're not outgunned." They turned down Calle Sta. Maria to a small church facing a pond formed by the stream flowing through the village. Melissa often came here when she wanted to think and to be alone. Tonight she wanted to be there with Raul.

"Melissa, it's not just a wider freeway, is it?"

"On the surface, it's more lanes for the Interstate, which they definitely want. But there's another objective, just as important to them. They want this village gone, eliminated. Totally torn down and taken off the map. In their straitjacket thinking the village is a stigma, a burr on their expensive saddle. They want no trace of a different culture, especially a non-white culture, so near their insulated haven."

"So we need to get with our neighbors to the north."

"Money can work in both directions, Raul."

"Come again?"

"We may have little of it here, but do you know how many millions have been spent on renovating homes in the Phillips Neighborhood? The same homes my father and his cohorts are so eager to demolish? Some of that investment came from the private sector; it isn't all public money. Banks have invested heavily in that neighborhood and they won't just sit back and watch those houses be torn down.

"We need an ally, Raul. Someone from the inner city who has connections into the power structure. You know what I mean: someone wearing wing tip shoes and a dark suit. A real member of the establishment who can be our mouthpiece. I don't have a clue who that might be, but we'd better look around up there and start working at it."

"Melissa, I'm mostly a researcher of statutes and rules, one who organizes material for others more gifted in speaking to our people's needs. That's what Peter did so well; he got them behind him. The people here aren't skilled at grabbing media attention. They are a quiet lot, and they make their own way."

"Maybe I can do that for you. With you behind me we can do this, Raul. We can find the people we will need in the Phillips area. This little village has crawled out of poverty and the chicken shacks, but today we need something else, Raul. We need an amplifier. Someone from within."

Raul thought for a moment and nodded. "You can find someone like that?"

"I have certain ways." Raul sensed an iron tone to these words.

"I want to hear about these ways."

"I'll tell you when the time comes."

They came to a small opening and sat on a bench, the bare branches of the trees silhouetted against the almond moonlight filtering down upon them. The only sounds were the gentle wind slipping through the trees, water lapping on the shore and the faint hum of traffic on the freeway. She curled her legs beneath her and leaned against him, her head on his shoulder, a smile crossing her face. Minutes passed in silence. The warmth of his hand on her arm, the firmness of his shoulder negating the need for words.

"Some day your father will throw you out, you know." he finally said.

She smiled, then reached and took his hand in hers. "Yes. Fairly soon, I think."

"Where will you go?"

She closed her eyes, his warmth flowing into her. "There is a place I will go. I know where that is, and what I must do. My heretofore dissipated life has turned a corner, giving me a purpose. If

I succeed, then there will be other purposes to live for, other hills to climb. If I fail, it won't be for a lack of faith, or in the people I trust."

Chapter Ten

Forrest Turley sat in the small lobby, rubbing his hands as he awaited his appointment. He chose this clinic not only because they specialized in the kind of problems he was struggling with; it was also located in a northwestern suburb of Minneapolis, far from his council ward. No familiar faces here. How many times had he been here, now? Was it seven? Eight?

His insurance policy had a fifty per cent pay plus a cap on mental health services, and two more visits would put him at the limit. The rest would be out-of-pocket if he wished to continue. The horrifying dreams and the stigma that came with this left him little choice. The other problem was finding time; city council work demanded a minimum of sixty hours a week, given council meetings, committee work and neighborhood gatherings.

He asked the staff at the front desk to call for him using another name. The name might be recognized by someone keeping up with Minneapolis politics. If that happened, things back in his ward could turn ugly. His problem defied easy explanation, especially one he could put across in a few simple sentences. He tried many times, working out some kind of spin to explain in a few words. But no matter how he phrased it or messaged the wording, he could never condense it down to something easily understood.

Well, how would anyone else understand it when he had so little grasp of the problem himself? The age of the thirty minute television sitcom, the fifteen second sound byte and most of what passed for mass entertainment conditioned viewers to expect easily understandable concepts, problems and quick solutions. Present the problem briefly, bring in the quick solution, then on to something else. But first a message from our sponsors.

He had faith in his people, faith in the way the inner city mind worked. But it was also a very mixed group, becoming ever more so, and they weren't all supporting him on the council.

Different disorders carry different stigmas. Post traumatic and situational stress syndromes were temporary in nature and weren't seen by the public as terribly embarrassing.

The schizophrenic problems, like paranoia and other dissociative disorders, were sometimes perceived as scary, or just odd, depending on how this illness affected you. Many very successful and well-known people were hobbled by horrible memories that haunted them in private, or experienced regular withdrawals from the real world. But unless the illness took over your entire personality, it could be hidden and expressed only in private.

But the sexual afflictions had to be concealed. There was still that singular Puritanical streak in the American character; something left over from the Victorian era, that cast a pall over these disorders. It demanded you conceal anything that deviated from sexual orthodoxy. They often began as one expression, then mutated into something completely different.

In the first six or seven sessions he floundered and stumbled, trying to find the right words, struggling to get a grip on the phantom-like images that flashed across his mind. "Describe that figure again," suggested his psychologist, a black man about his own age.

Turley was quiet for many moments. He was only twelve when this happened and his mother had been dead for three years. "It keeps changing," he said. "Never the same. Every time I tell you this…it's different."

"Tell me again what you saw the last time"

"…It was maybe nine in the evening. It was in the fall so it was dark by then. This shape, it was a man, he was big…broad sloping shoulders…

"Who do you think that might be?"

Turley shook his head. "I don't know, he was a big man…like my father, but, another time…that wasn't, I mean, it couldn't have been him."

"Your father?"

"That other dark shape…always at night, in fog…it was a small man…walking away from me, down the street."

"Tell me what you saw the last time."

"He..I saw him on the dark street, always at night, very dark."

"Was the street where you lived very dark at night?"

"Yes, always pitch black at night. It was a long block…only one intersection was lighted…the other corner had no light, always dark at night…pitch black…Old neighborhood, big trees hanging over the street." They sat quietly for five minutes. "I don't know, why does this man, this figure, keep changing? Why is he big one time and the next time I see him he's small?"

"Could it be the same person, Forrest?"

"But then…why do I see it like that? Why is there always fog, which is actually fairly rare? It's like some night scene in a Sherlock Holmes movie."

"Do you think it might be there to confuse you?"

"What?"

"You saw images of two men, one large, the other smaller, both in foggy conditions. It's possible you only saw one person, but your mind doesn't want you to know who that is, so the image changes from one episode to the next."

Their time ended and he drove home obsessed with these nocturnal shapes lurking on that gloomy, foggy street. Again he racked his mind, trying to remember more about his father, one whom he barely knew. He was a truck driver and spent many nights on the road. After his mother died two aunts moved in to care for him while his father was gone. He couldn't even recall having a conversation with the man; only a few vague memories when the man was angry with him and he raised his voice. He was home briefly, most of that time spent with friends at a nearby tavern, then back on the road and out of his life again.

He would return for a visit with the therapist next week. After that, when the insurance cap kicked in, he'd have to pay the full amount if he wanted to continue.

A frantic week passed with the city council business and Forrest Turley was again in the lobby. "Mr. Clark?" the receptionist said to him. That was his prearranged name.

After their usual greetings and the how-did-the-week-go questions, his therapist briefly scanned his notes and looked at Turley. He never used his desk but preferred another room with comfortable armchairs and coffee table. He poured coffee for both and sat back. "Last week you were talking about what appeared to be two images of a man, one quite large, the other one a smaller person, always walking in heavy fog at night. Have you thought about that any more?"

Except for council matters, he had thought of nothing else. "Dr. West, it must seem strange that I have so few memories of my father. That everything about him seems shrouded in mist. Could that explain why fog is always in the dreams?"

"We see many people whose vague memories are associated with fog. Fog is a symbol for the unknown. Movies have used this for years to create the effect of the brooding unknown, the mysterious, as in the Sherlock Holmes stories. It's not surprising it would appear in your images when you consider that you had almost no significant relationship with him. He was a very distant figure in your life and fog could symbolize that distance. But we don't know at this point if that image is your father or someone else. What can you tell me about this?"

Turley thought for several moments, then shook his head. "It was always those two, I mean, those two images."

"Do you think they were the same person?"

"How could they be the same person when one was large, the other much smaller?"

"Where were they going, Forrest? You may be at the point of answering your own question."

"What do you mean?"

"Where were the two images going? You saw them on the street. What did you do?"

"...I...followed them, a safe distance behind. It was a dark night, no moon...Black as hell."

"Go on."

"You could hardly see the houses and the big trees. I was afraid the man would see me and I'd be in trouble, but I followed him anyway. It was an old neighborhood with big, thick trees on the boulevard...I was behind the man, sneaking from one tree to the next. He was walking toward the dark intersection, the one with no street light." A full minute passed in utter silence, the images slowly coalescing in Turley's mind. "Then he turned the corner...he kept on walking. I thought maybe he was just strolling around the block"

"Go on."

"Slinking from tree to tree. I thought sure he'd catch me and I'd be punished, but I had to stay with him...I had to know."

"Had to know what?"

"...What the man was doing. Where he was going. I wanted to know where he went because he did this many times...He'd leave the house, always after dark, and just disappear into the night. He must have done that for a long time…"

"Why do you say that?"

"…Because…" Then his voice went soft, nearly inaudible. "Because it had to be my father."

"Why, Forrest? Why did it have to be your father?"

Almost a full minute passed in silence. "That night, when I followed him…he turned the corner, like I said…I stayed behind the trees and shrubs." Forrest closed his eyes and sighed deeply, slowly. Dr. West heard a tiny quiver in the way Turley exhaled. "He went to this house, another half block down the street. I thought he was just visiting someone he knew…Someone he worked with…Maybe a women he was seeing…I had to know…"

"What happened?"

"I thought he'd go up to the front door and ring the bell, or just walk in…but he didn't…"

"What did he do?"

"…He…went to the side of the house. Then I couldn't see him…very dark, big trees overhanging the yard, lots of bushes and shrubs growing wild…Big houses close together…There were lights on in the house. I went through the neighbor's yard…then saw him standing beside the house…he was…" He trembled and sighed heavily again. "He was…looking inside. I was about twenty feet away from him but too short to see inside…I climbed up a tree so I could see…" Another minute passed in silence. "…It was a bedroom…A children's bedroom…" Suddenly Turley leaned forward and covered his face in his hands. "He…he was watching the children undress…!" Another two minutes passed, then another, finally he sat back slowly and let his breath out. "My father…was a peeping Tom, Dr. West…That man got his thrills watching naked children!"

"You saw the children in the room?"

"Yes!"

Dr. West sat silently. "How did you feel?"

"Oh God!" he mumbled softly. "He might not have been much of a father, but I never thought he'd do this. I thought maybe it was a lady friend, something like that…but…" Turley's eyes were wide open, "I never thought he was doing…that!"

"What happened then?"

"I was numb, just sick. I was so embarrassed that he would do this…What if the kids in school found out about him? I wanted to vomit, to cry! I started to climb down, slowly…I just wanted to get away from there as fast as I could…then the branch I was standing on broke and I fell to the ground."

"He saw you?"

Turley nodded. "He saw me on the ground. Then he looked back in the house. No one inside must have heard the noise. He lunged at me. I saw him grit his teeth in anger, then he covered my mouth with his huge hand and dragged me away from there, down the street. I didn't know what he was going to do, he was so angry, he had to be embarrassed…He dragged me behind a garage. I was so scared I didn't know what he said at first, I thought he'd beat the hell out of me for sure, he had done that before…For several seconds he didn't do anything; like he was thinking what to say to me. But then he shook me, looked me right in the face and said, 'Okay, you little bastard, now you know what I'm doing, eh?' I just nodded. I remember he had his big hand around my shoulder and I thought my arm was coming off. I was shaking so bad I started to sweat. He said he'd kill me if I told his sisters about this…Then he paused…he looked at me again, and I remember what he said…He said 'Just so you don't say nothin,' that was how he put it,…'I'm taking you with me.'"

"What happened then?"

"Then he took me back to the same house, below the window, and…and he lifted me up…I saw…the children…" Another two minutes of silence. "He dragged me out to the sidewalk, down the block, then he said 'Now you're in this with me and you can't say nothin' to Emily or Sarah.' They were his sisters…I still see that sick grin on his face…He made me a partner to the sick thing he was doing…God! Little children, running around the house getting ready for bed…undressing…that was what the bastard did for entertainment!"

"And you lived with that knowledge."

"I don't know what his sisters knew, if anything at all. They were very quiet. I must have had a shocked look on my face for several days but they never said a word. He was away from home a lot after that…even more than before. But when he was home I had to go along with him on a few more of those sick ventures…He told his sisters we were just going for a walk. You know, that good father-son stuff. I was so afraid we'd get caught by the police, and it would all be out in the open...But then I thought that would be the best thing. I thought maybe that would end it all, even if my friends knew the truth, horrible as that would be."

"That experience, how did it change your feelings toward him?"

"Before that I was just indifferent toward him. He was hardly ever there, and when he was at home he didn't talk with me anyway. I didn't hate him, I just..." He shrugged, "I just didn't care, one way or the other. That was before all of this. After that I hated him. I lived in that house and hated my own father for what he did to me...and for what he did to those children, and to many others, I'm sure...I lived with that humiliation, all the time terrified that some day it would get out in the open...for six more years. I graduated from high school June first and was in the Navy three weeks later.

"I spent my leave time with friends on the West Coast. I came home only twice, the last time to get the rest of my clothes and leave for good. He must have been out on the road that day...I never saw him again. I don't know if he's dead or alive...To be honest, Dr. West, it didn't matter...then or now."

"How are you feeling now?"

Turley grimaced and shook his head. "Washed out...I don't know how you're supposed to feel when you've just revealed something that has been knocking around in your head for years. I still hate him. Hate him for what he was...and for what he did to me...I will say one thing for him: he never once...touched me...you know...in the wrong places...I guess he got his thrills from watching little kids undress...Dr. West, isn't that a form of abuse? I mean, to use them in that way, even if they never knew he was out there?"

"What do you think?"

"He invaded their privacy! He did something they wouldn't want anyone to do. What would those poor kids have done if they'd seen him standing out there, looking at them? I mean, they wouldn't know what he was going to do! They'd think he was coming in the house to hurt them, or to take them away. Maybe to hurt their parents, too. God, how awful! I wanted to..." A minute of silence as Turley sat rigid, knuckles turning white, lips pressed into a thin line.

"What did you want to do, Forrest?"

"...I wanted to kill him...!" he shouted, his hands clenched in front of him, eyes wide and glowing in anger.

"Killing your father wasn't the only thing you wanted to do."

Turley looked at the man for a long moments. "What else...what else would I want to do?"

"You were only twelve, not much more than a child, but you were older than the children he watched. What was it you wanted to do?"

For another five minutes Forrest Turley was back by that garage in the alley, terrorized by the strength of the man's grip on his arms and shoulders as he stared up into those flashing, angry eyes. He thought of the small children, of the harm he feared his own father capable of rendering to them.

His perverted desires were satisfied for now by watching them, but would it always be like that? Would the day come when his twisted impulses became stronger, no longer satisfied just looking at them, and drove him to enter the house, to reach for another level of satisfaction? To do whatever placated those warped desires trapped in his mind, shattering the lives of happy, innocent children?

"What did I want to do…? I…I wanted to protect them, to save them from this evil man…Whatever he did, I could never kill him, even if I wanted to. I wanted to turn him in, to have him arrested. But I knew he'd deny everything, saying it was just a child's fantasy at work. There was no evidence. He had forced me into it, but who would believe me? I would have been branded a pervert…So I gave it up…"

"Gave up what?"

"…Trying to protect them…the children. I failed…I failed to save them from him." He sighed heavily. "A few months passed and he quit pressuring me to go with him. He was gone, but I didn't do what I should have done."

"What do you think you should have done, Forrest?"

"I should have protected them, those children…I should have turned him in to the police…no matter what happened to me. I think he was capable of doing things more horrible than what I saw. Maybe he actually did, I mean, after he left me and his sisters…I could have stopped it…but I didn't."

"You were only twelve, a child. He was a man. He held the power."

"But I failed to do what I should have done."

"Forrest, you compensated."

Turley stared at the man, a searching look on his face. “How…how did I…compensate?”

“What did you experience around small children.”

“…Yes…yes. That’s what has frightened me, I mean…what I feel…”

“What is it you really feel?”

“I want to…to touch them…Isn’t that…? You know.”

He shook his head. “Visualize it, Forrest. Close your eyes and see yourself in the presence of little children.”

Turley closed his eyes and sighed heavily, his forehead glistening. “…Yes, I see them…five, maybe six…Like that night at the house on the dark street…”

“Is that where you are, Forrest?”

“…Yes…that’s where we are…me and him.”

“Don’t try to think, Forrest. Just look and feel. What are you seeing and feeling?”

A full five minutes passed as Forest Turley sat motionless, his eyes closed. The wall clock ticked softly, the silence touched only by a passing truck on the street. “You are seeing and feeling, Forrest, but where it is you are feeling? What part of you is feeling?”

The room was silent for another three minutes. Then his right hand slowly reached up from the armrest, then the left hand, his fingers spread, hands trembling. Suddenly his right hand grasped his chest, just over his heart, then the left hand followed and he leaned sideways, the armrest keeping him in the chair. He was breathing heavily, his forehead perspiring. Then he looked up at the therapist. "It wasn't that way…was it."

Dr. West shook his head. "What was it?"

Turley gazed at the floor, his mind spinning, reaching back through the mists of twenty-eight years. "No…what he felt was…" He shook his head. "Was only what happened…between his legs…What gratified that twisted mind…But for me, no…not that way, was it?…No, I wanted to…" He wrestled with the expression, to sort out the words as they came rushing like logs tumbling down a turbulent, swirling stream, wedging into a narrow opening. He looked down to his hands still clutching his chest. "No…no, not at all…Oh, God, it really wasn't…like that for me…!"

He slowly looked up at the man seated across a table from him. "I told you about my son, years after my father did that…then the boy and his mother were gone…that terrible day. There was nothing left to love but memories…Nothing I could do for them in the ER…they were gone by then…DOA, they told me…Then this all came back to me…and I thought I was a sick man…Twisted and sick…Just like him. What I saw there, inside that old house, years later, after my own son…died…it was him again, Dr. West; it was Allen. My son was in that house now…I had to…protect him…this time…to shield him against the evil I saw in my father."

"Was this what you felt that night at the Metropolitan Council meeting, when the children were in the back of the room?"

Turley nodded. "It was that same feeling. It scared me because…because of what I thought I was feeling, about the bad desires I thought I had toward them. But it was…it was what I said, wasn't it?"

"It's best if you say what it was, Forrest."

"It was like they were my own…They were children…whose lives would be disrupted again. Who'd have to move, find another place to live, start over with new friends, new schools, all because others wanted to drive their cars over the ground where they lived. I wanted to save them…to do what I couldn't do for…for those children my father wanted…and for what I couldn't do for my own son after that accident…It wasn't those bad feelings he had…What I thought I had, that I was like him. My mind thought it was that terrible drive that he had…"

"And your mind tucked those fears far away, down deep where you couldn't reach them."

"Until now."

"You only thought it was something bad, because they look so much alike. They can be mistaken, one for another. But now you know."

Forrest Turley crashed back in his chair and smiled thinly, arms hanging loosely. "God in Heaven…!"

Twenty minutes later Turley was driving south on I-94, his mind still reeling from the strain of the past hour's revelations. For the past three years he believed he harbored a warped, compulsive need for touch, and that had terrified him. His greatest fear was that those perverted drives would come out the way it did with his father, or something worse. A great fear the day would come when it brought him to another level; when he would walk the lonely, gloomy streets of the night, a solitary figure seeking private outlets for his twisted cravings.

He drove through the Lowry Tunnel and turned onto I-35W, glancing in the rearview mirror. Just the usual traffic for three PM. At the Thirty-second Street/Lake Street exit he turned east and steered back toward Lake Street and now he noticed it for the first time: a lime green Ford Taurus followed every one of his turns. He drove east on Lake Street and turned right onto Portland Avenue. The Taurus turned right. Goddamn amateur, he thought. But who was this? Why? The relief he had felt after leaving the clinic dissipated quickly, a sickening ball gathering in his stomach.

He passed his home and saw the driver glance at the house but kept following him. Turley turned right onto Thirty-second Street, drove one block and turned right again, this time without signaling, then glanced in the mirror. It was still there. He came to the stop light at Lake Street and waited. The Taurus was close behind. The driver had taken a clumsy effort to conceal himself with dark glasses and a hat pulled low on his forehead. Should he get out, go back and confront the man? It could be someone he knew.

The light turned green and Turley swung to his right again onto Lake Street. It was obvious by now the man knew where he lived. Well, what the hell, he thought, no point in continuing this chase. He turned right again on Portland, drove a block, then turned left on Thirty-first Street and then right into the alley where his garage fronted. He looked back quickly and saw the green car continue on south. No point in calling the police. The less attention the better.

Did this man know he was at the clinic? He strained his memory but couldn't recall seeing the green car until he was coming down I-94, and by that time he was two or three miles from the clinic. The driver had to be waiting for him near the clinic, the chance of finding him right in heavy freeway traffic was slim. Shit! Someone wanted to know about him. Now they did.

Minutes later he felt his intestines cramp into tight knots as perspiration trickled down his neck. Was he still out there? He cautiously peered through the Venetian blinds in his front room but saw only a long and empty street.

Chapter Eleven

He could have hired an auctioneer and saved himself a lot of time and work, but with their four vehicles already sold, there wasn't a lot of equipment and inventory left to move, so Vince decided to do it himself. It saved the auctioneers's fee. By now, the Bellands were in Florida, sipping margaritas by the seaside, nary the slightest worry on their minds. Their parting gesture was a late night call from Albert. "Vince," he said, "John and I decided that since you're handling the sale you should keep all the proceeds. I know we agreed to take half but, we'd feel better about it this way."

Okay, it's a deal. It meant another ten thousand, and for Vince that was fine. The Bellands wouldn't miss it. From their cut of the business sale, long years of investing, and stumbling into a huge family inheritance a few years ago, they were set free of need. One drove a new Cadillac and a dark green SUV, the other owned a monster Town Car, all fully equipped. Waiving off on the equipment might have been their way of shedding guilt about how it ended. The soothing sound of washing surf would soon dissolve any remaining cares.

Throughout the long day, trucks owned by his former competitors and others arrived empty and departed loaded with paraphernalia: boxes and drums of electrical cable of all gauges; piles of aluminum conduit, bins full of receptacles, crates of wire nuts, conduit benders, switches, outlets; an array of hand tools including drills and bits, wrenches, pliers, crimpers, solderers. The list went on.

Two of his remaining employees helped him as he wandered from one part of the building to another, stopping to talk with those whom he knew, watching what felt like pieces of himself being sold and hauled away. It was like presiding over your own estate sale. Eighteen goddamn years. He kept several of the hand tools, just in case he'd need them later. Somewhere. Maybe.

He put a modest price tag on the archaic computer and printer but it generated no interest whatever. It was an old model 386, a shriveled runt among today's hundred gig hard drives and their million-plus megs of memory. Technology had raced right on by at the speed of light. By evening it would be in the Dumpster.

When he arrived home he sifted through the mail—the usual unsolicited junk; something about winning a prize, just call this number, place your order for some damn thing or another, then a month later they'd tell you that you didn't actually win the big prize. But, anyway, thanks for whatever it was you bought from us!

"Go screw yourself!" he mumbled to the envelope.

He savaged the contents, flinging the shredded pieces into the waste paper can. So also, the damned advertising flyers met swift end. The bills accorded a little more respect.

Two other letters quickly gripped his attention: the first from an electrical supplier with whom he recently interviewed for an assistant manager position, the other for an electrical maintenance position in a plastics factory. He slashed open the first of these envelopes, then read the letter. It was nicely worded. Someone didn't want to make him feel bad, but it said that after considering the qualifications of all available candidates, we have decided to extend the offer to another person. It thanked him for his interest in the position and wished him success in his search for employment. He was not surprised. His retail experience was thirty years old, and he had no real interest in traveling that road again. He contacted them just as a fall-back.

The second envelope came from an ad in the Minneapolis Star Tribune. It was for someone to do mechanical and electrical maintenance of the machinery used by a firm manufacturing plastic products. Though he had not wired these same systems, he had designed the electrical schematics for at least a hundred similar units. He knew the operation of the system.

After reading the ad he reviewed his resume. It reflected his experience, but for this job it needed revisions. He labored an entire evening redrafting the skills summary to more closely reflect what the firm was seeking. Nothing wrong with massaging one's resume a bit here and there. After all, you're looking for a way to support yourself…and Ann. When he was done it looked good and he sent it to the address in the ad.

Two weeks passed while he waited, then came the phone call, from someone he assumed was secretary for the firm, since she was calling on behalf of someone else. A woman with the most beautiful, creamy-smooth accent he'd ever heard. It sounded Australian. That alone would make it fun working there. Keep her on the line as long as possible! These people often have great influence on business decisions. The interview went well and he thought they were on common ground talking about electrical designs. Except for one part: there was to be no discussion about compensation. That would be addressed in the second round of interviews, if he survived the first cut.

Like the other letter, this one was tactfully written.

"Shit!" he hollered to the walls, to a room that seemed so indifferent to him.

It had gone so well! He knew he had the skills they needed and he wondered how many others were in the running. What did they bring to the table, besides youth? He had responded with accurate information to their questions, but he just couldn't get to the point where they all could kick back and relax. That's when you know you're on the inside track.

Vince hadn't hired anyone in seven years and he'd done all the interviewing himself, the brothers preferring to defer to his judgment. To date he had been interviewed seven times and in every case there were either two or three company personnel present; one appeared to be the note-taker, while one asked the questions and another merely observed. A witness, he assumed, in case someone screamed discrimination, harassment, or whatever other grievance they might find.

His own style of conducting interviews for the business were as relaxed as possible and he kept no notes. Today these were distinctly serious, even somber affairs. It was all because of the discrimination laws. Every interview a potential source of costly litigation, win or lose. Times had changed. “Dammit!” he muttered, “How many other jobs are there like this one?” God, how you hate to see these go by the board! He slammed the letter on the table. Maybe he should give them a call and ask why he was passed over. He thought about that for a few minutes, then muttered no, they’d give him the standard response: Sorry, we found someone with better qualifications.

Five weeks ago, he filed a claim for unemployment insurance against his own company. He wondered how that would go, being a part owner. “You are eligible when you’re out of work through no fault of your own,” they told him. “Usually, this is due to a lack of work.” Well, when the competition stomps you into the ground there’s a definite lack of work.

The claim came back denied. The legal hodgepodge supporting the decision said that since he was one of the owners, shutting down was a voluntary decision, and being voluntary, it led to a disqualification, according to Minnesota Statutes at Chapter blah, blah, Section blah, blah, blah…Subitem blah, blah, blah…provide, in part…blah, blah, blah…How voluntary is it when other eighty per cent votes to close shop? He saw that he had fifteen days to file an appeal. Why not? It didn’t cost him anything. He took a blank sheet of paper. “I wish to appeal this decision,” he wrote, signed and dated it, and added his social security number.

Then came the day of the appeal hearing. In an ordinary hearing the employer is present, but the brothers would be whacking balls around the fairways somewhere, oblivious to all of this.

That was when he met Peter Hoffler, the appeal judge. Peter asked him a few questions and Vince sensed something in his bearing when he told him about the minority ownership and how the business came to be shut down.

A week passed and the decision arrived in the mail. The denial was overturned. He had four hundred and twenty-seven new dollars a week for up to twenty-six weeks! Wow! Taxable dollars, to be sure. Of course, Ann was mortified. "A government check is being sent in the mail?" she wailed. "I do not wish to have the mail carrier know of this!"

"I set it up on direct deposit. Just like you do with your salary."

"Well that was better," she answered. "But they still sent that decision in the mail, and in a state government envelope!"

It just came out. He laughed loudly, his eyes closed tightly as it suddenly welled up, before his usual response of anger could bottle it.

"Vince, I do not find this humorous!"

"For God's sake, Ann, the Post Office delivers zillions of pieces of mail! I don't think they pay much attention to that." That smirk just wouldn't go away.

The rest of the day was very long and quiet.

Tomorrow he'd pay a visit to the resource room at the Employment and Training Center. They had a nationwide computerized system of job openings. It would be a good idea to check that out, the unemployment people told him. In fact, he was required to check it out, they told him. Very well, sir. It might be a good idea to look in other states, too, just in case Ann should be offered a position...somewhere...Some day. Wherever. And where might that be? Fifty states and she'd move to any of them for the coveted job? Just check the Minnesota openings. Then write down the website address and you can do it all from home—the wonders of thc Intcrnct.

He picked up the Minneapolis paper and again scanned the ads. Good God! There are jobs of every kind. Why not? The Twin City unemployment rate hasn't been above four per cent for six years.

For a half hour he read through the ads. Assemblers, packagers, mail inserters, data processing clerks, information systems technicians, truck drivers, food servers by the dozen, medical insurance clerks to handle the mountain of paperwork, more information system technicians, telephone marketers-formerly called solicitors-till the public resentment built. There were ads for carpenters and every other building trade, medical assistants, nurse aides-five hundred dollar sign-on bonus, nurses. The medical profession was going bonkers. Was everybody getting sick? Or just getting older? Other businesses were screaming for sales people, computer systems analysts everywhere. He'd never noticed before how many listings there were. He sighed and rubbed weary eyes. Good God! Which way to turn?

Then he noticed something else: Most of the listings paid less then ten dollars an hour. "Shit!" he mumbled.

There it was!...Phone systems installers. The opportunity that ran him down, leaving him for roadkill on the highway of human progress. What a reminder!

He didn't notice it at first: It was a smaller ad, over in the lower right corner, from a company called ProFab. Where had he...? Wasn't that the company that built a small addition about ten years ago and Lakes did the electrical work? Yeah, a smaller outfit in Robinsdale that...what did they make? ProFab...oh yeah, circuit boards for computers, printers and TVs. Seemed like a well-operated business when they did the wiring contract. They were looking for someone to do circuit design and layout, full time with benefits, salary negotiable. Experience in electrical work required. They weren't too specific about the experience. Give it a good, hard try. Join an expanding firm and grow with us, the ad beckoned.

The longer he thought the better he felt. Yes! This was reachable. This was a good fit! Now he felt his hopes rising like a hot air balloon. Like a miner who suddenly finds gold in his pan. Better to grow with ProFab than sink with Lakes Electric. They wanted a resume. Good, he'd rework it again, just enough to reflect the design work he had done.

It wouldn't be too bad a commute: straight north on Highway 100. Like every other major city, traffic was becoming a shrieking bitch any time of the day; Route 100 wasn't any worse than the others.

Maybe those people pushing for that light rail system had the right idea. We just can't keep putting more vehicles to the highways, always adding to the glut. There's got to be an alternative.

He plunged into his resume again, a sharpened pencil in hand, feeling good about stumbling onto what just might be the best replacement for what he lost. Wouldn't have to stay there forever; but it would be a good place to pick up the pieces and get back to a niche in his own field. He was overcome with that good feeling of lightness; as if riding buoyantly on the crest of a beneficial wave.

Chapter Twelve

The accountant looked across Dave Behlen's big walnut desk, wondering, not for the first time, why he contracted to do the books for this wild maverick. He had known Behlen as a colleague for the past five years, and as his client for the past two years. During that time he'd intervened on four occasions to rescue him, already deep into another acrimonious clash with the IRS or else dueling with state tax officials. If it wasn't with them, it was another episode in his running battle with Social Security, the unemployment insurance people or bickering with someone about a worker's comp premium. "I can understand your feelings about government and its tax policies, most of us in business share those same concerns," he said to him, "but love them or hate them, they are there and they aren't going away. Don't ignore them. I've seen too often how they use their enforcement authority." And by the looks of today's session, Dave Behlen was flying in the face of the law again. It never ceased to amaze Brad how this man could constantly stress compliance with all tax and regulatory rules when his associates worked with their clients, always warning them of the dire consequences of noncompliance, yet harbor utter disdain for those same rules when it came to his own business.

He had called Brad into his office today to get approval for his latest endeavor. "I want to turn all my associates into independent contractors." That caused Brad to cast a hard look at Behlen. "These guys are all running their own show, they've been doing it for a long time, and I see no reason why I should continue paying my share for Social Security, plus the premiums for Unemployment Insurance and Workers' Compensation, not to mention the cost of health insurance. I'm tired of paying all those taxes, so find a way to make this happen for all seven associates. That's the bottom line, Brad: get me out from under the taxes."

Brad thought for several moments, pondering how he was going to pull him back from the brink this time. "Dave, that's the wish of every one in business, and these costs never go down, but iet me ask you a few questions first. Number one: who sets the associates' work schedule?"

"They do."

Brad looked at him. "You have no control at all over the time they spend working here? You don't control their hours in any way?"

Behlen shifted in his leather chair. "I give them the contracts, explain the goals and objectives we have to meet. I give them the time frames and the broad outlines about how I want them to proceed with each client, and any other specifics that may be involved. Other than that, they determine when they must be here and how long they stay on any given day. They all know what they have to do and how long they have to get it done and the resources available to them."

Brad nodded. "Suppose one of them wasn't coming in until noon and you became concerned that they might not get their work done in the time you allotted them. Would you ignore it because the associate knew the due date?"

"Absolutely not! Though they set their own hours, I'm in here by six, sometimes earlier, so I expect to see them at least by seven. In the case you cited I would demand to know where they'd been and what they were doing during that time. They all have enough work to keep them going seventy hours a week, usually more. It's entirely possible they were meeting clients away from the office. We do it all the time, and if that was what they told me I wouldn't be worried any longer."

"But you reserve the right to demand they account to you for the time in question?"

"Certainly."

Brad thought for a few more moments. "Okay, let me ask you this: who negotiates the contracts with your clients?"

"I do. I deal with every client myself."

He nodded. "Who determines the rate of compensation for your associates?"

Behlen paused. "Their pay is determined by the contracts they are assigned. They receive a per cent of the total fee. You must be aware of this—"

"Yes, but let's review this for a moment. These are the contracts that you negotiated, which includes the total dollar amount the client must pay as your fee, is that correct?"

"Of course."

"I see from the ledgers how much you pay your associates and the rate is usually about twenty to twenty five per cent. Do you determine the rate?"

"Yes, I do. What are you getting at?

"That would bc thc typical ratc payable to your associates?"

Behlen shrugged. "That varies, depending on the work and time involved."

"But would this be an average rate, Dave?"

Behlen squirmed restlessly as he always did when cast as the giver of information rather then its receiver. "All right, twenty-five is probably a typical cut for the associates. Look, all I want you to do is find a way. I don't care how you do it, just get the job done! That's the bottom line, Brad!"

Brad nodded. "We have to find a way that is legal and will avoid an audit. My CPA license and your legal liability both depend on that. As your accountant, I can't place either of us at risk. Let's take an example. You negotiate a contract for, say, a hundred thousand dollars. Is that a typical amount?"

"Close. Some are for more, some for less. So what?"

"All right, you assign one or more of your associates to work on this contract, the amount of which you have already negotiated with the client. Let's say your total expenses come to twenty thousand, so that leaves a net of eighty thousand. If the percentage paid to the associates is twenty-five, then would you pay them twenty thousand? Twenty-five per cent of the eighty thousand net?"

Behlen nodded. "In that example, yes, that would be their take."

"And you always determine the portion paid to your associates, even if that may be more or less that twenty-five per cent, depending on a number of factors? And you determine which associate will be assigned to each client?"

Behlen nodded impatiently. "Of course I do. I match every contract with the particular talents of the associates. I have to control who does what—"

"Understood. That Billings contract you had last year. As I recall, you started with one associate, then removed him for another. Is that correct?"

"I gave him the proper direction and time frames but he kept going outside of those parameters. I won't tolerate that so I took him off the contract, started him on another, then let him go about a month later."

"So you reviewed his performance, determined it to be unsatisfactory, initially changed his assignment, then subsequently discharged him."

Behlen held up a hand. "That's exactly what I did. Brad, the bottom line is this: I'm going the independent contractor route. Are you going to find a way for me to do this or do I need to find another accountant?" He squirmed in his chair, drumming fingers on the desktop.

"Dave, what I'm concerned about, for your sake and mine, is the issue of control. Legal independent contractorship turns on that matter more than any other. IRS has rules to determine if you have a valid independent contractor relationship with your associates. In my judgment, you don't because you still retain essential control over them. As I understand your operation, you decide who works on what contracts, the rate of their compensation and method of payment. You judge performance and take actions as you see appropriate, reserving the right to terminate. Do I have this correct?"

"You do. That is how I run my business and I believe every other consultant does it the same way."

"Dave, I know we discussed all of this when you became my client, but I have a duty to keep you in compliance with the tax laws and advise you if I see you heading toward possible problems. I see you headed in that direction and so I am advising you—"

Behlen shifted quickly and leaned forward, his elbows on his desk. "Brad are you going to do what I want done or not?"

"Dave, we have a serious issue here with the extent of control you wish to retain when you leave the traditional employee-employer relationship. Both IRS and the state tax people watch when this changes for any business. If you proceed with this plan, it's an open invitation for a tax audit and you are exposing your business to significant liability, whether it is with IRS, the state tax people, or any of the others. An audit from any one will trigger audits from the others. When they're done I believe they will say you continue to have the traditional relationship, and therefor you owe not only back taxes, which could come to tens of thousands of dollars, but they'll attach penalty and interest on top of the principal, which may well double your liability. There will also be back taxes your associates will have to pay because you're not deducting these. Do you really want to take the risk of incurring that kind of liability?"

Behlen glared at him and shook his head. "Brad, these tax people are cast-offs that couldn't make it in private business, so they end up bumbling around some government agency. I see this all the time! You, an accountant, can't be serious about their actually auditing me! And even if they were competent, what possible grounds would they have for slapping me with liability? Tell me that!"

Brad nodded. "First of all, they're not incompetent. Overworked maybe, stretched thin, but they know their business, and if they smell a fraud you won't have a moment of peace until they're done with you. You say your associates set their own hours, yet you also said you'd demand they account for their time if asked to do so. That's a strong controlling influence. You clearly determine when, where and how your staff perform their work. Loss of that control is the hallmark of independent contractorship. Be very careful; the tax people aren't incompetent as you believe them to be, Dave. As your accountant I must advise you that they will eventually catch this and if I steer you in this direction, then my license, as well as your liability, are both at risk."

Several moments passed in silence as Behlen first glanced out the window at the Minneapolis skyline, then he turned back to Brad, leaned his elbows on the walnut desk again and stared at him. "Brad, it's true I hired you to be my accountant and track the business's finances. But I hired you for another, equally good reason. Your job is to be my instrument, to aid me in doing what I see fit to do. When I make a business decision I expect you to find a way to get the job done. That's what it is all about: just getting the job done.So let me put it this way to you: find me a way around all this bureaucracy and red tape, and all the incompetent auditors, or you're no longer my accountant. Is that clear to you?"

The accountant thought for several moments. "Yes, you've made yourself very clear. You are placing yourself and your business at substantial risk, and asking me to be a partner to actions I cannot support. I have to advise you against doing this. I have now done this. If you continue in this direction I will end my professional relationship with you. I have served you by giving you my best advice, now I need to know your intentions."

Behlen glared at him for several seconds, his shoulders hunched over the desk, his forehead furrowed deeply. "You can't be serious about those tax clowns actually following this, charging me and making it all stick in court."

"I am, and I know they will. What are your intentions, Dave?"

"My intentions are to run this business the best way I can and I'll be damned if I will let those two-bit bean-counters get in my way! People that I do not regard as fit to do their jobs. My associates will be contractors because that's how I've decided to run my business, so don't stand in my way!"

"I won't stand in your way but I cannot support your intentions…I will fax you a letter of termination today, ending our contract as of five pm yesterday. I urge you to reconsider. For the record, we never had this conversation."

A tall, slender man with a rim of reddish hair looked up from a file on his desk and saw the accountant walk past the receptionist and through the main door into the hallway. He smiled grimly, opened his desk drawer, switched off a small electronic instrument and placed it in his suit jacket pocket.

Vince fumbled with the key, struggling to open the lock before the phone stopped ringing, despite the answering machine. When you're trying to convince half the world to hire you, phones never go unanswered. Third ring, one more and the machine kicks in. He hated returning calls. It seemed no matter how quickly you did it, the caller was either on another line already or had done a very quick disappearing act. Finally the tumblers gave way and he burst through the opening, grabbing the phone just as the machine was telling someone we're glad you called and your call is very impor—"Hello?"

It was a female with a honey-velvet voice he could have listened to all day, and, huh? Oh, yes, this was Vince Martinson. His heart was already throbbing. "This is Sheila, and I'm calling on behalf of Mark Wiley at ProFab." At the mention of ProFab his heartbeat arched over into whatever lies beyond very heavy throbbing. He shouldn't be sweating like this. He hoped she couldn't hear the pounding noise over the line. Try breath control. He remembered something about that during those prenatal parental sessions he and Ann attended. Maybe it would apply here. Shit, this was every bit as stressful as prenatal, but there, at least you were fairly sure of the outcome. "Due to a couple operating changes we've had to put off all hiring decisions for an indefinite period," honey-voice told him, Australian style. "We want to know if we reopen the circuit designer position, would you still be available?" A blend of two parts disappointment and one part relief; they hadn't hired someone else. Hell, they weren't hiring anyone!

"Yes, I'm still available," he managed to say, wishing he could stay on the line all day with her. She thanked him and promised to contact him when decisions were made. Then Creamy Voice was gone and there was just this huge big void. He suddenly felt terribly empty, abandoned. For long moments he stared silently at the tabletop.

So what happened to ProFab now? he wondered. A change of management? One of their larger contracts gone south? There were so many things that impacted hiring decisions. Well, shit! Nothing to do now but hang on. Hang on and wait. Wait for another call, another outcome.

There certainly will be other calls and other possibilities…wouldn't there?

Chapter Thirteen

Lynn Alveson rose from the bed, threw Dave Behlen's shirt over her shoulders, crossed the room and opened the wooden cabinet. She mixed two cocktails and brought them back to the bed where she snuggled up to him, casting aside the shirt. For the past three hours they frolicked in the suite paid by the firm of Wasten and Associates, a subsidiary of Behlen and Associates. He wrote it off as client entertainment.

"Are you sure this is a good place to be today?" she asked him. "The city council's holding a public hearing on the main level."

Behlen scoffed. "City Council! A bunch of clowns babbling endlessly about nothing. Lapping it up at the public trough." He shook his head. "Who cares?"

"Quite a few, apparently. It's an open forum on affordable housing and light rail. Big issues, you know, don't you?"

He shrugged "Of course. It's a colossal waste of our money. Affordable housing?" He scoffed again. "Pay the market rate or go back South."

"What does this have to do with the South?"

"All those unemployed people down there, all whining and crying for millions to waste on housing and that crazy rail system. They're all on welfare, you know. They come up from those Southern states to get better welfare benefits. Turn ‘em around and send ‘em right back!”

She found his tirades atrocious, yet the holder of those atrocious ideas oddly attractive. “I looked into this and learned if a welfare recipient moves here from any state with a lower level of payment they’re entitled only to that state’s lower level for the first year they are here. If they’re still on welfare after one year, and most aren’t, then they come up to the benefit level that prevails here.”

“Is that so? Then if those clowns in the Legislature had any sense they’d drop the payment below that of the lowest-paying state and keep it there! That would cure the whole thing in one simple step!” he declared with a sweep of his arm. “I suppose a bunch of those self-appointed advocates down there are screaming against that! ‘Oh, please, members of the Legislature,’ he mimicked in a falsetto voice, hands folded in supplicating fashion, ‘don’t be so mean to our poor welfare loafers.’ Can we talk about something else? I’m getting ill.”

“Sure. Light rail is also on their agenda.” She smiled.

He groaned. “Lynn, that first scheme they hatched, the Hiawatha Corridor, cost the city and county a hundred and twenty-three million. That’s only about a fourth of the cost! This other bit of lunacy, running a rail line across the poor neighborhood and down I-35, will cost the city and county at least two hundred million! For whose benefit? What’s the payback on all of this”

She cocked her head and looked at him. “It’s for everybody, Dave. For suburban commuters-like you and all the others out there. Think of it: you could all leave your Cadillacs and Town Cars at home and let someone else do the driving! It's utterly fantastic! I love it!" She sprung from the bed, grabbing his glass. "You need a refill, the state you're in." This time she went to the wet bar sans shirt or anything else while he admired what was so pleasurable to hold in his arms.

She returned and sat cross-legged on the bed, a coy look on her face. "Tell me, Dave, and be honest, does your wife have any idea what you're doing today?"

"I have a standing rule in my office. When a call comes in for me I'm always in conference, except to a few clients who know how to identify themselves. The receptionist takes messages from the others and I decide whether to call them back. I still pay a real, live person to answer phones, not one of those answering services. Only my associates have voice mail."

"Your wife isn't among the select clients?"

"She used to call every time she needed anything: a loaf of bread, milk, whatever. I told her she has a car, a checkbook, and a lot more time that I have, so use it and don't bother me."

"So she doesn't call you?"

"Hasn't called for a year."

She smiled and looked at him leaning back against the headboard. "Dave, do you love your wife? I sense that you really do want her, your sex life with her notwithstanding."

A stunned expression came over his face, then he hesitated. "Well…sure."

"You're here with me."

"Lynn, you're getting into something really complicated. Would you feel offended if I told you I wouldn't be here if Cheryl was anywhere near as responsive as you are? I know that sounds like whining, but I need your kind of aggressiveness, and I can't get that from her. She just doesn't have the same needs as I have. Yes, I care for her. She's my wife and my wife she shall remain." There was a strong downdrop to these last words.

"You care in the sense that you wouldn't want anything bad to happen to her."

"Lynn, I'm not a very sensitive man. I don't catch those subtle signals women send out. I guess my antenna just isn't terribly sensitive. I'm sure many men are the same. But that doesn't make us bad. I'm a good provider and work very hard to see that Cheryl and my family are well taken care of.

"It's important to me that they have a good, safe home and enough money to take care of their needs, and not just at the basic level. I give to them, and I give willingly. I paid for my son's law school education," he said proudly, then sighed just as heavily. "I suppose if my daughter ever gets her act together I'll pay for hers, too. I have this awful fear I'll be turning loose a monster if she ever gets a law degree like she's been threatening."

"You're a good man in many ways."

"Thank you. It's good to hear that now and then. I can't remember the last time she complimented me on anything."

"But I don't think providing for them is the only reason you throw yourself into your work so thoroughly."

"I have seven associates and nine support staff to look after. I care for my clients who are willing to pay me big fees to solve their problems. I want them all to continue eating their lunch."

"There are other reasons, too."

He pondered that for several seconds, then nodded. "My father worked in a box factory. For forty-one years all he did was run some kind of machine that turned out cardboard boxes. Forty-one years, all in the same place! He hit sixty-five and kept right on working. If his legs were cut off or his spine severed he would've crawled to work in a pool of blood.

"What he did wasn't hard work; he told me that. But I saw what it did to him. He became a walking zombie. Finally at sixty-nine the place closed down and he had to retire. Six months later they hauled him off to a mental hospital. Four months after that we buried him.

"The evening before the funeral I walked up to his open casket and there he was, all laid out in the same suit he wore to church every Sunday for twenty years. He looked...as if he was ready for this. I thought, 'God, what an awful way to live out your life. Dad, I'll do better than you did.' I promised a dead man I would have a better life than he had."

"Did it happen?"

Dave Behlen smiled. "Several years later my mother sold the house for fifty-three thousand. My three-stall garage is worth that much. To succeed I had to become very competitive. It didn't come easily or naturally, which must be a surprise to a lot of people."

"It might have seemed boring to you, but living the same routine every day might have given him a sense of order and control. Maybe what he was striving for was to know exactly what was coming next. Obviously, he thrived on routine and wasn't a risk-taker, even in small ways. Could it be he was actually happier than you thought he was?"

Behlen shrugged. "Could be. Then why am I such a risk-taker and cage-rattler?"

"Probably because you're trying to achieve what you thought he wanted but never had.You have wealth, you take risks and seek out challenges; three things your father either never had or avoided. Sometimes it scares me, the things you say and do."

"Really?"

She paused for several moments. "I've always felt that while you abide by most laws, I sense a lack of respect for rules that regulate business or that relate to public issues. You believe we should throw every issue where they will all be sorted out by laws of the free market."

He handed her his empty glass. "One more, then we'd better go back to work. Sure, I've skirted a few of those business rules, but then who doesn't? Most of those are put there by bureaucrats who know nothing about the real world and couldn't run a business if their lives depended on it and—"

She put her hand over his mouth and her voice was soft again. "Enough, Dave." She snuggled beside him, lay her head on his shoulder and pulled his arm across her shoulder. "We'll leave here soon, but...Please be careful, with all of this. I don't what bad things to happen to you."

"Nothing bad will happen to me. I'm not going to do something that will sink me, so—"

"It's what you overlook...This is going to sound really bizarre, but...I shouldn't try telling you this."

He looked at her just as she looked up at him. "Lynn, we've come this far and you started to say something, so please finish it. Whatever it is it won't make me jump out the window."

"You're crazy in a strange, wild, recklessly attractive way and..." She gripped his hand and placed it on her chest. "All right, I'll tell you what it is...I'm in love with you."

His reaction was two parts stunned, one part vaguely pleased that a woman this attractive could feel that way for him. He squirmed as he often did when faced with something he hadn't predicted or didn't know how to immediately control. "Dave, I've had other affairs, though they were with single men, but I turned from them, one after another. Then one day you came along. The wild guy, the American cowboy right off the silver screen, both guns ablazing. The one who says what he's thinking, does it all his own way. The real honest-to-goodness freebooter. I should despise you for doing what you're doing here, but I don't. Please don't ask me why, because I just don't know. You seem to be one of a kind, not like all the others I've known. But you must decide, Dave, what you are going to do...About us. I can't do that for you. Things have changed, Dave. It's not what it was when we started together."

They dressed in heavy silence; she brushed her hair, he fixed his tie. He opened the door for her, whispered something softly. She looked wistfully at him, touched his hand. Then he closed the door behind them.

The public hearing ended and the people were standing around, some gathering in small discussion groups, some corralling their small children to leave. A few had cornered members of the city council to get in the last word. Others sat and read the handouts. Forrest Turley slipped away, walked into the large hotel lobby and stood in one corner. At that moment one of the elevator doors opened and four small children burst noisily into the lobby, their embarrassed parents in frantic pursuit. Turley took an involuntary step forward, then abruptly stopped. It's still there, isn't it? Dr.West told you it wouldn't go away. "It will always be there," he told Forrest. "It will diminish in time, and you will learn to manage it. But you will always feel something. Remember the source, now that you've identified it. It will always be with you."

That was the greater share of the battle, he thought. He looked at the children now that the parents had regained control, and inwardly smiled to himself. He'd beat this damn thing! One way or another, he'd conquer that harrowing feeling he suffered for all those years, captive to its iron grip. It has to stay under wraps. Elections were fifteen months away and he wanted nothing more than to keep this out of the press.

He'd worked hard at being a good councilman and it consumed most of his time. The people in his ward, many of whom struggled every day against poverty, crime and the other scourges of life in a declining inner city, were his people. They were what got him up every morning and compelled him to spend hours studying the complex problems so he came to council meetings informed and prepared to talk intelligently about issues effecting his ward. He couldn't bear the thought of those people, many of whom he knew from his walks on the streets, all turning against him, driven by the stigma placed on illnesses where your urges and feelings got out of control.

As he was about to leave, another elevator door opened and a tall man with dark brown hair going elegantly gray entered the lobby with a slender, attractive woman with long, straight hair. Turley stopped when he saw them and watched as they exited the building and were lost in the crowd on the sidewalk. Where had he seen that man? He looked too familiar to be a stranger along with the hundreds of others nearby. Where…? Was that…? Yes! He was the one who testified at the Metropolitan Council hearing. That arrogant son of a bitch who preached about choices. His choices. He racked his memory but couldn't recall the name. Something about them didn't look right. He reached for his pager and dialed a familiar number. "May I speak to Peter Hoffler, please?"

Chapter Fourteen

He had been an unemployment insurance appeals judge now for six months, and though he had it written on his calendar, he'd forgotten his probationary interview was today. It was all very serious and somber, as probationary interviews are supposed to be. Though he heard the words, he kept staring out the window at the building across the street. Another daytime home to modern-day warriors carrying out the missions of their superiors while others of greater stature moiled away in bigger cubicles overseen by those of even brighter plumage who, in turn, bowed to the great moguls who had the corner offices with real walls separating them from the masses over whose destiny they ruled. Then he caught himself wandering and turned his attention to what the man had said, as best he could remember, anyway. "I'm sorry, you were saying..."

The man glanced briefly at Peter, then back to his notes. "I was saying that you will clear probation. You should consider that half of your decisions that were appealed to the next level were overturned.

Peter nodded. "Half...?. What is the average for the other judges?"

"About ten per cent."

"I see. Well, I have my biases, as we discussed three months ago. Single parents, particularly single female parents. I'm aware of this little hang-up, which is more than can be said for some of the others here.

"I think some of our older judges need a lot of training on social awareness. I overturned an initial denial of benefits to a single parent, a male in this case, who quit because his employer put him on the night shift after six months, but initially told him he was hired only for the day shift with no shift rotation. Day care is unavailable in the middle of the night, as some of our judges appear to be unaware, so I attributed the quit to actions taken by the employer and reversed the decision. Then Emerson, our sixty-eight year-old pterodactyl, overturns me, saying it was a voluntary quit attributable to the employee."

"You might want to talk that over with Emerson. Anyway," he said, sliding the form across the desk, "sign here and Human Resources will send you a letter."

"Well, thanks," Peter replied, hardly expecting any other outcome. He signed the form and thus with a stroke of the pen became a permanent, tenured member of the governing establishment.

He arrived home that evening, unsure what to expect, sensing a subtle change in the atmosphere of the house. Mary met him as he came into the living room, her eyes reddened, face drawn. "There is something we need to discuss," she began and from the tone of her voice he knew he was going to have a very difficult time with this. All he really wanted at the moment was a cold beer, but something serious and heavy was on her evening agenda.

"I need to make a decision about what I'm going to do," she told him as she rubbed her hands, trying to focus on his face. "I can't go on wallowing around in this…this pit. I've been depressed and this has been going on for a much longer time than you know, Peter. It started my first year in law school. You probably saw it as the usual fatigue all law students suffer, and I might have led you to believe that. I was unhappy struggling to learn the legal trade. Anyway, I plunged on, hoping to make the grade, but with a growing fear that I would fail, and I had no idea how I would deal with failure."

"I hope I didn't pressure you into thinking you had to complete the program because of me." He reached for her hand but she withdrew.

"No. I think law was a natural for you, only it wasn't for me. You found it much easier than I did. I didn't want you to think I was struggling so much. I didn't want my problems to be your burden. You already had enough of a load to carry, working for Advocate Services and paying my tuition. But it wasn't what I wanted, and I knew by then I would never make a good lawyer."

Peter looked down at the worn carpet, then up to Mary. "I wish you had told me about this…I never knew you felt this way."

Mary sighed deeply and he saw the lines in her face. She had aged a decade in four years. "There you were: Peter, super attorney, defender and legal light to the unfortunate, making a difference, using the tools of a trade in which I would ultimately fail!" Now her voice broke and she sobbed.

Peter sat back in his chair. Years ago he learned the silent wait worked better then anything else when she was burdened. Unlike him, her emotions were mercurial, unpredictable. She could rise to great heights, then suddenly plunge to the pits. He had no idea where she would take this, once the tears dried and she began saying what was on her mind. Finally she looked toward him, wiping away the last of the tears. "Do you remember Jane?' she asked. Oh yes. Jane was one of Mary's friends through high school and the pre-law years. A bubbly but singularly eccentric person, as Peter remembered her. "Jane always wanted to be a writer, or so she thought. She read everything about writers from Balzac to Michael Dorris; attended every writers' workshop in the Twin Cities; enrolled in writing classes at St. Thomas, Hamline, the U of M, everywhere else. She wanted to be a writer, Peter, but she never really wanted to write. She ended up producing nothing."

"I remember."

"I wanted to be a lawyer. I wanted to have that title; to hold in my hands the Juris Doctor degree. To be able to say, 'I am a lawyer.' It was all based on what I thought law school and practice would be. A myth. I am to law what Jane is to the writing profession." Again she buried her face in her hands and wept, her shoulders convulsing softly.

He wanted to go to her, but thought better. He waited another minute. "Mary, is it that you really don't want to do anything in law or that you just don't know what you can do without the license?"

She nodded, her face still buried in her hands. “An in-house lawyer, doing research, but not providing counsel for clients. That’s not what I want to do.”

“I can understand that.”

She removed her hands, sighed loudly and sat straight in the chair. “I don’t know any more…! With all the time I put in there I could have a Ph.D. in sociology, urban studies…whatever.”

Mary rose again, slowly and walked to the window, still sniffling, her voice calm and flat, her knuckles white, her shoulders bowed. “Emmy is playing with the neighbor girl. She won’t be back for a while.” She stayed by the window looking out at the houses that lined the street for generations. “There is something that I need to do.” He waited for her to continue while the seconds silently ticked by and she groped for the words. Her voice became softer, hushed. “Peter…I need to be on my own.” It took several moments, then the truck slammed into him. He could actually feel the impact. “I don’t mean divorce. I just need to spend some time by myself, with Emmy, I mean.”

“Mary, what’s wrong?” he asked, feeling every muscle, every organ and tissue tighten. “Have I done something—”

“No!” she snapped, then shook her head. “I’m sorry, I didn’t mean to be so sharp. I don’t know what’s happening, but after the bar exam it all rolled right over me, like a big floodgate. I need to break out of this pattern. I don’t like it, but I have this awful urge to…to be on my own…Where…you’re not here every day. I’m sorry, Peter.” An ironic smile crossed her face and she slowly shook her head. “Do you remember when we were dating how my father hoped you'd just go away? Now he'll think I'm the crazy one."

He thought for several moments as he rubbed weary eyes. "I'm confused. You didn't like the evening work I did with AS, so with this job I'm home by five-thirty but now you're saying it's best if I'm not here every day. I'm trying to understand what you're groping for."

She turned quickly on him. "I don't know! Can't you understand what I'm saying?" Her eyes glistened, her face tight and blushing as she slowly turned from him. "I need…I need to be apart from you! I am Mary Hoffler, not just the wife of Peter Michael Hoffler! There's a whole world out there and for four goddamn wasted years I pursued this illusion! I threw away four years to get what I didn't want, now I can't do shit with it! For once, I would like to reach out, just go where I want to go, just do what I want to do. Without anyone telling me I can't do it!"

Peter held up his hands. "Mary, please, it's never been my place to say what you can and cannot do. All right, I hear you." He didn't understand a damn thing. "I don't know what it is you want,' he sighed… "but I won't stand in your way."

"Thank you, Peter."

He gazed down at the floor, his voice soft. "I never thought you should study law merely because I did, or that you shouldn't change your mind and do something else. What I don't understand is why you didn't tell me this. It would've turned out better for us. I can't understand why this has to happen. Now you want to leave."

Mary nodded as the tears flowed once again and she abruptly turned away from him, gazing out the window. "I feel sick! I just don't know how I feel about so many things, you included. Yes, I overreacted and the bar exam can be retaken. That's not the point. I don't care if I ever take the damn test again! I hate the thought of it! I just have to get away and I don't know how else to tell you."

God, it's strange, he thought, what comes to mind when this is suddenly dropped into your lap. Of all things that could have rolled into his reeling mind, he recalled an undergraduate course in research methodology where the professor was explaining how systematic research seeks answers by isolating one factor at a time, tests the hypothesis, then moves on to the next variable and continues this until reliable results are obtained.

Is that how it is here? he wondered. You run smack into some goddamn wall, thrash around everywhere for answers, can't find any, so you set up a testing strategy? And the first variable you isolate is your spouse? And if that doesn't turn out to be the problem, what do you do then? Bring spouse back and isolate something else?

For another hour they discussed the logistics. In the end it was Peter who would make the move. "I'm not even thinking about divorce," she assured him. "It's a separation, and that's all. Emmy needs the stability of her neighborhood," Mary said to him. Peter had grown up surrounded by wealth and space but walked away from all of it and worked his way through law school on his own, living in what most would call a hovel. He learned to shrink his world when circumstances required that of him.

He walked to the door, then turned to her. "I will do this. I want you to know that I fell in love with you when you had no degrees, no credentials, to offer...Nothing has changed."

He would make the move.

Fifteen minutes later he was in a neighborhood coffee shop that doubled as a bookstore, drinking French Roast coffee—he needed something with real body. Its offbeat atmosphere fit his style and he was one of their regulars since the gutsy days he and his group gathered there, planning their demonstrations and protests against the wrongs of society perpetuated by that hated establishment out there.

Most of those in the group had gone on to more profitable pursuits. One was an electrician, another had become an accountant in St. Paul. Two others were designing webpages for a Minneapolis company and a couple others opened their own businesses. All had found their niche in that society they once condemned as corrupt, fascist, chauvinist or anything else that made them sound visionary, above the swirl of everyday life. He still saw a few of them here but the magic of those days was gone.

It wasn't very far from here where Peter made his decision to study law. It was one of those glorious days when he and his fellow protesters stopped traffic downtown on Robert Street to draw public attention to the treatment of Russian poets in the Ukraine. That was a serious breach of human rights! About four in the afternoon they had brought traffic to a halt and the police were unable to penetrate the mass of vehicles. It was a Divine miracle they weren't all killed, but how purely exhilarating it was to see such spontaneous support for their cause! This gross civil rights violation by the erstwhile Soviet government demanded international condemnation, and it would start here, on a clogged street in St. Paul!

The depth of concern over the plight of poets in far-off lands was measured in startling terms when the cab door of an eighteen-wheeler opened and out stepped the driver, a gorilla with bowling ball hands and a hateful expression on his wide face, which Peter assumed was directed at those Soviets. He grabbed Peter's jacket, and with a single blow propelled by two hundred and fifty pounds of raging beef, Peter went cartwheeling across the sidewalk, crashing against a building. The driver then calmly began directing traffic and soon the jam was cleared.

Peter looked up and saw Melissa walk through the door. She approached him and smiled, then sat at his table and ordered coffee without looking at the menu: Italian Blend. He knew this was the only place selling that bean. She'd been here before. How had she picked this very time and place to show up? Was she following him? She walked right up to his table, as if he was expecting her, but maybe she was always that assertive. There was evidence of that. "You're a long way from home," he said, trying to fathom her intent.

She smiled. "Suburbs bore me, Peter, and bedroom suburbs bore me even more so."

"Why do you live there?"

"I won't be there much longer. My father and I argue constantly about things in the village and my mother is getting upset. She feels caught in between us." Melissa shrugged. "She's right, of course."

"Where would you go?" For a moment he regretted asking her.

"I want to move somewhere around here. I like this old neighborhood. It has an atmosphere you don't find in any of those hyped up, scattered messes where Dad and Mom live. Maybe I'll look for an apartment somewhere near this place. Do you know of any vacancies?"

He thought for a minute before answering, then shook his head. "No," he said, not wishing to open that subject.

She looked at him for a few seconds. "Things aren't going very well at the village." He nodded. "Torres is getting a lot of people stirred up and they're turning against Cardenas."

"Then you'd better wallop Torres again. Cardenas is old, and though he has a lot of good sense, he isn't well tuned into the world of today. Torres is no leader; he's a very angry man with a lot of emotional baggage, and that can be damaging. I'd like to reinvolve myself out there, but I've taken on a lot of work with my new job and there just isn't time."

Melissa sat just around the corner of the small table from him and now moved even closer, their knees bumping together. "Will you please come with me to the next meeting out there?"

Peter thought for several seconds, then sighed. "I don't think I should go back, not now, anyway. You still have Montero."

Melissa nodded and spoke softly. “Yes, we still have Raul. He’s intelligent, he knows the issues, but he can’t assert himself. You know, Peter, for the first time in my life I wish I had a profession...I want to be a lawyer, to do what you do...what you did. I’d like to be able to step into the breech out there and get the people behind me...Just as you did.”

“You want to go into advocate law?”

“Yes. To me, that would be the highest calling. I would find it an honor to do that work, even if it’s near the bottom of the salary curve.”

Peter arched his eyebrows and looked back at her strange green eyes. “No, it’s not near the bottom of the curve.”

“It’s not? I thought—”

“It’s at the bottom. Do you have any real idea what being an advocate lawyer means, or are you just attracted to the idea of it?” For a moment he thought about Jane, the would-be writer. “Advocates are scorned by the legal establishment as wash-outs who couldn’t make it in private practice, though most could.”

“I don’t care what they think. I want to do something where my efforts will make a difference in the lives of at least a few people. I’ve no illusions about saving the world; it’s a little too big for that to happen. But I would like to have an impact in some tiny corner of it.”

“That’s as much as anyone can hope for. I don’t know how it looks to you, but from the inside, it’s really not a lot of fun. Not the way it used to be out there. The public distrusts you, thinks you’re all communists out to destroy our way of life. Businesses genuinely hate you and don't mind telling you so. Your clients think you're okay, but they don't appreciate what goes into meeting their legal needs. It's a pretty damned thankless job, then one day you realize there are more satisfying ways to earn a living. And more lucrative ways as well."

"You disappoint me; I didn't think you were into this for the money."

"What I'm doing now isn't for the long run. It's only a stop along the route to something else, and I don't know what that is at the moment, but I am in transition…in more ways than you know."

They finished their coffee. "Let's take a little walk," Melissa said. "It's such a nice evening."

They walked a block in silence, then Melissa said, "You have a lot of personal issues going on, don't you?"

"Like I said, many things are in transition."

"Really?"

He nodded. "Really. My wife wants a little more lebensraum…you know…living space. Without me in it…for a while, at least."

"You're giving it to her?"

"I don't see a good alternative."

"You're doing the right thing. It couldn't have been easy, but you're respecting her feelings, even if you don't understand them. My father could be a lot closer to my mother if he'd do that once in a while."

"Thank you. It's taken me a long time to learn this, but I've come to see that while we can make a difference in some small ways, people and events basically are what they are. We can't stop the world and send it off in another direction. Others more powerful than us have gone down that path and it always ends in ruin. Think of it; we've been served up Hitler, Stalin, Joe McCarthy. By the way, if my wife saw us here, walking down a dark street, she'd want more than lebensraum."

"Your wife has a small child to care for. She won't be patrolling around in the dark. Relax. So what is it you're saying, actually? That things have a way? That they are what they are, so forget about making any difference? That doesn't sound like the Peter I've heard so much about." For a moment their eyes met and in the dim glow of the street lights he saw enigmatic waves cross her face: a smile, regret, something else he couldn't decipher.

"A few years as advocate will teach you things about the world, and you will shed some of your old assumptions. There is a way of things. In some perverse way, foxes are what foxes must be; chickens are what chickens must be. They have a basic nature, so, despite all the lawyer rhetoric, maybe it's best if the chickens take responsibility to stay away from the foxes. You can keep them apart for only so long, and if the fox ends up dining on the chicken, well, don't blame him for it. That's part of its nature."

"That sounds like some kind of Darwinism. Do you think survival of the fittest is the best policy for time?"

Peter thought for several moments as they continued down Selby Avenue. "We're living in an era where, for whatever reasons, we don't apply the good sense and decency they did a generation ago. We lack the leadership we had then. I don't know why, but the best qualities of mankind aren't coming to the surface. This is reflected in our political leaders, absorbed as they are in partisan politics, but in our own behavior as well. Look at all the mindless violence pandered on TV in the name of entertainment. Parents obsessed with money and ignoring their families. It says something about the way we live. It screams "instant gratification.'

"Some day a far wiser generation will take the leadership. Maybe then we will return to a common sense approach to life and restore a sense of respect and dignity. But until then, yes, foxes will be foxes and chickens will be chickens. It's time I should go home. Thanks for listening to me."

They walked half a block in silence. Suddenly she turned and stepped abruptly in front of him, stopping him in his tracks. "Is that what you really think?" she demanded. "Ten years of practicing law and that's all it's taught you? What happened to the Peter Hoffler of five years ago? Did he just fade away, sidelined by some kind of warped but politically correct rhetoric? You sacrificed all of those principles and ideals that you believed would guide your life to…to what? To this dumb job you have listening to unemployment appeals?"

"I don't plan to stay with this—"

"Then what?" she shouted, her eyes blazing up at him, jaw set in firm lines. "Oh, I've got a great idea for you! Listen to this: since you now believe in all this Darwinism, you should join that group that my father runs with. Those smug, self-satisfied bastards who go around patting each other on the back for doing it all, the ones keeping society from falling apart by some horrid, liberal-sponsored fiasco. That's what they profess to believe! Survival of the fittest; the free, unfettered market; Laissez Faire for everyone! Survival of the strongest and damn the others! Sacrifice all on the altar of the free market, American style! Only the giants win; then they tear each other apart! Up until the moment someone out there in that free market takes a bite out of their ass! Then all those same pompous phonies run straight to the government, wearing their custom-tailored suits, demanding protection from the very same competition they so loudly worshipped! Wouldn't you just love to be a part of that crowd? You'd fit right in!"

"Melissa, I—"

"Is that the sort of people you want running our public affairs? Are you satisfied that the public interest is best served by those who hold those narrow views? Those who are bent on forcing their own agenda onto everyone, because it's either profitable or it soothes some religious zeal they harbor? This is the kind that my father surrounds himself with, and they would love to grab the reins of government and twist it into something serving only their needs, and then call that the workings of the market! And you would let them take control, then walk away from it saying 'Oh well, foxes are foxes and chickens are chickens and the chickens just better take care,' or some other bullshit like that?"

"Listen, please—"

"Is this the world you want your daughter to grow up in, and raise her own family? You said there is a lack of common sense today. Well, you're right and the most pitiful thing about it is that I'm looking at the reason we have this sorry mess! It's because people like you have lost the courage and will to stand up to these people. You are the reason we have so many thugs and flakes running our society!" She jammed her hands into his chest, nearly pushing him off his feet. He felt the air forced from his lungs. Then she brushed past him, bumping his shoulder.

Peter watched her walk quickly down the long block, turning the corner and disappearing into the night. For several moments he just stood there, stung by her sharp words, struggling to collect his scattered, broken thoughts. He still felt her knees against his. Sensations he hadn't experienced in two years. Now he knew how much he missed that simple, female contact.

In less than one hour he had alienated two women, and for opposite reasons. One had said, in effect, 'leave,' while the other was demanding to know why he left. Well, where to go now? Home to the empty rooms? He thought for a moment, then turned and headed back to the coffee shop. The little place on the corner of Western and Selby was his haven from turbulence, as much now and as it was in the past.

Chapter Fifteen

It was still an odd, alien feeling being home in mid-afternoon when the mail arrived. Another one of those daytime rituals, along with ignoring the afternoon TV talk and game shows he abhorred. How many years passed since he'd been home during the week-days? Thirty? Vince watched through the front window as the postal carrier dropped the day's serving into his mail box. He didn't want the driver to see him. He didn't want his neighbors to see him at this time of the day, either. A quick dash down the driveway and back. One of those quirky things you do at times like this.

There was the usual assortment of junk mail and unsolicited debris headed nonstop to the waste basket, several bills to be paid…an envelope from Great States Electric…Now his heartbeat quickened, a spinning mix of fear and hope. Like sitting at the defense table watching the jury coming back to the courtroom.

Great States had been by far the best of the interviews he had to date. How many, now? Was it ten? Twelve? Whatever. He'd lost count. But this interview had gone extremely well, better than any of the others. Yes, they were glad he applied, indeed they were; he had the skills they were looking for. Wiring up computer systems? Not to worry. That was just one branch of Great States and this job was for estimating and layout design, which was mostly what he'd done for the last twenty years. Everyone was relaxed; the coffee flowed and they talked about past projects, for some of which they'd been competitors, a few of which they both lost out in the bidding. They talked about the idiocy of some of the state and city codes and all the other concerns and aggravations that beset modern-day business. "Vince, we were really sorry to hear of Lakes folding up," someone told him. Oh, yeah! Come on, when did a company ever grieve over a competitor going in the tank? Still, they had a lot in common and the hour passed quickly. Thanks so much, he was told. Really appreciate the interest.

He threw all the other envelopes on the table and ripped this one open with a finger, ignoring the letter opener lying nearby. The logo of Great States was familiar; he'd seen it many times…In his former life. He settled into a chair and, holding himself from rambling through the letter, started reading from the beginning, his heartbeat rising heavily. "Thank you so much for your interest in…There were several well-qualified candidates like yourself…After careful consideration we have decided…" He closed his eyes and let the letter drop to the floor. For five minutes he didn't move, nor did a coherent thought come to him. He sat silently with his chin in his hand and heard the clock ticking off more time from his life. Hours, days, years.

For a moment he wondered who they hired. Some twenty-five year-old with a tenth of his experience but willing to work for far less? There was a time when a job candidate's experience was valued, and he always did when hiring someone. Beyond a minimum level today, it seemed to be a liability. Goddammit! He thought for several more moments. Jeff Martin was Great States's operating manager, one who interviewed him and whom he knew well. He was one of his old lunch mates from times gone by. Why not give him a call, take him out to lunch and ask what happened? There was always that chance…He rose slowly and walked a few paces, hands in his pockets, staring at the kitchen floor tile, thinking hard. Then he stopped abruptly and lightly thumped his head against the door jamb. Dumb idea! Just plain dumb! Wake up, Bozo; it's the age of litigation. All they'd tell him would be the same platitudes they put in the letter.

He still hadn't heard back from ProFab and his interview was four weeks ago. Dammit, these delays were frustrating!

He grabbed the Great States letter and slammed it on the table, his hand stinging from the impact, then he swept it on the floor. He stood and wandered from room to room. He came back to the kitchen and sat for a few moments. What really happened to the old days? Back when you could keep your livelihood till you decided when to pull the pin, not when someone far away pulled it for you, without a second thought or the slightest remorse. It's hard to follow the trends today, he thought. Some of the old rules of economics either didn't apply any more, or did so in some oddly altered form.

What he found strange was when you perform well you expected continuity under the old rules. Today, some holding company finds you attractive and you're bought out just like that. Back in the eighties he held stock in a company in northern Minnesota that manufactured snowmobiles. Things went well for several years, their payroll grew and profits were strong. Then one day a North Carolina firm learned about them and sent agents to visit the site. "We have a most favorable impression of your business," they told the owners. "There is great potential for further development." What they wanted to develop was promptly disassembled and hauled down to Charlotte. The rest stayed behind to rust in an abandoned building and the workers were left to file their unemployment claims. Following that, the stock prices for the surviving company greatly improved. The old law of supply and demand might be alive and well as ever, he thought, but the new atmosphere of heightened competition defined success in terms of the Dow and NASDAQ indexes.

Great States…Gone! He sat silently at the table for another half hour. ProFab…It came to him gradually as the minutes ticked their way into history. It was one of those moments of truth, when the light of clarity burns brightly. ProFab would be the end of the line. If they didn't extend an offer, and he'd accept thirty thousand less if necessary, he'd have to turn his back on construction. There would be no other offers. He would have do what was always there: retail. Over the counter selling at a third of what he had before, maybe closer to a fourth. How brutally heavy it was, all this waiting.

"Ann would just shit!" he shouted. Ann the great curriculum director, seventy-seven thousand a year and expecting no less in the future for any reason.

"Why can't you just slide right over to another firm and pick up where you left off?" she kept asking. Bright in a bookish way, but oddly naive about the world beyond the walls of learning. Would he have to sell his skills at a fraction of the rate that he used to charge to install? Would he soon have to deal with his former competitors as a clerk? What would they think when they saw him behind the counter? Vince was mulling over this prospect when he heard a car pull in the driveway and the rumble of the garage door opening. He tightened up as Ann stepped in through the side door, not a happy look on her face. Let her lead off.

She sighed heavily and glanced at the clock. "A budget committee is meeting tonight. I have to be there." she said tersely.

"The district has a business manager. Maybe it would be a lot easier if you just stayed away from all those—"

"The future of the curriculum is at stake!" she snapped. "This isn't just a budget issue all by itself."

"How bad is the budget?"

"Four to five million," she answered, slowly pacing the kitchen floor, her arms folded.

"It was only three million a month ago."

"It wasn't addressed quickly enough. Things escalated, but it's manageable. I want to be sure the cuts are passed around so instruction doesn't bear the brunt of the hits."

"I thought the board made those—"

"We recommend and give our reasons," she said, sighing audibly. "There are two board members who have the old one-room school mentality and think teachers are overpaid. I have to be there to address these concerns. You can grill a steak or go out if you'd prefer.

I have to leave." With that she disappeared into the bedroom for fifteen minutes, then emerged wearing another outfit.

"You have to change clothing for a board meeting?"

She sighed as she brushed past him. Then she saw the letter on the table. "Well?" she demanded.

He shook his head. "Same as all the others. No cigar for second place."

She breezed past him toward the garage door. "I don't have the time to discuss this now but later I would like your explanation as to why you consistently fail to obtain work that is so similar to what you have done. Vince…I cannot understand this! There is just no logical reason for what is happening! It appears to me you are not effectively marketing yourself. You have the skills and you have the experience, so what is the issue here?"

Now he sighed loudly. "Ann, it's not how much experience—"

"I don't want your explanation now!" she interrupted, holding both hands before her. "I don't have time! But we will discuss this tomorrow." She turned quickly, stepping into the garage, then stopped and turned back to him, standing in the doorway. "I'm sorry if I…" For just a moment she wore a curious, perplexed expression as the words seemed to jam in her mouth. She shook her head slowly, her voice softer now. "We can discuss this later."

"You asked for an explanation, now you don't want it?" he demanded, his voice rising, his face flushed.

Again she stopped at the door and turned to him. She raised her hands again, as if they were her voice, then dropped them quickly.

"We will discuss this later!" She turned abruptly and the door closed behind her. He heard the car start and back down the driveway as the opener closed the door.

Market? This coming from someone who has never attempted marketing a single, goddamn thing in her life? Then...why did she suddenly stop with that strange look on her face, as if she had a second thought? About what? What the hell's going on here? He wheeled back toward the table, grabbed the Great States letter from the floor, ripped it into shreds and flung them, the tiny pieces scattering across the tile floor. He stood quickly, his thighs nearly overturning the table, then lurched to the sink and grabbed a cup, one Ann inherited from her mother. His lips tightened as his arm went back, the cup held high. He envisioned it: shreds of glass exploding on the counter, the sink, all across the floor. "Shit!" he yelled. "Leave it for her to clean up!"

It was as if the plug was pulled, standing there, cup still raised over his head. He felt the rage drain from him. Then he placed the cup on the counter, turned and walked out the door. Screw the neighbors if they see me!

Ann glanced at the gilded clock on the bedroom fireplace mantle, sighed and laid her head back on Carter Newman's chest. She felt the warm, gentle flow of air from the fireplace heatilator, the faint taste of his fine white wine still on her tongue. "You've been rather quiet tonight," he said.

She took his hand in hers and stroked it. "Too much, all at once. The budget issue will not be resolved easily and we'll have to make major staff cuts. Unfortunately, the home life is becoming impossible."

"I know things are difficult but you've never really explained what's going on with him."

Ann was silent for several moments. "Carter, why do I behave one way around you and like a completely different person when I'm with Vince? When I'm with you, the gentler side of me comes out. I speak softly, take time to think, feel so much more confident of what I am saying and doing. Here I feel comfortable, as if…I don't know. Don't ask me if I still love him. Right now I don't know if I ever did. Love burns strong with the sweet flames of youth, Carter, but then come the middle years when it has to change and grow. He tries in his own way to do things right. Basically, he is a well-intentioned man, but it appears he has given up.

"Being around him seems to bring out that critical, judgmental side of my personality, and I know it comes across badly to him. I did this again today. I felt the anger rising, then tried to get control of it, before hurting him. The words just jammed in my mouth, I couldn't say what I wanted to say to him…" She paused, holding her head in her hands. "I harbor a certain amount of anger, and I aim most of that at him, then he gets angry. It doesn't bring out the good that is within me, or within him, and that makes it very hard to go on, day after day, year after year. Would it be a great sin if I just told him that I want both of us to be happy, and for that to happen we must not live together? If I leave him, it won't because I no longer love him; if I stay with him it won't be because of a great love for him."

Ten minutes passed in silence. She turned slightly and placed her glass on the small table, then set his glass beside hers. She lay back against his chest again, her hands reaching down, across his thighs, and her pulse began racing. Slowly she turned and rolled on top of him, his face in her shadow, pulled her blouse up, her breasts brushing against his hairy chest, and that same surging, throbbing desire, appeased just an hour earlier, now came roaring, rushing back to her. She pressed her hands behind his head and pulled it forward, her lips meshing tightly into his, her tongue sliding into his mouth. Now she felt the surging tumescence from his groin pushing against her legs, against the swollen, throbbing, heated flesh, the raging flames of her desire fanned once again, rising, spiraling toward that Nirvana she shared with him. Her breathing was heavy, coming in throbbing surges, their rhythms rising, falling together, rising again in a pulsing tandem, toward that crescendo of ecstasy that her whirling mind told her could be shared only with the man lying beneath her heaving, thrusting body.

Forrest Turley Finished his coffee, set the mug on the side table and again dived into the stack of reading material in front of him. It was standard fare: a hundred pages or more to read and attempt to digest before the next council meeting. Bills to pay by the city; an easement for power lines to run across someone's property; two new office workers to approve for hire; purchase of a thousand yards of some kind of gravel for repair of a city parking ramp. All the crunch and grind of keeping city government going. You get elected to jobs like this and they actually pay you a salary for giving up sixty or seventy hours every week. He thought about that for a moment. It was his life.

The telephone at the side table rang and he reached for it. The last two calls were from constituents in a boil over a zoning amendment allowing additional multiple unit dwellings to be built too nearby. We don't want all that extra traffic, they told him. Those buildings help pay the taxes, he reminded them. Well, we still don't want it, they said. Um. Wait till tax assessments are mailed next year. Who was upset this time? He listened for several seconds.

Then his blood turned cold and he froze. His breath stopped.

The voice was that of a male, middle-age, as best he could determine, muffled somehow, probably with a cloth over the mouthpiece or by some electronic device. "We know about your little problem, Mr. Turley," the voice said. "The Deming Clinic—"

"Who are you?" Turley demanded.

"My identity is not important, Mr. Turley. What is important is a very vital issue coming up for a vote."

"I'm voting the way my constituents—"

"If you do, you will never serve another term. You will not be able to walk the streets of your ward. You will be an outcast."

"Don't try using threats, whoever you are—"

"Just remember this call when you vote next month, Mr. Turley. If you don't, life won't be worth living." The line went dead.

He looked quickly at the caller ID window but it merely read "Anonymous."

He called the phone company but was told a trace was unreliable due to the short duration of the call. Who was it? he agonized. He racked his memory for a similar voice, somewhere, but nothing came to mind. The caller sounded well-educated, judging from the speech pattern. Who knew about his treatment and how did they find out? Dammit! He rose quickly and paced back and forth, then glanced out into the street. There wasn't a phone booth anywhere near his house and the dark streets were empty.

He gripped the back of a chair. Would these slimy bastards carry through on the threat and spread the word all around his ward? Would he be a pariah in his own neighborhood? Anyone serving more than a month on an urban city council received threats, that went with the territory, but most were hollow, someone venting their feelings. He knew the pattern: it would all start a few months before the election. Feed the voters just enough at a time to kindle their interest, then gradually let it rise to its peak just before election day. He had made his position on light rail very clear: before his own city council, transportation committee, the Metropolitan Council, a committee at the Legislature and countless gatherings with his constituents. Now what to do? Find a good reason to change your vote and ride out the heat? He shook his head. Either way you lose, Forrest. Vote it down and you'll face the public outrage. Vote it up and some son of a bitch out there will destroy what is left of your purpose for living.

Chapter Sixteen

Peter Hoffler leaned back in his leather chair and gazed out the window at the people scurrying along Grand Avenue. The leaves were losing the last of their autumn colors and would soon give way to the blasts of November winds that would strip the limbs bare for the long winter that lay ahead. The darkness of evening was arriving earlier now, and with each passing day the sun backed farther into the south, casting the bookstore across the street in a lengthening shadow of his own building. The grass that was green a month ago was now cast in a uniform dun color, receding into dormancy and soon would be smothered beneath a blanket of snow and ice.

For nearly four months he had been a partner in the law offices of Brown and Dailey, a small firm in St. Paul's Victoria Crossing area, with no specialty other than civil and family law. No high profile criminal cases for Brown or Dailey. Those sticky discrimination and labor law cases were left to other agencies. Pretty conservative stuff, but it was a step closer to what he wanted. Six months in the unemployment insurance appeals business taught him he had little chance to use his skills to make a difference in the lives of people. Still, his time as appeal attorney wasn't misspent; it just wasn't spent terribly well.

Then one day he made a major decision that marked a watershed in his life. He went against his deep-felt principles and joined a private law firm. It was a small one, just two older partners on their way into retirement and one younger associate along with three clerk typists, or administrative support, who spent their days cranking out documents on their word processors. They employed a paralegal who did all the footwork for the three attorneys.

Ironically, the firm came looking for him, which was rare for anyone in Peter's line of work. Over time he developed a relationship with Brown and Dailey that became quite cordial, considering what brought it all about. A former female employee of theirs came to him while he was with Advocate Services, claiming Dailey had discriminated against her in a recent performance rating. She claimed they were just "out to get her." Some doubts about her already set in after his initial interview but he contacted Dailey, then met with her again. Her record contained several anecdotal incidences, which brought vague responses from her, but still she insisted Dailey terminated her because she was female, and was, therefore, guilty of sex discrimination. "If Dailey wanted you gone due to your sex," Peter asked, "why did he hire a female to replace you?" He never heard back from her.

In the aftermath, Brown and Dailey decided maybe advocate attorneys weren't so bad after all, or at least Peter wasn't, anyway. During the following months he had other opportunities to collaborate with both Dailey and Brown on civil matters that were quickly resolved. Less than a year ago they approached him about a possible associate position in the firm. That was before Whitman and Pollard told Peter what's what for the future. A few months passed, a few more discussions, then their associate left and the rest was history.

Peter was trying hard to balance all of life's demands, and he told the partners he'd work fifty to fifty-five hours a week and no more. He would start between six and seven am so his evenings were open for family. Fatherhood was going to have its priority, though Mary and Emmy had lived without him now for four months. Those hours were fine, Brown and Dailey said. They never put in more than that themselves. Unlike a lot of other law firms, they hadn't kept pace with the American obsession with litigation.

What made up his day was just the usual run of mundane legal work. He wrote wills for estate settlements. He waded through the unending array of property transfer documents and real estate closings. He obtained easements for someone who wanted special access onto, over or under someone else's property. He did title searches for home buyers. He researched city building codes and settled debts—for those who could pay-the others went to his former employer. All of this made up the daily fare for more than a half million others just like him.

With all of this, he learned something: most of his clientele were owners of small to medium sized businesses or other private parties with legal problems to solve. Business owners were the very sort with whom he had earlier crossed swords. What he discovered in working out their issues was that he liked these people. They weren't the brassy, arrogant bastards he used to clash with. They were simply well-intentioned people fully prepared to pay thousands of dollars to resolve their issues. The first check paid to Brown and Dailey for his work came to three thousand two hundred and nineteen dollars. Wow! All of that for about twenty-two hours of his time. Only about half of that went into his account; the rest went to keep the doors open and paid the staff, plus a little something to Brown and Dailey for the retirement years. He was being paid to work his butt off for a client, unlike AS, where an equal or even greater amount of labor brought the same size paycheck as the time before.

The clients kept coming through the door and sending him checks for his good services. Having that kind of control wasn't a bad thing.

He had a fine rosewood desk and credenza which he moved from the middle of his private office to a window for a better view of Grand Avenue. The office was fairly large, about sixteen feet square, with walnut wainscoting and a light green carpet. Worlds apart from the tin-roofed rat traps AS rented. If he kept up at this pace, he estimated, his income would be thirty thousand dollars higher than last year.

"Have I sold out?" he once asked Raul while discussing affairs at Nuevo Del Rio. "I came to a fork in my road and I had to make a change. I will always have a tie with Cardenas and the village. I will do what I can for them, but I can't turn from my family, as I did with AS. I needed a change and the redirection of Advocate Services, faddish though it was, gave me the needed thrust." In a few months, when Brown and Dailey departed for retirement, he would become full partner, along with two other associates whom he had known for several years. "We will take on new challenges, Raul, ones avoided by the departing duet, including employment and housing law. Think about it, Raul. There may be a place for you here."

The break with Mary came four long months ago and he still wasn't adjusted as well as he expected. His small apartment, six blocks from their house on Virginia Street, still seemed alien to him. At times he was glad to have the privacy, to do what he wanted, and to stroll down to his favorite coffee house where he occasionally found someone he knew from times past. They had their own careers now and time was short for them. He could linger there as long as he wished, away from the confines of the small flat. Freed of the daily responsibilities of fatherhood, he could work on client files at the cafe, or bring them home and prepare stacks of documents for their word processors. Law was not a paperless endeavor, all the hard drives and e-systems aside.

Among the few pieces of furniture he took with him was the desk where she had slogged through four years of law school. Sitting there, her intense frustration and anxiety was almost palpable, like a musk odor. Why hadn't she just told him? It hurt to think that she fought her own silent and desperate battle, often when he was just a few feet away.

He shook his head, trying to shed these morbid thoughts and get on with his work. The fifty-five hour per week arrangement with Brown and Dailey assumed a normal family life. Separated from that, he was investing closer to eighty hours every week. He kept up with his workload; even created more of it.

Truth to tell, he was running like hell to fend off that crushing, penetrating sense of loneliness that surrounded him as soon as he stopped working. When marriage turns into an emotional roller coaster life becomes unsettling. "I crave continuity," he once told Raul. "I reach out for that comforting feeling that what I have will be there tomorrow, and all the tomorrows. Our generation imposes too many interruptions."

He made weekly visits with Mary and Emmy and noticed her mood was lighter than before, her eyes brighter, a spirit to her words he hadn't heard earlier. That made him feel happy for her; it made him sad that it came because he was not there. In one corner of the room was a table piled high with books and notes written on yellow legal-size pads. "I'm going to try it again," she told him. "It may take several months, and that's okay. Emmy is too young for me to be out of the home."

He noted the titles: tomes on corporate law and tax rules: dull as hell but those were the nemeses that brought her down. Emmy lumbered out of another room, looked at Peter, then darted straight for Mary. He felt a sharp pain and it stabbed deep into his soul. "Daddy's here," Mary told her and she came to him, more slowly. He crouched down and reached for her, then picked her up and set her on his lap, wrapping his arm around the small, soft bundle and he felt something warmer than anything he had experienced since leaving their home. She was nearly eighteen months old and learning to run better than she walked. "I have two months left on my apartment lease," he said. Emmy cuddled in his lap; she was too young to follow adult talk. He could have stayed there all day. All night.

Mary nodded and took a deep breath. "I can see that you're happy when you visit us and you're lonely when you're alone, Peter. It's hard to describe, but it would be best if we stayed apart, at least for a while longer." She came to him, took his hand and looked up to him. "I love you, but something very important is happening and I must follow that for, well, for however long." That was met with a quizzical look. "Look over there," she said, pointing toward the table. "When you left I was depressed, to the point of being immobilized. I couldn't tolerate the idea of studying law ever again. I was angry and hated the very thought of it. But something started happening to me about two months ago. It wasn't anything that I did, no sudden, great moment of clarity. One day I walked past these books, looked at the one on corporate law. I sat down, opened it to one of the bookmarks and began reading. Just like that. I've been doing it every day since then. It was as if a light came on in my mind. Some long-dormant machine suddenly started running again.

"I know what I need to do; I have a direction, Peter, I just need time. I'm sorry, that wasn't what you wanted to hear, but I'm trying to be honest with you. I couldn't go on carrying all that depression. I was afraid where that might lead. You're a good man, Peter. Please don't forget that. Are things okay with you?"

"Yes, things are okay." Okay, as in falling off a cliff with the bottom racing up toward you. He told her he was taking home tons of work. He didn't tell her why.

He walked the six blocks slowly, shivering slightly in the chill of evening, entered the cramped apartment, wandered around for a few minutes, no more than four steps in any direction, looking out at the overgrown shrubs obscuring the windows of the house next door. He tried reading a novel for fifteen minutes but the words went off into the abyss, the thread of the story lost. He threw down the book and rose, and was startled to hear the doorbell ring. He hadn't had a single visitor in four months. Who would be at his door this time of the night? He opened it carefully. At first he saw only the profile against the street light. It took a few awkward moments for this to register in his mind. How or where had Melissa gotten his address? She always seemed to know where he was. They exchanged a clumsy greeting and then he let her in, glancing quickly out into the street before closing the door. "I hope I haven't disturbed you," she said.

"No, I just came home."

"Yes, I know. You were with your family."

"Melissa, are you keeping tabs on me? You always seem to know—"

"I'm your neighbor now. I took an apartment last week, a small garret over on Nina Street. It's an old place, smaller than yours. I rather like it."

Nina was a short street two blocks from here. "Well, welcome to the neighborhood. Don't leave your door unlocked. There's always that one per cent, you know."

She walked slowly about his small living room and saw the files on the desk. "Is this all you do now? Your new job?"

He nodded. "It is, yes. It's been quite busy lately." She idly picked up a file and opened it. "Ah, we have this confidentiality thing, you know."

"Oh, shut up." She looked directly at him. "Don't you trust me?

"Certainly. It's just that—"

"You trust my judgment?" Well, yes, he did, from what he knew of her. He had this feeling he was being led somewhere. "Do you still believe that bullshit you told me about a month ago?"

"What was it about?"

"Some silly-ass thing about foxes and chickens."

He groaned silently. "You really don't want to start that argument again. You stomped away from me in a piquish fit when I said that."

"Raul may have a partial solution to the freeway issue, if he could only get some heavier support."

"A partial solution? Would you like to sit down?"

"No, thank you. He has researched other highway projects where communities stood in the path of proposed construction. He has also held discussions with officials at various levels and seems to gaining some headway on a plan that would route I-35 around the village." She explained the plan Montero presented earlier to the county commissioners and to citizens of the village. "This would mean building two to three miles of new southbound lanes to the west of the present roadway. It's less expensive than completely reworking the roads out there and it's an alternative if we lose the rail issue and the freeway is widened."

Peter thought for several moments. “It’s workable as far as the road itself goes, but it doesn’t give your father and his group what they really want.”

“I know,” she answered softly. “He and some others won’t rest till the village is wiped off the map. They have been schmoozing politicians at every level, wining and dining them, all the time hating their guts just for being what they are. Aaron Young is talking with people in Minneapolis and has started something for the inner city people, but his health is not good and he tires easily. You’ve spent time in the Phillips Neighborhood. You know how much redevelopment has occurred there and the millions spent in refurbishing houses. Has the Peter Hoffler I’m looking at totally abandoned the people he knows and cares about in the village?” She stepped in front him and took his hand in hers. It felt warm, as it did with Mary only an hour ago. “Raul has made progress, more than I expected, but he doesn’t deal well with politics. Neither does Reverend Young.”

“Neither do I, Melissa.”

“Much better than they do.”

“Melissa, if I go back there now, everyone will think I have returned to the same role I played earlier. Then when I tell them this it will erode their confidence in Raul, and that will mean the end of everything we’ve all done out there.”

“You’ve stepped away but don’t you still care what happens to those people? For all they have done to build themselves a home and a life of their own? You’ve been separated from Mary for four months." Now she gripped his other hand and held them tightly in hers, her strength surprising, the warmth of her hands flowing into his. For a moment he looked into her clear, green-colored eyes and felt something, an odd swirling, like sand stirring from a placid river bottom, as it had that night at the village when she laid her hand on his shoulder. But as quickly as it came it deserted him. "Do you want to lose what you've done out there as well as—"

"As well as losing Mary and my daughter?"

She held his hands, then turned slowly, bringing his arms around her as she backed up against his chest. "Peter, I don't know what you think of me, but I'm not someone who lacks inhibitions and throws herself on everyone else. The boys in my high school class thought I was a prude. Can you imagine that?"

"Yes, I can, actually."

"Thank you. I know some day you will find your way back to Mary and to your daughter, because that's what you want and it's what your family needs. She thinks she doesn't need you now because she's working her way through a lot of issues. They're complicated, very subjective, best understood by other women. Most of us pass through phases like that, great or small; only a few are spared. The bar exam didn't cause this; it was only the catalyst that opened the door, then it all came out. She will come to you later, but right now I need you. I had a terrible row with my father and that's how I ended up here. Just hold me, please."

Something inside told him no; something else inside him said yes. He felt the warmth of her back pressing against his chest, against his arms and his hands as they clutched her firm, slender shoulders. He still knew little of her past life but he sensed she knew men, in many different ways. There was a kind of enigmatic innocence about her often accorded to one who clings to their values and takes the blows delivered by the rest of the world.

Now it came back, that swirling, pulsing feeling, the bottom again stirred from its torpidity by her closeness, bringing back memories of a lost time, of an age when flames burned brightly, fueled by youthful innocence and intense desire. The river was churning, whipped into a cloud of murky, powerful thrusts and whirls. His searing circuits heaved and pounded by the overload. It seemed to him he lost his hearing, her words were not coherent. "I want the every best…whatever that may be," Her voice came swirling out of the spinning vortex. "If you cannot go back…I will understand and we will…hoping that the powers that be will see…We must all see the light of reason, before judgments spanning great distances are made! Let's just share these moments, can we?" It was more than mere desire for her; it was a longing that rose, pulsed, reached back to times lost in memory.

She turned slowly and his hands were behind her, sliding down her slender frame to the curve of her hips. She tilted her head back and her lips brushed over his, then down again, up and down, side to side, they meshed—warm, soft, inviting, beckoning him to a time that seemed so distant; a better time, when feelings could be overt and - they could revel in the pure, simple pleasure of each other. A shared ovation once bestowed upon him and his beloved by the hallowed sanction of the Holy Christian Church.

Chapter Seventeen

Those who claim expertise on death—a dubious assertion for one still among the living—describe a phase through which survivors often pass when they feel a powerful urge to sever themselves from much of what connected them to the deceased. Homes are sold, careers and work locations often changed, new social lives formed. There can occur that need to dissociate with one's past and find a new life.

Following the deaths of his wife and son, Forrest Turley went through a period when he felt compelled to sell off everything, the house, the furniture, and start all over. He thought it would all be a constant reminder connecting him to his loved ones and it would only bring back the pain to for him suffer time and again. But in the end, after passing through that part of the grieving process, coupled with his own judgment and some advice from a council member, he decided to keep it all. There would always be reminders; something that would trigger another episode of pain. He couldn't bring himself to turn away from his former life and the loved ones who made that life for him.

So tonight, on an overcast November evening, he sat at the dinner table where he had shared meals with his departed wife and son. Tonight he was with others whom he had come to know and trust. A few days ago, Melissa called and asked for him to meet with her,

Raul, Cardenas and Reverend Young. Coffee cups were scattered around the table and Melissa was telling them about her recent visit with Peter, leaving out some details. "He's going through a crisis of his own," she said. "He and his wife are separated and he has also left Advocate Services."

Turley and Young arched their eyebrows. "What happened?" Young asked.

"A philosophical change; political correctness in a conservative environment. He disagreed, then soon after received a nicely worded letter about a great future somewhere else."

Turley sighed heavily. "They've lost a good man, but times change. Where is he now?"

"He floundered a bit at first, but then joined a small law firm in St. Paul. This was a good change for him, though his wife is still going through her own emotional tailspin. We must go on without him. He wants to help, and he will consult with you, Raul, but he believes that returning in any capacity will weaken your position with them. It's disappointing," she shrugged. "Anyway, Raul has developed an alternative plan if the Legislature votes down the rail appropriation."

Raul spread a large map across the table. Turley and Young leaned forward as he described the layout. "If the freeway wins out, we might still be able to save the community." He described the plan to swing the north and southbound lanes in an arc west of the village with the present northbound lanes serving as a frontage road to the new businesses to be built north of the village limits.

Aaron young studied the plan and nodded. "This would only require construction of about two miles of new road, plus the two off-ramps. That's much cheaper than acquiring all that village property for the lane widening and the building demolition."

Cardenas looked closely at the plan. "Have you talked with the Dakota County commissioners?"

Raul nodded. "There was cautious support, but not wholehearted endorsement. They're concerned about the cost of purchasing the land needed for the new lanes. They won't raise the mill levy under any circumstances. They took a lot of heat the last time the taxes went up. The board has no interest in eliminating the village, if for no other reason than the loss of property taxes when the freeway takes acres of land off the tax rolls. This would eliminate the cabinet shop and Dahlenberg pays more than thirty thousand a year in property taxes."

Cardenas raised a finger. "Raul, the cabinet shop pays taxes, yes, but new businesses built along the frontage road, wouldn't they pay more taxes? This is a one-mile stretch of businesses, once they're all up and running."

"Not necessarily," Raul answered. "Mr. Behlen's plan calls for a freeway turnoff directly in the middle of the village that would extend east to the Bellwood security gate. An interchange of this size takes fifty acres off the tax rolls, and another thirty-five with the road into Bellwood. If you subtract out what taxes the paved-over land would have paid, the difference becomes much less.

"My father's usual reaction to a project like this is to scream about the cost to the public, tax increases and what not, but with this issue he doesn't care as it benefits him." Melissa said. "He wants the village eliminated, wiped off the map, no trace of a Hispanic presence anywhere near his exclusive retreat."

Reverend Young was silent for a moment, then said, "Raul, does your plan relate at all to freeway development north of here, from the Minnesota River to Minneapolis?"

"Construction will be in the median from Nuevo Del Rio to south Minneapolis where the median disappears. From there, overhead rails would be installed. A great deal of money could be saved if we attach the commuter stations to the existing overpasses, rather than building stand-alone stations." He turned to Turley. "We will need your support, both here and in the village."

Odd, awkward moments of hesitation as Turley sat silently, staring at the drawing on the table, but something in his expression, in the tight, drawn lines of his face, caused Raul to look long at him. "You…you referred to supporting this portion of the plan, Mr. Turley. The part effecting the village…You do still support light rail for the city…don't you?"

Again that stiff, strained silence as Turley sighed deeply, fighting some internal struggle. Now Aaron Young looked at him. "Forrest, is something wrong?"

More seconds of silence, then a slow nod. "There is another dimension in all of this. In all large scale public projects there is a gap between the time the Legislature makes the appropriation for the matching funds, and the time when construction begins, which can be more than a year later. During that lag period the costs rise and whatever was planned and approved earlier must be either cut back to stay within the limits of the funding, or local tax dollars have to make up for the rise in costs. That usually translates into another tax hike. "We've gone through the lag period for the Hiawatha project and costs inevitably rose. There have been discussions about cutting back on the number of stations on the route and the number of train cars to purchase. There are quite a few people very upset about it. This will happen also with the 35 corridor project, and voting it in will mean the public will have two rail projects that need to be cut back significantly. I know what can happen: widespread disillusionment sets in and enough folks ready to stir the resentment and call for a referendum vote. If it goes down, and it will if it comes to a public vote over paying for greatly increased costs, it's going to be very bad thing for those who would make use of the rail lines, many of whom will be my constituents."

Three people around the table stared hard at him in disbelief. It was Aaron Young who found the words first. "Forrest, you…you aren't withdrawing your support for the rail plan? You can't be serious!" Young glanced to the others, his eyes wide in dismay. They just stared at Turley who sat silently, staring at the table, not even seeing the drawing in front of him.

"Mr. Turley,' said Melissa, "I don't understand. Without your support we lose the benefits of rail and also the homes and businesses of those in Senor Cardenas's village. If Raul's idea is not accepted there will also be the loss of many homes bordering the present right of way in your own ward.. We can't..." she again looked at him, "Mr. Turley...what went wrong...?"

Turley was silent, and it seemed as if time came to a stop in the small room. Finally Manuel Cardenas turned slowly to Melissa and Raul. "Could I ask the two of you to leave for about a half hour? This is something Reverend Young and I should talk over with Mr. Turley. It would be best if just the three of us were here"

"There is a cafe half a block up on Lake Street," Turley told them. Raul and Melissa rose slowly, glancing at Turley, Young and Cardenas as they left the room and stepped through the door.

When they were gone Young again turned to Turley. "Forrest, something has gone very wrong. This is the most important issue you'll ever face on the council!"

"I've told you I'm concerned about the costs—"

"No, something else caused you to pull back. The cost matter alone wouldn't stop you...Did someone else talk to you?"

He looked up quickly at Young. "What...? No, it's just that...well," he sighed heavily, "there are many competing causes before the council now for funding. We can't underwrite them all."

Young kept staring at him. "Of course not, we never could. It all comes down to priorities. But you've faced that many times without reversing yourself."

Now Young turned slowly to Cardenas and as he did so Turley's eyes followed him. Cardenas looked softly at Turley and smiled. "There are always priorities. We have many problems at my village, too, and I have to sort them out with my council. But here...ah, something bad has happened." He looked at Turley. "Can we help? Is there anything Reverend Young and I can do to help you with this business?"

Turley shook his head. "No. No, but thank you for the offer."

Cardenas turned back to Young who said, "Forrest, some every serious matter has come between you and your constituents and has caused you to change your vote on a very vital issue. We can't turn away from this, not now, with everything at stake! Please, what has gone wrong? What terrible thing could cause this?"

Forrest Turley looked straight at Young, then to Manuel Cardenas, then a very long look at the table in front of him as the clock on the mantle softly ticked away the time, seconds, minutes. Young stared at Turley with a stricken expression. Finally Turley took a deep breath and exhaled slowly, drumming his fingers on the tabletop. "You are all my friends...So you must know. For the past several months I have been seeing a counselor at a clinic, far enough away from here, so I thought. Someone must've learned about it. I was followed home one afternoon. Then came an anonymous phone call about the vote."

Young sat back. "Behlen set this up. He hired someone to do this. Were you able to trace the call?"

"Probably came from a pay phone. I could hear traffic in the background. We don't have evidence that Behlen was behind it. I have enough other enemies and any of them could have done this. Dave Behlen is not alone in his opposition."

"But that's not what you're thinking, is it?"

Turley shook his head. "No. But there's still no way to trace this to him. He's too smart to get directly involved in dirty work like this."

"What would anyone do with this information?" Cardenas asked. "Is this, you know, very bad business for you?"

Turley looked at the two men and nodded slowly. "For years I blamed myself for something that happened, when I was a child. I kept telling myself I should have done something…but I didn't. They were little children. It was bad for me, all those years after that, but I thought I had it under control. Then the accident…when they both died…and it all started coming back. Like some horrible nightmare. It took a long time, but I finally learned it was my father's doing, not some flaw in me. He had this strange thing about small children." He told them what he saw that black night and what his father did to him. "I never thought guilt could be such a horrible burden. I had to get rid of it."

"But it sounds as if you did," Young said.

"Yes, and now I can live without all of that extra baggage. But…because of what it was, involving small children, and now that someone else knows about it, things can be distorted and any spin put on it, then they spread it around everywhere. I've been threatened before, but never so personally, and now I don't know what to do."

Cardenas rubbed his chin. "If this happened to me I would just let everybody know the truth. Then it would be all right."

Turley smiled thinly. "Yes, Senor Cardenas, in your village that might work. You are all of the same race with a similar background.

But this is a very big urban area, a racially and ethnically mixed inner city neighborhood, and they don't all see the world the same way. Not everyone living here is so forgiving, either. There are many publications that circulate through the inner city neighborhoods and these people, whomever they are, could use any of them to spread whatever twisted version they wished.Yes, I have support in my ward, but like I said, I have my enemies, too, and they read those publications."

Young glanced at his watch. "The three of us should set a time to come together again. Right now we need to decide what to tell Raul and Melissa."

A north wind swept over the city, a harbinger of what was soon to come. Raul and Melissa walked beneath the trees, stripped of the leaves that blew loosely in the street, the knarled branches casting an eerie Halloween silhouette against the glow of city lights in the dark evening. They walked for a half hour, her hand in his, Melissa telling him that one way or another, she was going to bring Peter back. "He won't take your place, Raul. He refused to do that, but he can make it easier for all of us, and that we do need."

Raul sighed again. "Melissa, right now, after what happened at Turley's house, I think we're just whipping a dead horse. I don't know what caused him to back away, but that is plainly evident."

"No, Raul, we—"

"We can't do this without Turley's support. He votes no and that will convince every other supporter to do the same and it will be dead in the water. Why would the others risk supporting it when the one whose ward would receive the most benefit votes against it? He backs out and they're spared the burden of justifying the costs." He slowly shook his head. "I don't know...maybe I should take the offer I got last week."

Melissa looked up at him quickly. "Offer? What offer was that?"

"I didn't say anything to you because at the time I wasn't very interested. I thought we still had a chance here. Now I'm sure we don't...Two of my cousins have part ownership in a law firm in Phoenix. They've offered me a position."

"I see. Doing what?"

He hesitated, taking a deep breath. "...They specialize in economic development, mostly land purchases and property development."

"Oh, you would be working with all those developers, is that right?" She abruptly released the grip on his hand.

"Yes, that is what they need."

"Uh huh, well that should be nice for you. I mean, wow, you could negotiate leases and contracts for brand new shopping malls! Pave the legal way to build more discount stores and casinos for people to piss away money they don't have, or build another featureless bromide of a strip mall that no one needs! Maybe another no-brainer entertainment park! Help the politicians brag about all the new part-time service jobs they created! You could prepare the way for one more overpriced and underbuilt housing development, spreading the hell and gone to the horizon! Chop up those old, outdated neighborhoods; lay down another eight-lane thoroughfare so we can all drive faster and get to the next mall thirty seconds sooner! I mean, who needs those old-fashioned neighborhoods where people know each other? It's the twenty-first century, people, so get the hell out of the way of progress! Is this really what we need in this country? More, more, more, more?"

"Yes, Melissa, it does seem to be what people want. If not, then why are these being built everywhere—"

"Because this is what's served up as progress. As if this is the only goddamn way to go and there just are no alternatives! Look at it, Raul; over here we have a strip mall, over there is a cluster of single family dwellings; clumped right beside all of this we have apartments or condos. Scattered here and there are the discount stores and in some suburbs you even have warehouses and manufacturing, all in the same goddamn place! You don't even have sidewalks in most of these developments because it's assumed no one would ever attempt getting around by any means other than auto. They plan and build as if pedestrians no longer exist! There is no community of people living together; no central gathering places, nothing that brings people together. Everyone is an island onto themselves. These creations are nothing but profit centers on the spread sheets of the holding companies far away! And you want to serve up more of that?"

"It's the wave, Melissa. The trend, and I don't know how you change its direction—"

"There are alternatives! We need people like you and Peter to flesh out that vision. Peter talks of urban infill: redeveloping the inner city areas to make them more liveable and less vulnerable to crime. Most of that older architecture just cannot be replicated and it's infinitely better than those pressed wood and concrete slabs they throw together in the suburbs.

"Government shouldn't use its brute force to stop outer development. My father's dead right about one thing: people must have the right to make choices, and if that sends some folks to the outlying area, then let it be so."

Again she gripped his hand in hers, more tightly than before, and he winced. "It's in our nature to crave open space. We have these conflicting needs for space, for movement, and for unlimited choices. But at the same time, we feel an equal pull to come together, to form communities with enduring relationships where the welfare of one actually is the concern of at least a few others. Where someone will say to you, 'Hey, I haven't seen you for several days. Are you okay?' We pay homage to the idea of rugged individualism and to that knock-'em-dead Laissez Faire notion; yet we want just as badly to know that somewhere out there someone cares for us. We seem to have this need to expand and contract, all at once.

"Please reconsider, Raul. You won't be happy down there. You'll be back in a year. Where will you go? To the big firms downtown?" She scoffed, biting off her words. "You tried that once. Sorry, you're just not the image they want to put out to their clients. You want to be a token Mexican? Someone they put in the display window to appease Affirmative Action? Would you like to join big government and try making public policy? Good luck! What's left?" They walked another half block in silence, then she shivered as a damp wind whipped around the corner of a building. "November's not my favorite month. Let's join the others. I have this awful fear that something bad happened to Forrest."

An hour later Melissa checked through the Bellwood gate-she kept her swipe card-and stopped in the wide driveway of her father's house. She talked briefly with her mother who pointed to the lower level. "Very critical basketball tournament."

"Excellent," Melissa said as she walked down the open stairway to the spacious room with two fifty-inch wide screen TV sets, both aglow with seven-footers racing up and down the courts, her father dividing his time and emotional energy between them. His favorite college teams, juggernauts in the Division One circuit, were playing separate games and both were leading by several points, as he fully expected. They'd better be seeing each other in the NCAA finals. If not, the coaches' heads will be in the gutter. He saw her approach and glanced sideways, pointing at one of the TVs. "First year coach," he said, referring to one of the inferior teams, "Can't cut it in Division One. Get rid of him. So how is your emancipation going?"

Without answering she crossed the room, grabbed the two remotes and pressed the power buttons. Behlen gasped and sputtered loudly and half stood, his mouth wide. The audacity! Critical moments on both courts! "Oh, settle down," she said, pushing him back down in his chair. "You can read about it in the paper tomorrow."

"Those games were close and playoff—"

"Never mind! I have something wonderful to tell you."

"Really? What is that?" he said, casting her a wary eye, still staring in disbelief at the blank screens. "Tell me but first turn the games back on."

"No. Now listen to me. I came out here to tell you that I'm going back to college and have a plan to finish in less than eighteen months. Aren't you glad I finally have some direction in my heretofore dissipated and undisciplined life?"

"Ah, I don't know. Am I? What are you going to study? Would you please just turn the games on again? I can hear you just as well…"

"No. Sit still and listen. I'm going to major in economics. I want to learn how businesses operate." Cheryl came down the stairway and stood behind him at the bottom of the steps.

He stared at Melissa for several moments, his mouth half open. "What?"

"You heard me: business economics."

"Melissa, you have never shown anything but contempt for business. What brought—"

"I want to better understand the economics of private enterprise. Maybe some day I will have my own business."

He leaned forward at the edge of his seat, shaking his head, struggling with what she was telling him. "Economics…You actually want to study business?" He started to rise out of the chair.

"Sit down!" she demanded, pushing him back. "Yes, that is exactly what I said."

He nodded, still mulling over this shattering prospect. "Not social work? Not psychology or any of those usual things? Business?"

"Business."

"Business…All right," he shrugged, all enthusiasm draining from his face and voice, "if that's what you've finally decided to do." He still had that guarded look etched on his disbelieving face. "Well…Hamilne, Macalester and St. Thomas all have fine programs and—"

"Yes, I know. You will pay for it, and I do appreciate that, but I thought I'd save you some cash. I've already enrolled at Metropolitan State University."

Another stunned silence. He tilted his head to one side and looked up at her still standing directly in front of him. "Isn't that the one in downtown St. Paul?"

"Yes, and it's right on a bus route from my little apartment that I rented, you know, after our last discussion about the world" Her apartment was a small garret just under the roof of a three story building, but it was pleasing to her tastes. "Metro State might lack the prestige of those others, but it's a good school and I'm sure when I'm done there I can just as easily pursue my other goals."

"You're sure you don't want to attend St. Thomas or Hamline?"

"Thank you, but I'll be attending a very fine school. And by the way, I have this wonderful part-time job at a coffee bistro just down the street from my apartment. You should come there some day. Oh, Dad, you meet the most interesting people there! Some day I'll tell you all about them"

The tournaments disappeared from his mind, crowded out by fearful images: writers, poets, misfits, radicals of every stripe, all gathering in this coffee shop! And she's working there?

He rubbed eyes suddenly gone weary. "...You mentioned ah, some other goals—"

"Yes, I have that planned out, too. After graduation I'm enrolling in law school. Just like Kevin. Imagine, Dad, I might be an associate in some powerful corporate office, and with your help I can get it done in three years, possibly a little less. Won't that be wonderful?"

He contemplated that prospect for several moments, trying to crank up his faltering courage. "Could I ask you what your plans might be following law school?" Melissa could sense the trepidation in his words. God only knew what horrid images were boring through his tortured mind. How do you reconcile legitimate business interests with...poets and radicals?

"Of course. I think I will help wealthy clients clear the legal path so they can build wonderful shopping malls, strip malls, nifty new housing developments, all in the outer suburbs. That would be so exciting and meaningful!"

His eyes now glazed over, long fingers drumming the armrests. He shook his head. "Melissa, this goes against everything you've ever done. Everything you've ever believed in."

"But Dad, just think of it. I could be sending out intimidating letters, all written in complicated, scary legalese, sent to those poor people who just won't understand that they must get out of the way of modern development. You know who I mean: folks with those foolish ideas about keeping their little homes, neighborhoods and businesses. Oh!" she shook her head and stamped her feet, balling her fists. "Those people are just so unreasonable and unfair, don't you think?" She swept her arms out in wide arcs and shouted, "Bulldoze 'em all down, I say! Make way for progress!"

Dave Behlen just stared at her for several seconds, wishing he could get back to what he was doing when this storm broke loose. Those were big games. If they lost, their schools would lose millions in tournament revenue. "Melissa, I don't believe a word you're saying. You want me to think you're going to be a lawyer and actually do what you described?"

"Why, of course. Isn't that what you would want? You certainly did with Kevin."

"I just happen to agree with his choices. Look, the absolute last thing we need now is another radical lawyer running around, pushing government to get involved in everybody's business."

"So who said I was going to do that?" she asked, feigning a hurt expression, her lower lip curled.

"Why don't you just say what you're planning to do? You know you want to be one of those…advocates, or whatever they're called, like that…Hoffman, Hoffmeyer, whatever his name is. We don't need his kind."

"Oh, I see! We don't need those like him but it's perfectly all right to join up with some powerful machine that uses its muscle to push others around, so long as it's in the name of economic development, job creation, business expansion, private sector development, or something along that line, all promoted by well-mannered people dressed in pin-stripes and wing-tip shoes!"

"I would rather see someone working to expand the scope of our free market than for someone to chase around, screaming for more regulation and trying to frustrate every legitimate attempt to give the buying public what it wants! That's the bottom line, Melissa!"

"And what if Kevin actually changes his mind one day and has the audacity to say, 'Dad, I'm tired of serving these people. I'm going into advocate work'"

"Because I know my son and I know what he values. It's what I passed on to him! That's reason enough to feel perfectly comfortable with his future!"

"Oh, I see. As long as his choices agree with your narrow values he gets your full support because you told him what's what many years ago and he went along with it all! Well, you told me what's what a few years ago, too, and guess what? I didn't buy into it! All those preachings about how it all fits together according to your views and that there's no other way. About who belongs where and exactly why they should stay put. That's what I threw out! So where does that leave us now? Can I expect the same amount of help you so willingly gave Kevin, or do I go it alone? Because if I have to do it that way I will."

"Melissa, why can't you just…reconsider what you're telling me. If Kevin had told me he was pursuing the same plan as you, well, I guess I just wouldn't…"

"Just wouldn't what?"

He held his hands outward, struggling for the words. Those games were well into the forth quarter by now! Then he felt Cheryl's cold stare behind him. "Melissa, can we discuss this at another time? I just need to—"

"We will discuss this right now!" Behlen's head jerked around as Cheryl walked slowly across the room, stopping alongside Melissa in front of him. He thought there was a slight quiver to her voice. "Your father, the poor and silent man that he may have been, was a great believer in education, though he had little of it himself. You told him you were going to college and he praised your decision, even though he didn't have a clue what colleges were all about. He only knew it would lead to a better life, and he never once set foot on a campus. But whatever he may have thought to himself, he didn't stand in your way.

"You told him you were going into business. Well, your mother told me that he had some pretty definite feelings about people who run businesses, and you know very well he was jacked around. Still, he didn't oppose you.

"Our son decided he was going into law and you didn't stand in his way. Now we've been told that our daughter has her own goals, and she arrived at these decisions the very same way you and Kevin did. Our children are adults and we taught them to make their own decisions. Melissa just made a major one…and if you want to know the truth, I support her." She glared down at him for a several moments. No trace of a quiver in her voice now. For some reason he seemed to be sinking deeper into his chair. "Melissa, you enroll at

Metro State, if that's your choice, and we will pay the tuition till you finish. After that, you attend law school, wherever you choose, and we will pay that, too." She turned toward the stairway, stopped, then swung back to him. "And if anybody has questions about this they'll have to see me!"

An hour later Melissa was flitting about her apartment, hanging pictures and rearranging the few pieces of furniture she owned, listening to a CD. Cheryl was sitting in the living room reading a book, looked up and smiled slowly to herself. Dave Behlen sat numbly in his chair, slumping even farther into the cushion, staring dumbly at the two screens, both live again. Then he heard the final horns, only seconds apart. The two misfits in Division One suddenly got hot, sinking three pointers from beyond the circle. The great goliaths went down in the final three minutes, right along with lucrative TC contracts. The favored players stumbled off the court, stunned, heads hung down while half of the crowd went berserk with joy.

An announcer was frantically trying to interview one of the losing coaches who barricaded himself in the men's room. They heard him throwing up, contemplating a future suddenly gone very bleak.

He turned mournfully away from the screens and again rubbed weary eyes. What is this world coming to? he agonized silently. When people have the audacity to walk right up to you, just defy every shred of common sense and reason, then throw it all right in your face? Just stand there and rub your nose in all that collectivist crap! And you pay those coaches the top salaries in the business, give them the biggest budgets, the best athletes money can buy! Then they throw it all away to some low-ball teams. Just cannot understand the bottom line in all of this!

Chapter Eighteen

Once again, that singular time of the year: The Holidays! The annual collective mania, the mad scramble of Christmas spending, was about to begin amid endless splattering assaults of advertising and good cheer. Ho, Ho, Merry Christmas! We're all open 'round the clock now to serve you even better. Come charge with us. It hadn't been Vince's favorite time of year since he turned fifteen and was told he'd have to pay for the gifts he gave. That took the magic out of it. It was a time made for children and young families, but the glow of those earlier years faded without the family gathering as a cushion and that meant Vince and Ann rubbed up against each other.

For two weeks Vince struggled in a quandary about protocol: do you buy your spouse a Christmas present in the same year you separate? "Goddamned if I would!" said one he knew who had gone through a bitter divorce. Another man exchanged with his ex-spouse every year but their relationship was far more congenial. "She just married a rich guy and I have my freedom," he told Vince. Everyone was happy. Vince and Ann were somewhere in between the two poles: neither the terminal bitterness of the one nor certainly the cordiality of the other. Ann came to his rescue flatly declaring this was not a good year to be traditional. It also saved him a hundred bucks or more.

It was early afternoon and Vince was again sorting through piles of correspondence and copies of resumes he had so hopefully sent out into the business world. It was amazing how many times he retooled that document to fit what he thought were the interests of those doing the interviewing. For one employer he stressed his work in circuit design and layout; for another it was cost estimating. Another was interested mainly in his experiences as contract manager while two others were seeking someone knowledgeable in the electrical codes and layout A large firm wanted someone experienced in personnel administration. He was strong for the first four, but a bit light for personnel work, but what the hell? So he hadn't hired anyone in seven years? Shoot off a resume and see what happens.

Nothing happened.

By now he was becoming inured to rejection. Maybe after fifteen or twenty turndowns your hide gets thicker and each letter impacts less than the last one. When he filed his unemployment claim they told him he should be prepared for rejections. Really? he thought.

Yeah, really, they said.

Yeah, really.

He came across the resume he sent to ProFab three months ago. They had only called him that one time, saying hiring decisions were on the back burner for undisclosed reasons. He had a feeling about ProFab. Somehow, some way, his senses, instinct, whatever was still operating, told him this would be his last shot in the electrical contracting business. All the previous turndowns were forming a pattern he couldn't avoid any longer. He was on the edge. Out at the margin. A turndown from ProFab would be his final verdict, a final and distant judgment about the value of his skills on a market he thought he knew so well.

He drummed his fingers on the table and thought for several minutes. Desperation overwhelmed him last week and he left an application at Builders' Market, a discount outlet selling building materials, supplies and every conceivable tool and gadget on the market. One hundred and fifty thousand square feet of sprawling floor space and twenty acres of parking. That was in addition to about ten acres of lumber and other durable supplies too large to stock indoors.

After completing the application he walked up and down the twenty-eight aisles. Good God! How does anyone ever know what they have in stock, much less where it's all located? It was twelve miles from his home and a vendor Lakes Electric hadn't used to purchase supplies. It would be something to fall back on. A last resort.

Above all, he had to know where he stood with ProFab. This was pivotal to everything else. He dialed the number. For Christ's sake, keep those fingers still, will you? A woman answered, another creamy smooth voice. "Ah, may I speak with Mark Wiley, please?" he asked.

"May I ask who's calling, please?" He gave her his name. "And what is the purpose of your call?" GODDAMMIT, he hated that!! He never allowed that kind of filtering at Lakes Electric. He repressed an urge to say it was none of her f——'n business and patch me through! Can't say you're inquiring about a job. Those calls were bottom priority and you'd be ditched for sure.

"I need to discuss an estimate with Mr. Wiley. It's urgent, please." He hoped creamy voice wouldn't ask which estimate. You couldn't be sure how much these people who answered phones knew about the business. Some of those folks had their finger on everything and you could never fake your way past them. Others could be replaced by a relay switch.

"I'll put you through," she replied.

"Thank you." Past the first barrier.

A cold monotone voice came on the line. He didn't seem that way during the interview, but that was three months ago. Crap happens. Vince identified himself and the reason for the call. "Thought you were calling about an estimate," he answered, his voice still flat, cold.

"Sorry, but I didn't think I could get through to you otherwise. I'm following up on the interview I had with you last August—"

"Which one?" He heard a beep on his line: another incoming call.

"Ah, for the circuit designer—"

"We aren't hiring for that right now."

"I see…Ah, do you think you will in the near future? If so, I'd like to keep—"

"Check back in a couple months or so."

"Sure—" Click.

Dial tone.

Something must've gone bad for them, or else Wiley became a ten karat asshole in three months. Was this the end of one road in his life? He checked the Caller ID window. Builders' Market.

An hour later he was in the outer office of the Human Resources director, wondering what sort of personality he was about to encounter now. The office was on the second level, above the entry area, looking out over the entire realm, aisle after aisle, as far as he could see: customers pushing carts, lugging big cardboard boxes, navigating the aisles with four-wheel carts loaded with two-by-fours bristling like guns on a warship, customer service staff scurrying about, the PA system going almost constantly. The whir and hum of daily commerce. Wiley's abruptness was still fresh in his mind. One of his kind per day was enough.

Then the door opened and out came a short, rotund man in his late forties, wearing a cherubic smile beneath a thick shock of red hair. Vince got to his feet as the man approached. "Tim Horvack," he announced as they shook hands. "Glad to see you, Mr. Martinson."

He led Vince to his office, a rather cramped affair compared to some of the suites he'd been in recently. The smile was not that cardboard-like mask he'd seen so many times. He expected at least one other person in the office, the observer or the notetaker, but it looked as if Horvack did it the old-fashioned way.

"I've looked over your application and resume, Mr. Martinson, and I think you'd fit in with our team here." He went on to explain how the service teams worked; there were several throughout the place. There were information booths everywhere, one for electrical, others for plumbing, carpentry, flooring materials, windows, anything you wanted, someone was waiting to help you in a booth.

"All new personnel start by stocking shelves," he said. "That's their opportunity to learn the layout and for us to observe them interacting with customers. We have the location of all merchandise in our computers and that gives them time to learn how that operates. You may have noticed we have small stations located throughout the store. Either you or the customer can call up a certain screen, enter the general title of the object, pipes, for example, plumbing supplies, wiring, and it will show the aisle and section number. After a few weeks you'll rely less on that system. It's mainly for self-service."

They discussed the job for another half hour, though it only seemed like minutes to Vince. "We start new members at eleven dollars an hour and it goes to twelve once you're off the ninety-day probation and assigned to a booth. Medical benefits are available at that time. Profit-sharing and vacation times are explained in the employee handbook." Tim Horvack leaned forward, chunky arms atop his desk. "May I call you Vince?"

"Certainly."

"Good. Vince, can you start with us next Monday at eight am?"

He sat stunned for a few moments. Oh, shit! Now what? Okay, okay, let's think this through: the ProFab job's probably gone in the tank. For now, anyway. Did his skills go with it? Are we down to retail? Some little voice said y'all better grab it! Then another little voice said no! Forget it! This is ridiculous Retail? Never!! "I'd be glad to, Mr. Horvack."

"Great! Come to my office first thing Monday. I'm sorry about your business but you'll find others here who've had that same experience. They make good consultants." That was the title given those who worked the booths.

A half hour later, after Horvack arranged a tour of the store, he left the giant building and weaved his way out past cars, trucks, vans, SUVs, vehicles of every description, dodging loose carts customers neglected to shove into the corrals. Well, now what? He didn't know whether to laugh or cry; to dance for joy or just puke. He was rejoining the ranks of the employed! A bona fide member of the American workforce once again!

When he filed the claim they told him that an already employed person always looks better to a prospective employer than someone unemployed. Okay, we just took care of that little problem. In a way he was actually anxious to get started Monday…OOOOOOOOHHHHHHHHH Jesus!! Something he noticed about the people in the booths, men and women alike: They all wore polo shirts with the store logo but…some wore aprons…OOOOOOOOHHHHHHHH God! Ann is just going to have a force ten shit fit when she hears about that! No! Wait a minute. Think, man!…Just tell her about the polo shirts. No! Better yet, don't say a damned thing…no, that's not going to work, either. She's been to those places, she sees what everybody wears, even their socks, for Christ's sake! Besides, you'd have to bring the shirt home for washing and you can't sneak that in and out of the house. He almost turned the car around. No, no, that won't work, either. Oh, just let her bitch her way through it, flail away at each other for a few minutes it'll all be under the rug. Same as always. She'll make a big flap over the wage, too. Eleven bucks an hour, going to twelve. Tell her it's twelve. Christ! A year ago a buck meant nothing; now it's almost ten per cent.

God, he thought, how many times had he bought supplies from a clerk somewhere, knowing you were paid four, five times what they were getting, and you never thought for a moment you'd be there yourself. Well, shit, isn't that capitalism for you, American style? One soars to great heights while another falls head-first into the tank. Laugh when you win, cry when you fall.

Ann arrived late, as he expected. Another marathon school board meeting about the budget. Her face was tight, her voice tense, but she had been that way now for several months. "Worse than before?" he asked.

She thumped her purse on the counter and sighed heavily. "Our pupil count fell below projections for next year so that drops the average daily attendance numbers."

"Sounds bad."

"The business manager says the deficit will reach five million. Yes, that's bad, but it's still manageable."

"When does it become unmanageable?"

"I don't know," she snapped.

"Your job is still on high ground?"

"Yes. I offered my assistant as part of the cuts for next year if it comes to that."

What a noble act, he thought. Put someone else's head on the chopper, then say you'll really miss them on their way out the door.

"Did you hear from that place today? ProFab, wasn't it?"

So the battle is joined. "I don't know what happened, Ann, they wouldn't say, but they're not hiring anybody."

Ann looked directly at him, her eyes boring through him, that same tight-lipped expression she used when facing anything she didn't understand. "And why are they not hiring now? They advertised for a...circuit...designer, and you're saying they aren't filling the job?"

"They're not and I can only guess as to why. Things can change very fast—"

"I just don't understand! Why did they bother to advertise the position? Or did they hire someone else? Did you ask them about that?"

Her ignorance of private business never ceased to amaze him. Twenty-plus years in education and she knew less about the business world than any first year teacher or the average sophomore. "Ann, it could have been a hundred things: new management, a new competitor comes on the scene, you lose a large customer. Something changed, that's all I know. They don't go into the details when that happens."

She glared at him, then spun around to the window. "Well, what are you going to do now?"

He took a deep breath..."I accepted another offer. It's only temporary, but it will do till something better comes along."

"And where is this?" she demanded.

"...Builders' Market."

She thought for a moment. “Is that one of those…discount stores?”

“Yes,” he answered, watching her facial ticks start up again. “I will be a consultant in the electrical department.” Leaving out the stocking duties for the first thirty days. “For now, it’s the best I can find.”

“I just don’t believe this! A job working at a discount store? This represents the best you can find? You have more than twenty-five years’ experience in contracting and building and this is the best you can do? A CLERK IN A STORE?”

The sharpness and volume of her voice cut and shattered the air and he fought to keep his own voice from rising. “And I’m closing in on fifty-two, Ann. They can actually see that in the interview, you know. That doesn’t make me a very attractive candidate for a job close to what I did. That’s not fair, but that’s the way it works out there.” Hold your voice down. No need for both of us to lose it and shout. “I can’t remain unemployed forever and have only ten weeks of unemployment benefits left, and I need to save those, just in case I’m laid off again.”

She was silent for a few moments, looking down at the kitchen counter as she gripped its edges, her knuckles going white. “You had at least a dozen other interviews, all for estimating, designing, all the things you’ve done, and you couldn’t land any one of those? This…this just absolutely defies understanding!”

He fought back an urge to throw something on the floor. “Ann, I know this seems terribly strange, and it did to me at first, but you don't have any idea how much specialization has occurred out there. It's getting like medicine or law, not at all like it was when I started. Then you could get by being a generalist, but not now. There's more specialty calling for more advanced training or experience, and it increases every day.

"When you've been sealed away in a job for twenty years or more, as we both have, then suddenly you need to start all over again, it's as if you've just woke up after a twenty-five year sleep, walked out of your cave and tried to make sense out of what you haven't seen for that long. The first thing you learn is that you can't just pick up where you left off. Do you remember that musical we went to a couple years ago—"Brigadoon"? Every morning when they wake up it's a hundred years later. That's the way it out there now."

She was still looking out the window, shaking her head. Now her voice dropped. "So what are they paying you at this…this store?"

"…Twelve an hour."

She stood stock still for a moment, her shoulders hunched, then turned slowly toward him. Like a predator turning on its prey. Her voice was still low. "You said…twelve? Twelve dollars an hour?"

This was like two dogs circling each other in the pit. "Yes, Ann, that is what I said. Twelve an hour. They also have profit-sharing and 401K, so it should come out to thirty thousand the first year and more after that." He knew that was stretching it a bit. "I know how that looks to you, and I wish I could explain it better, why it has to be this way, but I don't really understand it myself. All I can say is that in the past two months I have learned a lot about how the world runs today and how much it has changed since I set up the business. In a way it's like walking out of a nice, warm house directly into a blizzard."

"This...this place, you're working in some kind of information booth, I gather?"

For a few minutes he thought this part of it might be headed off. Wrong. "Yes, that's what it's called."

"I see. They wear aprons there, don't they?"

"Yes, they do."

She turned back to the window, her fingers again gripping the edge of the counter as she slowly shook her head, her knuckles were still white from the strain. Permanent finger marks on the bottom of the countertop. "This is a clerk's job. You work behind a counter!"

Oh, Christ! he thought. "No, it's a consultant job," he said, his voice now rising. "You use your knowledge to help customers solve building problems—"

"Vince!" she shouted, her voice topping his, "This is a job high school graduates do! People with no more education than that! What on earth are you doing wearing an apron and doing clerk's work? And you tell me this is the best you can do, with all your experience in the building trades? I just cannot believe this!"

Now his own voice rose several clicks. He felt his vocal cords straining. "Ann, I'm not proud, but I'm not ashamed of it, either! I represent a large company in its dealings with customers, and that job requires a lot of electrical knowledge as well as a few people skills. This is not something they give to a greenhorn right out of high school! All they do is stock shelves. Last summer you were offered an internship in a glass manufacturing firm. I think it was part of that school-to-work program. Why did you turn it down?"

"I was extremely busy that summer," she snapped.

"You've said that every year. That wasn't the reason, was it?"

"Certainly it was. I am the only curriculum—"

"At the time you said this was a 'factory,' some place that employs the ones who didn't go to college, the bottom half of the class. You didn't want to identify with that crowd, so you stayed in your academic cave and told them you were too busy."

Suddenly she swung around, grabbed her purse and walked quickly to the garage door. She turned back to him, her lips set in an even line. "I have some shopping to do. I will be back later."

"Well, since we're both pissed off, why don't you just stay here and we can scream at each other. It would feel good!"

"I will not attempt reasoning with you in this mood you're in!"

"Reasoning? Who in hell is doing the reasoning here? Who's the one getting stiffed left and right out there in the real world where you don't dare to take a step—"

"VINCE!" she shouted, slamming her purse on the counter. He hoped something inside it would break. "I will not…I refuse to discuss this…" Her crimson face was twitching in rage. For a moment they just glared at each other-two belligerents separated by a deep, bitter chasm. He heard his heart slamming. "This is a waste of time! I do not care if we ever discuss this again!" She jerked open the garage door, stepped through and slammed it behind her, four walls shaking from the force.

For a few minutes Vince stood where he was, his emotions churning from swirling, break-her-neck anger to something only a little less savage. How can an educated person, age forty-seven, be so goddamn naive about the world? Cloistered all those years in the halls of education. Insulated from the crunch and grind of commerce and industry. "Shit!" he yelled to no one, picking up a wooden napkin holder and flinging it against the far wall where it shattered in a rain of splinters, falling on top the stove. He was shaking in rage only now released from the reins of self-control. Hateful images seethed inside him. "Goddammit! She wants to argue, then she runs away from it! Discuss? What the hell does she know about discussing anything?" Finally he sat at the table and rubbed his eyes, forcing the seething anger to drain away.

Minutes passed in silence, then he sighed and glanced at his watch: four-thirty. There was a small bar and grill a half mile down the street. Ann hated the place. He liked its down to earth ambiance. Right now a big, juicy hamburger, French fries and a cold beer would wash away all the rage and that other emotional debris. And if he wanted to enjoy a little more than a single beer, well, what the hell? This was as close to independence as you've been for more than twenty years, man. Enjoy it!

Forrest Turley finished his dinner; another box-meal concoction. His culinary skills were minimal. He looked to the stack of papers waiting him on the desk: A joint powers agreement with one of the suburbs to construct two transit hubs. It was one of those projects that crossed political subdivisions, thus the need for joint powers agreements. You have to share the clout. There was a contract award for refuse disposal, a new bus shelter near the University of Minnesota and an update on a park and ride study project. Keeping the gears of city business churning. They pay you sixty-two thousand a year to do this.

He sat down and dived into the stack. One does not come to the council meetings unprepared; a few of his constituents were always in the sitting area. He began studying the first document when the phone rang. Many thoughts raced through his mind as he sat there. He was expecting a call from someone about one of the items in the stack and maybe another regarding a question about street resurfacing. He reached for the receiver.

Thirty seconds later his stomach was spinning again, twisting as he dripped cold sweat. God in Heaven! Someone must have gotten into his records at the clinic! How? Certainly they take precautions with all the sensitive material as they have in their files. Dr. West wouldn't leave his case folder laying out in the open. But they used computer files and if some bastard hacked their way into them, the potential for damage was horrendous. "The score was tied six to six," the voice said, and he was coming to bat. "Last of the ninth inning." He knew the city council was close to an even divide over the rail project, five to six votes for each side, so the whole issue might well turn on him. His constituents wanted it funded; someone else wanted it to go down and they held devastating information in their filthy hands. Information that could destroy everything that still had any meaning in his life.

He dropped the receiver on the cradle and struggled to regain his thoughts, his heart thundering against his tortured ribs. Wait! Think of it this way: the issue comes, as they all do, stands its time front and center, then it dies and goes into history's dustbin. If he killed it with his vote, how long would the tempest really last? Might the repercussions be less than he always assumed? Just a month, maybe? How many would either remember or care enough to make his life miserable any longer than that?

He remembered something a history professor told him years ago: people have a tremendous memory for major events. Just not tremendous for very long.

Chapter Nineteen

The March wind rattled the windows as Lloyd Dahlenberg eased himself into the old leather chair in his Spartan office at Dahlenberg Cabinets. He sat back for a few moments, hands clasped behind his head. Three more just completed his training program, having passed their tests in trigonometry and geometry. He needed them. Business was on the rise. In the past year fifteen new houses had been built in the area between the village and Bellwood. All of these were valued well above those in the village, but still at a fraction of the Bellwood rates.

Like many of the village residents, he was wary of all that new development so close to their village limits and what impact this would soon have on their property taxes. Sewer and water lines weren't given away as gifts; the bill had to be paid. But for whatever else growth brought, there was one big plus: it seemed everyone in that new area wanted his custom-built cabinets. Not those in Bellwood, mind you, but he was giving thought to how he could better position himself to meet demand from other home construction that would inevitably occur nearby. Big and old though this building was, it served his present and anticipated needs quite well. It was situated on land large enough for a big addition, should that become necessary.

Somewhere in the stack of unopened mail should be his annual property tax statement. For the past year or two, the rates for commercial and industrial property in this area had remained fairly stable, though the same could not be said for residential taxes. Even the modest two and three bedroom ramblers in the village had seen increases in excess of twelve percent over the past year. It was the age-old struggle between commercial and residential interests: the burden went one way until the burdened shrieked loudly, then shifted to the other till they screamed louder yet. After that they switched places and repeated the process.

Sure enough, there it was, with the blue and white logo of the County Assessor's office. Always such a goddamn a welcome sight. He slit open the envelope and unfolded the contents, one of those forms printed on continuous-feeding—"JESUS CHA-RIST!" he muttered, feeling not at all guilty for his transgression. He scanned it again, just to be sure his little outburst was justified. It was. Thirty-eight thousand dollars? Shit, it was twenty-nine thousand-and-some last year.

What the hell happened? He'd made no capital improvements to the property in the past year, save adding a bathroom in the production area, but a toilet was no damn reason to jump the taxes. He dropped the report to the desk, then picked it up and looked at it again. He wasn't hallucinating: thirty-eight thousand one hundred and twelve dollars. "Up nine thousand dollars? In one year?" he roared. Who cared if his secretary heard him. "With no real goddamn improvements to the property?"

For several moments he just sat there, trying to contain his surging rage with a system that had grown into an anarchic maze of hopeless subjectivity.

He flipped through his Rolodex, found the number he wanted, then pounded the phone keys, as if they were responsible for all of this. "Dale!" he snapped into the mouthpiece. He'd known county commissioner Dale Brown most of his life and thought of him as a friend, but when it came to taxes and various aspects of county business Dale was as much fair game as any other official. "I have to ask you a question." All the statements had been mailed yesterday so Dale was braced for the annual barrage. "Do you think it is beneficial to society, in general, I mean, to have people trained for well-paying jobs?"

"Lloyd, I know what you're—"

"Now, do you think it's a good idea for me to train people who are not otherwise too well-educated so they can work in my business and thereby earn a downright decent living, pay taxes to build up their own community and stay off welfare permanently?"

"Yes, Lloyd, you know as well—"

"That really helps our society, doesn't it? You know, welfare reform and what not."

"Sure, Lloyd, now—"

"Dale, did you know that the amount of my tax increase is almost exactly equal to what it costs me to run my training program for a year? Did you know that?"

No, he hadn't known that.

"Do you think I should close the school and use those dollars to pay for my property tax increase, which you and the rest of the board levied?"

No, he wouldn't want to see that happen.

"You don't think that would serve the greater needs of society, is that right?"

Oh, no, not at all.

"Dale, did every other business in this county get stiffed as bad as I did-?"

"Lloyd," Dale broke in, having heard the same argument from others during the past eight years he had been a commissioner, "you read about the cuts the Legislature made in state aid to local governments. We opposed those but the Republicans thought they knew better, wanted to cut taxes in an election year so they'd look good to the voters. So we either make up the difference in county assessments, or else make steep cuts in city and county services. You know how the voters howl like hell when either of these happen. They want it both ways, Lloyd. You know that."

"Yes, but I want to know if other businesses around here got hit as hard as I did."

"All businesses on Main Street in Nuevo Del Rio had an increase. You're the largest so obviously you had the biggest increase."

"I don't mean just the village. What about others on the north end of the county? I can't believe they all got an increase like this. What the hell's going on, Dale? There haven't been any property improvements here since the new storm sewers went in three years ago."

"Within the village, no, but there were assessments for the new houses built to the east of you. Demand is rising in that area, and this jumps the value of your own property. I'm not saying this is completely fair or logical, but you know how the assessments—"

"Jesus, Dale, if this isn't changed I'm folding up the shop! I don't run this outfit just to raise money for the goddamn county!" This kind of banter was common to them They'd been friends since the third grade; struggled with the same teachers, smoked their purloined cigarettes behind the bushes, vied for the attention of the Prom queen, only to see her swept up by their team's all-state quarterback, leaving them to contemplate their bad fortune down at the pool hall. They'd played on the varsity baseball team, Dale was the pitcher and Lloyd was catcher, just like it was now with taxes.

"Well, what can I say, Lloyd? Businesses on the north end of the county are older, nothing new has been built there and much of that property is aging. The fringes of the older suburbs are showing their age. Twenty years ago we thought those were high fashion. The city's sprawling outward, Lloyd. All the growth in this county has been on the south end. What else could we do? We get a drop in federal and state aid while sewer and water lines have to go into new developments. Appeal if you want to. I'll certainly listen to what you have to say."

It went on in this vein for a while longer, both understanding each other's position.

The following day Dahlenberg went to the county assessor's office. It's all public information; one just needs either the patience of Job to wade through the reams of property listings or a friendly clerk who could get you there much sooner. He knew one of the clerks, having dated her in high school and even thought about getting serious but went into the Navy instead, served his country and had fun times overseas. All the while she was having fun times stateside.

He sat down and plowed through the assessments for the southern end of the county. As Dale said, the little businesses on the village's main street received hefty increases, and these would be burdensome with their small cash flows. Some of the newer homes to the east of the village, between Nuevo Del Rio and Bellwood, had greater increases in valuations but still nothing nearly as large as his own.

Then he noticed something else: a great deal of vacant property nearby had been recently purchased, all of it close to or adjoining the city limits of the village. Some outfit called the Glendale Corporation. Probably some goddamn property development lash-up buying off parcels of land, hoping to make a quick profit on the turnaround. "Grubby bastards," he muttered. "Raise the prices and the taxes for the next buyer." Just a personal bias on his part.

Then he turned to the property in the Bellwood Addition. Compared to his home, the rates for those six hundred thousand dollar palaces were staggering. Then he went to the next column and did some calculating. "Son of a bitch!" He did some more figuring. He brought his hand calculator. "What the hell…?" Though the assessed valuations were very high, as he expected, the largest increase in

Bellwood was just a bit over three per cent from the previous year for homes that had been there two years or more. "Three per cent! And I'm hit for a thirty-one per cent hike?" His erstwhile sweetheart copied twenty of these statements for him.

An hour later he closed the books and sat back, his earlier outrage draining away. There seemed to be a pattern here. No large tax increases for business property on the north end of the county; only on the south side. Most of that was either adjacent to, or within, the village limits. True, there was development in the area surrounding the village, mostly to its east, but those nouveau riche bastards in Bellwood got off with less than three per cent! It seemed the development just to the east was the reason for tax increases throughout the village, but not in Bellwood. What is this Glendale Group? Who runs it and why are they buying up these parcels of land? The age-old trick: someone won't sell to you? Okay, you buy up a chunk of surrounding land, do a bit of development and what do you suppose happens? Yeah, the assessor pays a visit to the area, sees all the splendid improvements and raises everyone's rates, including the poor schlock who wouldn't sell to you, but now he'll unload it. He can't afford to get walloped like that again next year.

He drove home, muttering about the inequity of it all, entered the house and went directly to the phone and snapped the receiver off the cradle. He abused the keys again as he dialed Peter Hoffler's number.

Chapter Twenty

Ann's meeting was set for two-thirty and at two-fifteen superintendent Richard Mathiew met briefly with his business manager, Ervin Bertz. "I want you here as a resource person," he told Bertz. "You know she had a history of contention here."

Ann held a grudging respect for Mathiew and his policies, but her despise of Bertz was barely masked and well known among the administrative set in the district. Their antagonism reached back several years, the cause of which sank into obscurity for Bertz, bit still festered in Ann's often fevered mind. Both egos were gigantic, easily bruised, and unforgiving.

Bertz was aware of Ann's ambitions as well as her history, though he held no similar aspirations. He was the district's financial officer and preferred to remain just that. He had seen enough of the stresses imposed on superintendents from every direction and this long ago blew away any longings he may have held for the position. Let the boss take the public's bullets. Mathiew's salary was thirty thousand above his, but after all taxes were applied to the difference, he concluded, the glory came at great cost.

At the appointed time they opened the door and Ann walked in. They sat around a small table in one corner of the office. She looked first to Mathiew, turned a withering glare at Bertz, then back to the superintendent. "Ann," he began, "as you are aware, we have struggled with a serious financial crisis for the past two years, and every time we thought we turned the corner something else happened and it became worse than before. Final figures are in and our average daily attendance is less than we expected." Budgets for state funding are based heavily on this forecast, then extended out two years, with commitments made for salaries and other ongoing expenses.

"Now we have a whole new set of issues. The school's share of health insurance cost will rise more than twenty-five per cent next year. We hadn't planned on such a large increase, even with the current provider. But they no longer carry the same policy and the next lowest priced one was well above last year's rates. As a result, we have to cut deeper than expected and take actions unforeseen just a few months ago." He paused for a few seconds, as if gathering his thoughts. "Ann, we have no alternative now but to impose substantial cuts in curriculum administration."

The room became deadly silent and Ann sat stock still. Mathiew was still leaning forward, while Bertz sat silently in the background, as far back as he could be. A clock on a side table ticked softly.

Finally, Ann spoke. "I have anticipated that it may come to this. I am recommending that we eliminate Morrie Russell's position."

"The board seriously considered that, until we learned about the insurance. At first we thought the twenty-nine retirements in June would take us out of the woods but now that's not enough. We will need to trim another twenty-one, some of which will be office and administrative, others from the instruction staff and three will come from maintenance. It may be mostly symbolic, but I have requested that the board reduce my salary by five thousand for next year and Ervin agreed to a three thousand dollar cut. That's not a great deal when set against a four million shortfall, but it lets everyone know we will share in the cuts, not merely passing them on to others…" The room was terribly silent. Mathiew's face was etched in stone as he straightened himself. "Ann, I have the unpleasant task of telling you that we find it necessary to eliminate your position rather than Russel's."

Time and motion hung suspended. Everything in the room seemed to freeze. Ann, seldom caught short of words, struggled with what she had just been told. For Bertz the tension in the air was palpable. Ann was intensely jealous that his annual salary was seven thousand dollars above hers. The cretin would be there when I was gone! When she found her voice it came soft, subdued. "Who will take over all of my responsibilities?"

"…Morrie Russel will have to do it as best he can."

A second meteor ripped through the heavens and crashed into Ann. "Morrie is not experienced in curriculum development." Her words came stronger than she anticipated.

"He will need to learn as fast as he can. It's not a desirable situation, and I'm sure you understand that. Every year we become more and more dependent on Internet connections to control costs and stay current with technology and he has the computer skills we need. It was not an easy decision, Ann. You've contributed a great deal to this district."

Ann shook her head. "Richard, I attended many board meetings but this was never discussed. When was this decision reached?"

"The recommendation came out of the finance committee in a meeting you did not attend. It was brought before the full board last week. You left before the vote was taken."

Again she fought for the words that seemed to jam somewhere in her throat. "How…how are you going to continue meeting state curriculum standards?"

Richard Mathiew sighed but looked straight at her. Bertz seemed to retreat farther into the corner. "We will arrange for assistance from the state. There are no workable alternatives. It's far from ideal, Ann, but we have no other choices. You heard what the Governor has stated: no increase for education in this biennium. I'm sorry to have to tell you this."

"What happened to the request we sent to the state for special needs funding?" Ann authored a grant several months ago asking for additional funds to defray the rising costs of special education needs. A new state mandate required them to provide reading and other remedial instruction to developmentally disabled children at a state institution nearby. The state offered only minimal funding and the district was obligated to cover the additional costs.

Adding further to the burden, the district was seeing an influx of refugees from African nations. English-as-second language classes were developed from monies set aside for other purposes. Mathiew shook his head. "It died in a legislative committee."

They spent another fifteen minutes discussing her separation package and completion of projects she had underway. Then she left the office, walked stiffly down the hall, unconscious of where she was going, bumping into a dead-end by the janitor's closet. She turned absently and walked in another direction, finally reaching the door leading to the parking lot, looking straight ahead, seeing no one, hearing only vague sounds from those nearby.

On her way home she ran a red light, and was nearly broadsided, leaving an angry motorist raging in her wake. She drove on numbly, as if drugged, taking no notice, staring straight ahead. Twenty years in education, ten as a teacher, ten more in curriculum, and this was how it ended: in a thirty minute meeting with the superintendent and that other dolt. A job carrying a seventy-six thousand a year in salary. Gone! Morrie Russel was to carry on her work? A mere computer wonk? Not even half-educated in what she did!

Her stomach started churning. Of all those board meetings in the past year when budget was on the agenda, how many had she attended? How many had she left early? What now? Start over again and drop back forty thousand or more in salary? For ten years she struggled up the administrative pay grade to reach a level twenty thousand a year above the top salary for teachers. She gripped the wheel as she drove through the afternoon traffic, racking her memory, trying to remember an opening somewhere. It no longer mattered where. She'd check the Internet and her trade magazines.

As she turned the corner onto Bruce Avenue and approached the house a trembling emptiness as she'd never known before suddenly gripped her.

An hour later Vince arrived and, without even seeing her, sensed tension in the house. The air was thick, full of a quivering, vibrating charge. At first Ann just glared back at him from her study and he thought he might have made another tactical error. "Well, it happened!" she snapped as she stood and slapped the magazine on the side table. It slid off and fell to the floor.

"What happened?"

"What do you think?"

"I don't...Oh no! Not your—"

"Yes, Vince!."

"They just told you now? Today? You told me there was a budget problem but that—"

"But that I was safe? So I thought! I don't know how much that cretin Bertz had to do with it but somehow they think Russel can handle it all by himself."

Vince shook his head. "In all those board meetings you attended, they never once mentioned cutting your position? They don't make decisions like this on the spur of the moment."

For several seconds she stared hard at the floor as a silence hung in the room. He saw the strain on her face. "This...ah...it was, in fact, discussed at finance committee meetings which I...ah...was, was unaware...ever...ever took place." She was wringing her hands and looking at the floor. "Ah…no one ever told me this was happening. The final blow was a major hike in health insurance costs." She sighed heavily and rubbed her eyes. "I don't know what else went into it. They have made their decision and I'm out of there."

She paced quickly in the small room, reacting as she always did when confronted with difficulties: her lips tight, her back straight, shoulders erect and squared. He stood and watched her pace, noticing her heavy breathing. "Where do we go from here?" he asked.

She continued pacing nervously. "There will be other curriculum jobs."

"Within decent communing—"

"I don't know!" she snapped. "Right now I wouldn't care where it was! Moving is not out of the question. It now appears that a major portion of our income will have to come from me. Certainly the job you have could be found almost anywhere."

Vince slowly exhaled. Let the slings and arrows pass quietly. Oh, Bullshit! Why do that? "Ann, I can't find work like that just any where, it—"

"Vince, it's a clerk's job! It seems to me you've gotten rather comfortable over there and have given up any serious attempt to regain work at your former level. I do not understand that, nor do I find it acceptable! You have most of the mornings off, why aren't you still out there seeking more appropriate employment?"

Seeking appropriate employment! He knew they were headed for another blow-out when her lips were set in that tight line and she resorted to that stiff, officious wording. Dammit, that was getting on his nerves! "Ann, since starting there I've had three other interviews, all at the level where I was. The project planner and the other for the estimator both went to someone else; I can't control that, and age is a far bigger factor than you think. I never heard back from the one for the layout designer, even after calling them four times. Obviously they're not too interested or they would have called by now. What more do you think I should be doing?

"I can't force someone to hire me, no matter how much experience I have. One thing I've learned is that long experience is more of a drawback than an advantage. I know that seems strange to you, Ann, you haven't gone through this, but you find yourself casting off a lot of old notions about how things are supposed to work. You think 'wow, I've got all this experience, no problem shifting over to another firm.' So you start in, and what happens?"

He looked but she betrayed no comprehension, her face a mask of rigid, stony lines and steady, glaring eyes. "There are two things that I need to do," she said. "I will look into my legal options concerning their actions. There is reason to believe this may constitute discrimination. They retained a male, and two males made that decision. I shall discuss this with an attorney in the near future."

"Ann, they had to cut deep. Don't forget this guy has two sets of skills—"

"And he is far less qualified to properly research and carry out my responsibilities! This clearly suggests liability on the part of the district."

Vince shrugged and sighed. "Do what you will."

"I shall." Another long pause. "There is another matter which we need to discuss. It concerns our future."

Vince could feel his viscerals tighten. He almost felt the floor sink beneath his feet. "What do you mean, 'our future'?"

"Precisely that. I have thought seriously about this for some time and I have concluded that it would be best for both of us if we lived apart for a period of time."

He felt as if she had hurled a giant boulder into his chest. He turned to face her but when he opened his mouth the words wouldn't come out. "You…you're saying we should separate…? With everything else happening? But why?"

"I am extremely dissatisfied with many aspects of our relationship, not the least of which relates to how you have handled your employment matter, choosing to accept what is little more than a clerk position at a discount outlet—"

"Oh, for Christ's sake, Ann—"

"Acceptance of such a position tells me you are not concerned with how this jeopardizes our current living standard and eliminates any upgrades as well. We have had two incomes for many years. You must realize that we have not had a normal relationship for five years or more. Our communication patterns have deteriorated to the extent that we merely occupy the same house. I find this totally unacceptable. It would be best, for the foreseeable future, for each of us to pursue a separate path. Perhaps at some later date we will revisit this issue."

He could only stare at her. "Revisit this issue'? he shouted. "'Get out of here and we'll revisit it later'? You said you thought seriously about this. You didn't talk seriously about it…Not with me, anyway. But you've just gone off somewhere, all by yourself, and made the decision for the two of us, is that it?"

Her shoulders dropped and her voice suddenly softened. "This is in the best interest of both of us. I am very sure of that, Vince."

"By your decision! And yours alone! We have a problem, so you go off in a corner, make the decision all by yourself, then come back and announce it as final? Is that the way of things?"

Ann held up her hands, her voice still soft, the hard lines in her face giving way. "Vince, please, just take the time to consider what I have said. This is not a snap decision on my part, but I am confident this is the right course of action. Any further discussion at this time would not be productive."

End of story.

A half hour later Vince was sitting alone in a restaurant, a slice of pecan pie and a cup of coffee in front of him. He looked around, saw all the families, the couples, friends, people gathering, sharing the company of each other. He was the only solo occupant of the room. Why was there such a contrast between this and the way it was with Ann? What was he trying to do, make himself feel worse than he already did? Across the aisle a man and woman about his age sat facing each other, their fingers intertwined atop the table, talking softly, happily awaiting their food. In an adjacent booth sat a young couple with two children, all intent on consuming their pie, the parents talking softly. Everything under control.

Years ago he and Ann brought their children here. He saw a couple in their late sixties or seventies talking to each other. How did they manage to get that far? How had they succeeded where he and Ann failed? Did they somehow bridge across a chasm while he and Ann fell into the abyss? How wonderful to be where these people are, enjoying each other's company.

Will I ever again come here to enjoy someone's company? Or am I doomed always to be a solo occupant of a booth, reduced to a spectator watching the interplay of others living happier lives? He hadn't felt this alone, this hollow, in years. And where would he go? What was to be his next address? For how long?

He wondered if his waitress sensed his feelings. She was so polite, had such a warm smile, always nearby for a coffee refill. Solos in a restaurant are a pathetic sight, he thought. They communicate a solitary message. It was in the way she looked at him. They must become good at perceiving the mood of others. Could things have gone wrong in her own life? She wore no wedding ring.

In a way Ann was right, he thought, as he worked his way through the pie. It hadn't been a good marriage for the past five years or more. They both longed for the intimacy and comforts of men and women being together. What was it that made people do all those neurotic things when they passed through their forties? he wondered. Couples that seemed to enjoy effective, loving relationships, willing to accommodate for each other's idiosyncrasies, grant a little space when it was needed?

Then came the forties and the storms broke loose. Had all these people gone through those years, surviving what was killing his marriage? All that was well before was gone. All that remained was that churning bitterness, some surging sense of lost opportunity, an empty thrashing about, first this way, then charging off in another direction. Everything becomes wrapped in a cloak of discontent that turns to anger and alienation. Why must this be aimed at one who was so dear and close in the better times? Hadn't they read the danger signals when they started coming? Was it too late?

She dialed his number from her study. "It's done," she said. "He's leaving." They talked for a half hour, mostly about what lay ahead for her. "I've had an awful day but still have a good feeling about the future." They talked briefly about him, about his plans, his life. She never seemed to notice, but he always brought it back to her.

He had everything a woman could want: wealth, time to do what he chose, status in social and political circles. He owned a condo in Miami Beach and an eight hundred-thousand dollar center-piece in Bellwood. A hundred thousand dollars worth of autos in the garage. All of this danced pleasantly across the stage of Ann Martinson's mind.

Chapter Twenty-one

The streets surrounding the soaring granite gothic housing the Minneapolis city hall buzzed with vehicle traffic and pedestrians as they made their way in and out through the massive doors. TV and radio remote units were parked in a strip down the center of Third Avenue and others scrambled to find parking space and feed the meters that stood like sentinels along every street. Every day saw a steady flow of citizens into and out of the building as they conducted their affairs with the city's bureaus. Today the vehicle and foot traffic was especially heavy. An important vote was on the council's agenda.

For a decade or more the hearings and debates raged and flowed. Information was offered up by those wanting additional freeway access. The automobile is clearly the vehicle of choice, said the freewayists. We live in a democracy where the supreme voices shall be those of the people and not those of the statists and others advocating primacy of government.

Others took the stand, citing the millions invested by banks and other sources in the inner city housing. Much of that investment will be destroyed, said the rail advocates, splitting up neighborhoods, leaving many residents still without affordable transportation. How do inner city resident access living-wage jobs in the suburbs? Are residents of the inner cities always to be on the move at any time the more affluent desire a wider path through their neighborhoods? "I want to go there so you must get out of my way, and that's the bottom line?" Look at the successes of rail in other cities, they said: Portland, Buffalo, San Diego. Look to Europe; their history is centuries greater than ours. Maybe they've learned something. Build a freeway, they said, and no income derives from its use, but maintenance begins almost immediately. The top layer quickly erodes under the onslaught of the ever-growing vehicle traffic. Light rail partially pays for itself in fares, and that's millions more than what can be said for any freeway. Maybe toll booths are the answer? Oh no! said the freewayists. No toll booths!

On and on raged the debate, through three public readings in the city council and the same for the county board of commissioners. Mountains of data and testimony for one side, and mountains of equal size for the opponents. Today it all came down to a final vote of those elected by the populace to serve their needs in the high councils of government.

The main issue today was the question of financial contributions by the city of Minneapolis, together with Hennepin County, for construction of the proposed light rail line. There had been several amendments, but the final draft provided for some cost cutting by having the new line use the present Hiawatha Corridor tracks through downtown southeast to the Franklyn Avenue station. This eliminated one hundred and fifty million dollars of additional demolition for a second rail line through downtown Minneapolis. From Franklyn Avenue the proposed line turned southwest, passing through the Phillips neighborhood, and joining Interstate 35W at a station to be built at Fortieth Street, then paralleling the freeway to a terminal point south of the city of Burnsville, a total distance of about twelve miles.

The amount at issue totaled one hundred and twenty-five million dollars, which if approved, would require the State Legislature to vote on the additional one hundred million in state match, which made the state eligible for two hundred and twenty-five million in federal matching funds. That brought the total to four hundred and fifty million, including the land, demolition, grading, track laying, train cars and stations. All other associated costs, including the transit villages and new businesses expected to follow the rails, would be borne by the private sector.

The vote represented something much larger than one rail line; it signaled a watershed change in transportation policy for a major urban area.

Forrest Turley took his seat at the U-shaped bench and glanced at his watch: nine-twenty. Council meetings started at nine-thirty.

He glanced anxiously at the growing crowd. As a chamber for the elected council of a major city government, it was a very small room. Looking at this colossus of granite that occupied an entire city block with a bell tower soaring high above the copper-plated roof, one envisioned a council bench placed magnificently atop a riser straddled by towering marble columns in the fashion of ancient Roman forums.

But behind the twin wood and glass doors was a relatively small room with eight or nine rows of seats split by a narrow center aisle. The council bench was separated from the public area only by a one-step rise and a small wrought-iron railing. The wall paneling was grooved mahogany, much in fashion twenty-some years ago. It reminded Turley of churches built in the seventies with their stark, utilitarian architecture. Yet in this inauspicious little room matters of public policy were deliberated, impacting the lives of nearly a half million citizens now living within the city, and that of millions more as their judgments arched across distant spans of time.

He glanced to the audience that he judged at about seventy or more, mostly inner city residents, primarily female, many bringing their small children. Most of those lived in his ward and looked to him to vote for them, for light rail. He recognized a few faces; some of these folks would be relocating if the vote went the other way. As usual, three TV cameras faced them in front of the iron railing, their power and coaxial cords snaking across the floor.

He saw the small children watched by their parents, most too absorbed in the commotion to become restless and noisy this early. Usually they held still for fifteen to twenty minutes.

It hadn't gone away, had it, that feeling now swirling, churning in the gut? It would never go away. It was much like alcoholism, Dr. West told him. Always there, always waiting in the wings. "It will be very difficult, seemingly impossible at first, but you must persist, Forrest, knowing you can overcome those urges. You must do that, or in time they will grow and overcome you."

Even in these moments he was feeling the struggle within but looked away, down at the agenda, while he felt the tension build, then soar. The children out there were only part of that ripping, searing anxiety. The rail issue was several items down on the agenda. They would come to it in a half hour.

He knew there was a near equal split on this issue. His vote could make the difference. Well, what the hell, he thought. His purpose in seeking election was to make a difference for his constituents. In those early, innocent days he had no idea what price might be paid for his judgments. He expected pressure: the irate phone calls and rude letters went with any elected position. But he hadn't factored in a threat so deeply personal, one bent on destroying his reputation and what that meant to his future. This was his only real life. He thought about that and he felt his stomach tighten into sharp, needle-like cramps that quickly swelled into cresting, throbbing waves of agony.

There was always the chance of another member or two switching their vote. But who would that be? What if they voted no and he did also, sending the hope of affordable transportation down the drain for his people?

Today his would be the last of the thirteen votes, so if it was a dead issue by virtue of seven nays when it came to him, why put your neck in the noose and vote for it? Yes, it might be a dead horse by then. He winced as another wave of cramps seized and wrung his stomach into a knot. Oh God, let it be a done deed! Seven votes, whichever way, when it comes to me!

The cramps became twisting knives slicing at his viscera and he leaned forward to ease the stabbing pain. If it was still alive at his turn he could kill it, then incur the enmity of thousands of his constituents who would remember this on election day next year.

Their memories weren't any longer than they had ever been; there were just more activists out there to remind them.

He could vote aye and bring this to his people, assuming the Legislature voted for the matching funds, as seemed likely they would. Then the story would unfold, wouldn't it? The media, short attention span though it may have, would serve up another feeding frenzy to its audience. Could he walk his streets after that, stop and talk public affairs with his people? Would they notice him, or would they look the other way to avoid him, a pariah existing among his own people?

Last week he thought of a plan in the event the threats became real. It seemed like a sound plan at the time…Now he wasn't as sure. It would be a very great risk.

For a few brief seconds the horrific agony let up, then came another sharp, tearing wave of pain, seizing his breath. He fought back a blinding urge to bolt for the bathroom down a hall behind the chamber. A sharp crack of the gavel, hitting him like a vicious migraine, and the meeting came to order. His breath was coming in heaves and he leaned forward again, hoping his suit jacket would hide the throbbing of his chest.

The council made its way through the first sixteen items, mostly reports from the standing committees. No issues raised by anyone. Turley stole a quick glance at the audience again. That tall man, the one with the dark hair beginning to gray, very well-dressed, rigidly sitting apart from the others. He wasn't looking at anyone, just staring straight ahead, an impatient look on his face. The high lord of the manor towering above the mundane affairs of the peasantry.

It was the one he saw at the hotel. Then he turned and whispered something to someone sitting beside him, a tall, slender man, bald with a rim of chestnut hair. Must be one of his associates he dragged along. There was a strange, inscrutable expression on the other man's face as he turned away. For a brief moment or two, Turley felt the man's eyes lock on him. He violated one of his cardinal rules: never make eye contact with anyone in the audience. What was he trying to tell him? His neck became hot and damp beneath the buttoned collar. He wanted to tear off his tie and toss it at them all, rip off his jacket and throw it on the floor. He felt sweat roll down his arms and chest and gather under his belt.

The committee reports were acted upon without comment. They were awaiting the only real item. It was listed as number nine for the Transportation and Public Works Committee. In these blistering, seething moments there was no past and there would be no future. There was only this flashing, searing moment in time. He was ill. His shirt was soaked. His stomach was rolling, churning, and he was nauseous, his breath still coming in shuddering heaves. God, it must be obvious to everybody! He tried sitting back in his chair but the stabs of pain came even sharper so he leaned forward again, as if studying the papers on the bench. He noticed the president staring at him now, an inquiring look on her face. He forced a cracked smile and nodded slightly to her. Get on with it, Madam President, please!

Then she introduced it and outlined the council's previous hearings. She said the vote today would determine whether the city and county would say no and end the issue for now, or vote aye, telling the Legislature they were prepared to put serious money on the table. That was still no assurance of a second rail line, which was supported by the more liberal members of the Legislature, for that body also included an enclave of conservatives who saw only wider roadways in their future. The governor would sign the bill, if it survived the Legislature and came to him. What a waste of your career and your life to vote it up here, suffer the inevitable backlash, only to have the conservatives in the State House vote it down!

Press the button and a small red light would flash signaling the president you had something to say before voting. Press it, now! Say you're increasingly concerned about cost escalation during the time lag. What you told Cardenas and the others, it's what you believe…isn't it? But it was too late for that now. The time for debate had passed.

And then it began.

The first vote was a no followed by a aye, as he expected, one being from an affluent area on the city's south side. The second vote came from a woman whose ward was adjacent to his own and on the rail line. That was followed by two more no votes from the north side, far from the proposed line and of little benefit to their constituents.

Three to one against it. Were the swing votes out there today?

The vote from member number five was a no, as was the sixth, both conservative men from high-income areas in the city's southwest corner. Turley knew their position: ignore the inner city. Two more and the matter was dead on arrival.

The next two came from wards close to his, they were both affirmative and his gut tightened. Five to three against. The next four would be a mixed bag. He had no idea where they stood and they had switched positions at least three times in the past two years. One of these came from a blue-collar industrial area which a bus route was to connect with one of the rail stations. Turley breathed a sigh as the first of these voted in favor, but another, from an older area on the north side of the city, voted no.

Six to four against.

God! he thought, was it actually going down before it came to him? Two more ahead of him.

The next vote came from a woman who had not been vocal. She was in her first term and seemed mainly interested in gathering professional sports teams and building stadiums for the city. She represented a ward close to the proposed line and connected to it by bus. Oddly, her home was in a wealthy corner of the ward and he wondered how she was ever elected. She says no and it's a done deal without his vote.

"Aye," she said.

Rails and stadiums. Some combination.

Just one more no vote and the entire matter was dead for at least a year.

Member number twelve was an older man who seemed to struggle and agonize over every issue before the council, even the most minor housekeeping items. Turley wondered how much longer he could remain on the council, carrying a burden like that. He was from an area west of downtown and not in the rail's path. It would seem he had little interest in the question. Vote no, Turley thought, and my choice is irrelevant. There was a long, thick pause as the man seemed to sway for one final time, the strain of decision weighing heavily upon his lined face. Then he let out a very audible sigh and cast his choice.

"Aye."

Twelve votes down and it was dead even. For a brief moment he wondered what the history books would say about this day.

Philosophers call it an existential moment. There are no guidelines; no structure; nothing to tell you right from wrong. It comes down to a choice made in a black, unfathomable abyss. This was his life, this council. Remove it and living would become a bleak burden, haunted by memories, and powerful urges he would have little incentive to restrain. They would let it all come out, wouldn't they? Then it wouldn't be long before he faced the blunt questions, the withering glare of publicity as the media went on another hyped up witch hunt.

No, it wasn't worth the agony! Kill it now, weather the criticism for the short time before it all faded away. Use the escalating cost issue and how all of this could not be paid without raising taxes. That would resonate, except among the poorest, who didn't pay taxes anyway. Let it surface at another time, a year or two down the line.

By then there would be new members here and the whole matter could easily die in committee, never coming up for a vote.

He felt the eyes of the president narrow in on him. He felt the hot eyes of the seventy-some souls in the audience. He felt another pair of cold eyes bearing down at him from a corner of the public area, aloof, looking above those around him.

He slowly straightened. There would be other times, other chances. It would live to surface another day. Suddenly the racking pain disappeared. It was all so clear now! He gathered his breath, turned and looked at Madam President.

Then he cast his vote.

"...Aye."

Two hours later Turley walked out the main doors of city hall, numb and weary, looking anxiously around him as he turned down Fifth Street. Just the usual bustle of city traffic weaving its way past the bottleneck of construction fences. Most of the public came only for the rail vote and left soon afterward, though he noticed the slender man with the chestnut hair stayed till adjournment. There would be the usual phone calls tonight, some thanking him for his support and far-reaching vision. Others just couldn't see how in the name of God anyone in their right goddamn mind would have voted as he did! And they'd tell him so.

"Mr. Turley?" came a voice from behind him. It was the man he saw looking at him in the chamber. "Richard Jamison," he said. "Could I speak with you for a minute?"

"About the vote?" Turley asked.

"Something more than the vote."

"You are the one they appointed to bring me down? I had a couple phone calls, you know." He looked straight at the man who appeared to about his age, but there was a strange, steady quality in the man's eyes that kept Turley from walking away.

Jamison looked at him for a few moments. "I'm not aware of any calls."

"I thought you would know that."

"What were the calls about?" Jamison cast a wary glance around him.

Turley studied the face again, but the man made eye contact without wavering and his voice seemed natural. "I don't think you need to worry about your boss seeing us here. He left an hour ago."

"I have a fair idea where he is."

"So do I. What is it you want to see me about?"

"Are you free for a few minutes?"

"I'm meeting a friend for lunch in a half hour."

"A trusted friend?"

"That is the only kind of friend I have. He is a minister at one of our city churches. I still haven't heard what your business is with me."

"Mr. Turley, I work for the man you saw next to me. I was an electronic communications officer in the Army. Does that interest you at all?"

Turley mulled that over for several seconds. "It might. Let's go over to Clary's. Reverend Young will be along shortly."

Clary's was a blue collar eatery four blocks away from downtown, its ambiance a bit earthy and not frequented by the City Hall types. It was out of the usual track for the local business people as well and Turley liked the privacy it afforded him. They took a table in the back. "Okay, Mr. Jamison, what's on your mind?"

"You made history today, Mr. Turley. What you did took courage."

"It certainly did," Turley nodded. "Thank you."

"I don't have much time, so let's get to the point. I'm sure you've noticed that Dave Behlen is a very intense man when he wants something. The freeway matter is an ego thing for him. Driving your own auto versus using common carriers. He hates losing, and losing to those whom he considers below him in the big hierarchy is unthinkable. Despite the vote today, he won't give up. He has a group that will likely file an injunction to stall the project for as long as possible. The longer he holds out the more the costs will rise. Then he'll have the matter reopened and claim that the added costs will lead to a tax increase. Given the vote today it wouldn't be hard to pull a seventh member over to his side."

Turley looked up and saw Aaron Young. "Excuse me for a minute." He approached Young, took him aside for a minute, then returned to the table with him and introduced the two men. "Yes, you were saying…?"

"You want him permanently out of the rail issue. I want to recover more than fifty thousand in fees from an earlier project. Three of us are planning to leave and form our own operation, but we need what he's holding back. A few months ago he decided to make all his associates independent contractors. He stopped paying Social Security and all the other taxes, yet he controls everything as he did before."

Turley nodded. "Not the hallmark of independent contractorship."

"He owes the three of us more than one hundred and forty thousand. You might also be interested in knowing that he's been in an affair for several months with a woman who runs a business on our floor."

"How do you know this?" Aaron Young asked.

"Like I told Mr. Turley, I was an Army electronics officer. That's a nice title given those who were trained to eavesdrop." Young nodded quietly and rubbed his chin.

"That wouldn't be a tall, slender woman with honey-blond hair, would it?" Turley asked.

"It would. So the question is this: How do we confront him so he can't simply deny it? I can't go to him on this. He'd fire me on the spot and see to it that I was blackballed from every other firm in town."

Turley fixed a steady eye on the man. "So you're saying we, Reverend Young and I, should approach him? Is that what you're asking?"

"If you don't, you will have him to contend with for as long as rail is an issue. You will never have that for your constituents. I can't say if he was involved in those calls you received, but if he was, Mr. Turley, be prepared for the worst. Outwardly, he's very smooth and diplomatic, extols all the family value rhetoric we hear now, but in his private life he has the morals of an alley cat. Ends are important. Means are not.

"So what I'm saying is this: my colleagues and I will take care of what he owes us, but he must be made vulnerable first. That's where you come in. He doesn't want a divorce. It would be very expensive and he's worried it would hurt him professionally. Given today's culture, I doubt that would happen, but that's how he sees it. Think it over." He gave them each a business card. "Call me at home." Then he rose from the table and left.

For a full minute they sat silent, digesting what they'd heard. Finally Young stirred in his seat. "You think this guy's leveling with us?"

Turley paused, then nodded. "His whole future rides on this; he's taking a terrible risk. We're not going that far. We'll still have our jobs when this is done…at least I hope I will. That says something to me. Would you do what he's willing to do?"

"I don't have much to lose. Not at my age. But this man puts it all of the table. Would I do this if I was him? Would I risk everything I had…? No, Forrest, I wouldn't have the courage. I Haven't had two nasty calls and next year's election facing me."

Turley pondered the prospect for a minute, the hum of a room full of customers providing a safe cover. "Aaron, sometimes you have to take a risk for what you believe in. I cast my lot today. Now I'll have to follow it, wherever it may take me. For six years the council has been my life, but it's that way only because of what I think I am and what my constituents think I am. There are those few times in our lives when we must put our beliefs on the line and act on them, whether that drops you off at the gates of Heaven…or kicks you into the fires of hell."

Chapter Twenty-two

Ann Martinson stepped into the kitchen, placed her purse on the table and sighed. It was just after five and she was returning from a visit to the office of Early Childhood Education at the Minnesota Department of Children, Families and Learning, mercifully shortened to CFL.

A few days ago she was searching Internet websites and pulled up the page for CFL, scrolled down and clicked on job postings. She came to the listings for the various educational specialists for level one, two and three and noticed the top of the salary range for a level three specialist was less than ten thousand below her salary…her past salary. She muttered something scathing about injustices, but a specialist wasn't what she wanted. Her expertise was in curriculum and that's where she would look. Nowhere else. Either that, or her ultimate goal.

She scanned several other announcements, clicking and scrolling, clicking and scrolling, then she came to it: Written in modern techno-lingo, it read: "To develop a curriculum of higher education options for secondary and middle school students. Key audience is students of color, low income or with no post-secondary education. Curriculum must include interactive features and will be tailored for use on the service office web page."

The prospect of a state-level job like this appealed to her. True, they were asking for both secondary and middle school experience. She had developed most of what was now used for the secondary level and somewhat less for the two middle schools. She paid scant attention to the part about web page development. She could claim some experience of this kind; just don't elaborate about it on the resume. That seemed to be a small part of the job.

It still rankled her bitterly that Morrie Russell now had her job. He was to absorb what she learned over ten years about curriculum development? She scoffed, turned back to the description and read it again, then pondered for a moment, about the part dealing with students of color. Her district was still less that two percent nonwhite but swelling with the influx of children from the various African nations. She was glad she had tuned up her resume to address this matter before turning it into the CFL office.

Ann read the description again and thought for several minutes. Students of color or not, this was a fit. A good fit. It had been a frustrating and disappointing month, having been interviewed and turned down for two more curriculum positions, one in the Twin City area, the other in an outstate community fifty miles from her home.

The first of these interviews went very well, and she left there buoyed with the belief she would be selected. They must have done some inquiring for they knew about her work in the district. It was in one of the northern fringe suburbs, and possibly they felt she wouldn't relocate within the school district. She assured them she would, of course, mentally measuring the distance from there to Bellwood, close to twenty-seven miles and most of it through of the worst traffic the Twin Cities had to offer.

The other interview, in a small, rural community west of Minneapolis, hadn't gone as well, right from the start. They asked the same question and she answered yes, but must not have sounded very convincing to one of the seven, who was the school board chairwoman, and her word carried weight.

But this was a good fit, the one with CFL, even if it wasn't for the long run. Ride it for two years, she thought. The doctorate will soon be in hand, then keep scanning the districts for curriculum directors or, more hopefully, a superintendent position somewhere. One with a Ph.D. and years of her experience would be a solid prospect. It could be anywhere now, even a distant, rural area. She'd accept what was offered and wait for a larger district to open, be it in the Twin Cities or some other metropolitan area. There was no need to restrict the geographics.

Many superintendents were retiring before age sixty-five, for good and sound reasons related to shifting demographics that placed new but unfunded demands on the education system. That was compounded by a public growing progressively moody, and aware, but largely indifferent to the impact these changes had on their school systems.

Today she hand-delivered the resume to the office of the director for early childhood education. While there she talked with several others in the labyrinthine agency. Network, let them know you're in the job market. It never hurts to keep those channels open. She walked out of the building in fine spirits.

Now she was alone in the kitchen and was suddenly overcome with a strange feeling. This was a very big house, and made even bigger with the absence of Vince. And quieter as well. Vince was not a TV watcher, often had scathing things to say about the networks, so he usually played music, anything from Andrew Lloyd-Weber to Garth Brooks to the Rolling Stones. Nor was she a TV addict. The demands of her studies and those evening meetings kept her away from the wide screen. "Why have we invested fifteen hundred dollars in anything so utterly useless?" he once asked her. For the children, she told him. Now it sat empty.

Years ago, the family visited the Kennedy grave in Arlington where everyone stood in reverent silence as the eternal flame flickered in the gentle wind. Later, they visited the Lincoln Memorial in Springfield, Illinois, walked the circular hallway and came to the wall mausoleum containing his family, then looked to the right where the former president was buried, encased in cement deep beneath the marble floor. Both had that same, hushed quality she felt now. The bones of their marriage were entombed within these walls, permeated with that same all-encompassing silence. She paused for a moment, then shook the morbid thoughts and walked slowly down the hallway to her study.

Vince's moving day carried a dark threat of rain as he and two of his friends loaded the truck with what little he took with him. "Travel light," one of his friends told him, one who had gone through divorce a year ago. "You'll move two or three times before settling in again." It was good to have these guys with him on that day, men he had known for several years. He could always shed a tear after they left, if he felt the need. They weren't Ann's friends.

It took less than an hour to load. "Go ahead," he told them. "I'll follow with the truck." When they left he went back into the house. It was hardly any emptier now than it was an hour ago. Amazing how much you accumulate living twenty-plus years with someone, especially when that someone tends to be acquisitive by nature. Jesus! All those years, and it comes down to this!

He went into the family room, the one with the wide screen, and glanced around at the fireplace, the shelves full of photos, trophies from long-ago victories when his son's softball team won the district championship. But he saw nothing. At the moment he felt nothing. Shouldn't you feel something? He was dreading moving day; fearing he would lose control of his feelings. After all, this was the day when a twenty-four year marriage came crashing to the floor, nothing more than a pile of twisted splinters from what was once a proud structure. But he felt nothing at all. All those long years and now you don't even have a single damn feeling or thought about it? Nothing but a vast, pervasive numbness.

That was only part of what he was feeling. The rest was a terrible sense of failure. Because they both knew that whatever their problems were, however their aspirations may have differed and clashed, and no matter how impossible it seemed at the time, in the end it could have been avoided. Saving it demanded patience, tolerance and some rationality, all in short supply when emotions take charge and better judgment steps out the door.

"Damn!" he muttered to no one at all. He shook his head, trying to drive out the demons. Then he turned and walked out the front door, locking ten years of living there behind him. He drove the truck out of the driveway and down the street, wondering if any of his neighbors saw him or knew what was happening. Today you could be gone for a very long time in this neighborhood before your absence was noticed. It hadn't been that way during their earlier years.

It only took a half hour to unload and put the few sticks of furniture in their place, where he knew they'd stay put. Vince wasn't big on continual moving and shuffling of everything. Ann would be up all night moving pieces here and there, rearranging, shuffling, arranging again and again. There were several other boxes yet to unpack, but that would come later. This was supposed to be a somber occasion, he thought, but they were all laughing, as if this was some sort of weird party! Maybe it was just the irony of it all. With Ann, moving was a dead serious affair, like almost everything else. It all had to be planned out, down to the last detail, and everyone had to perform their role as assigned. Exactly as assigned. This was not a time for humor. You stayed at it all night if need be, working at a furious pace. "Military movements were done with less rigor," he told his friends. Pop open another beer.

He often wondered how Ann, not one inclined to physical activity, found the stamina for those marathon efforts, while he, accustomed to outdoor physical work, would be exhausted by early evening. He could imagine what nanosecond precision a move to Bellwood meant.

When the unloading was done they sat on boxes on the front porch and again opened the beer cooler. It had been a long time since he enjoyed this loose sort of camaraderie, and it came on a day when his life was dumped on end. As he sat with the others enjoying his beer and their company, it occurred to him that he no longer had to endure Ann's withering glare when he returned home after being with them, and that "I do not approve of your associating with those men" admonishment he was certain to hear. The last time that happened, about six months ago, he stopped suddenly, turned to her and said, "When did every aspect of my life become subject to your approval?" It got very cold in the house. "You criticize me for not expressing my feelings. So I do, then you give me hell for doing it!" His next several meals were taken at Subway, Arby's, the little pub down the street.

When they left with the truck Vince stayed on the porch as the rumbling thunder shook the air and the wooden porch floor trembled. Nature delivered on her promise. The thick raindrops thrummed loudly on the old roof, the water roared out of the downspouts, jetting across the yard. He sat there and watched the houses nearby blend into shimmering, watery images as the deluge continued, the water spilling off the crown of the street and crashing against the curbs, surging and tumbling like whitewater into the drains. He finished his fourth beer and reached in the cooler for another. “What the hell,” he muttered. “I’m not going anywhere.”

As he gazed absently into the watery curtain he wondered who lived in all these old houses. Might there be a woman about his age, maybe one whose own life was dumped end-up, just like him? “No commitment,” he mumbled. “God, No!” Still, everybody needs a playmate.

Another hour passed as Vince sat on the porch, more empty beer cans in a sack on the floor, the rain continuing its assault, drumming steadily on the roof, splashing and flowing down the street, as if Nature was laughing at this singular figure perched on a box. Was it laughing with him, sending down this torrent symbolizing the cleansing tide sweeping the beach of what was to be the rest of his life? Or was the downpour sent to hide what was welling up from deep within, washing away the tears flowing down his grieving face?

Chapter Twenty-three

On a warm morning in June Vince walked into the law office of "Hoffler and Nordmeyer Inc.", the green lettering embossed against a white background. Wow! he thought entering Peter's new office with wide crank-out windows overlooking the shops along Victoria Crossing. He was handed coffee in a glass cup bearing the firm's name. "I'm impressed," Vince said, looking at the cup as Peter settled in his high-backed leather chair, an amenity left from his former associates.

"Thank you. I understand you have a new job," Peter said, then noticed a slight grimace on Vince's face.

"Well, yes, I started as a customer service rep at Builders' Market a couple months ago. It's not for the long run, but it will have to do for now. I never thought I'd end up on the opposite side of the counter. Last week one of my former contractors came in while I was there. He's kind of blunt, and I suppose he just wasn't thinking, but he said, 'How in hell'd you end up here?'"

"That must have been uncomfortable, but what you're going through is more common that you think. I've dealt with a lot of employment issues and learned that people at all levels of age, skill and education often start over when their primary job is gone. I have seen this happen to factory workers, to skilled machinists, professionals, office staff, management, technicians, engineers and even bankers caught up in some sort of changeover. I knew a man who rose through the ranks of computer engineering firm and became his company's director of technology. Two hundred and fifty thousand a year plus profit-sharing and stock options. One day he came to work and ten minutes later he was told the company had just completed an overnight merger and he and more than three hundred others were out of a job."

Vince smiled. "It's good to hear I'm not alone in this. I also see things have changed since you came here."

Peter nodded. "We have a five year business plan. We plan to broaden our scope; my partner and I are looking to add a third attorney within the next few months. We'll keep our current specialties, family law, and civil matters, but we'll also be involved with housing and employment law. I'd like to discuss this with you later, but I need to advise you that your wife told her attorney to put the action hold."

Vince straightened quickly, his eyebrows arched as he leaned toward Peter, gripping the armrests. "Put on hold? What…? Ann told this to her attorney?"

Peter nodded. "That's what he told me."

Vince sighed quietly. "In her professional life she's uncompromising and rarely changes her views, but in her personal life she can be all over the board. Here today, somewhere else tomorrow."

"I could send her attorney a letter stating we wish to have her decision within, say, thirty days, but that's your call."

Vince closed his eyes and thought for several moments, shaking his head. "I can't imagine...Agh! Let it ride for now," he grunted. "Contact her attorney in a couple months."

Peter nodded as he scribbled notes on a yellow note pad. "I could have done that over the phone, but I want to talk with you about another matter. I recall you telling me that you had some experience reading electrical codes and translating these into company procedures."

"I did the legal work and dealt with lawyers, city councils, all the various government units. It was the usual kind of thing: easements, variances from the codes and working with the zoning office. I learned to deal with the legal system. I have no formal training in law, but developed some understanding of terminology and procedures."

"Would you be interested in work related to this field?"

Vince arched his eyebrows again and leaned forward. "In the legal field?"

"Lawyers often avoid social law because of the pitfalls in prosecuting claims. I've had years of experience and see a niche for us. We plan to add one paralegal and a legal assistant to do the leg work. We can hire legal assistants without training. It involves obtaining documents from the court clerks, verifying authenticity of records, getting statements and signatures on documents and copying a lot of paper. It's not an eight-to-five job; some of it's done during the evenings when clients are at home. They're not always cooperative. I'm only asking at this time if you are interested in further discussion. No promises, you understand. We may also become reinvolved in the light rail issue, and that would involve a lot of work for a legal assistant."

Good God! Vince thought. He came expecting to hear the divorce action was rolling smoothly onward and he'd soon be thrust back into bachelorhood. Now he's told Ann's putting on the brakes, then that a new career might be on his horizon. This was too much to sort out. His mind was reeling.

Was she having second thoughts? What if she wants to stay with me? My God! Do I want her back? To live as we lived the past ten years or more? Sensing no warmth and struggling to give any in return? To endure that prissy, irritating stiffness, her social ambitions and the biting criticism? God, I'm free of all of that now! It's great…! Still, there was that void, that hollowed-out feeling beginning just a few days after I moved.

Now another change of jobs? That was what they told him when he filed his unemployment claim: two or three career changes often follow in rapid succession once the long term job attachment is broken. He wouldn't rise to wealth on a legal assistant's salary, but Builders' Market wouldn't get him there, either. He'd hate to tell Tim Horvack he was leaving when he'd been so understanding. Horvack was the first to throw him a lifeline. But, one must set one's priorities. "Sure, Peter. Let me know when you're ready to move on this."

Forrest Turley's quiet contemplation of the meeting minutes was interrupted by the phone ringing. The Caller ID window showed an unfamiliar number and no name. "Goddamn telemarketer," he mumbled as he snapped the receiver off the cradle. Instead of the pause followed by the script, he heard a voice only recently familiar. "Our lovebirds are at the Clarkson. Want to learn something interesting? Bring your pager."

It was mid-afternoon and hotel lobby was busy. Turley saw him in a far corner. "He registered a half hour ago with that same honey-blond," Jamison whispered softly. "All we need is the right room number."

Turley nodded. "How do we go about getting that?"

Jamison looked around quickly, then pulled Turley farther down a hallway away from the crowd. "We're taking a hell of a risk, and if this doesn't work we're out of here fast. Did you bring your pager?"

"I did." They exchanged numbers.

"There are seven floors and the second is used mostly for conferences, the third floor has the cheapest rooms, so I'm assuming they're somewhere on the top four floors.You stay down here and watch where they go from the bar. If they get into an elevator, hopefully alone, see where it stops and page me. I'll take the stairway up to five and wait for your call. If there are others on the elevator with them we'll call this off. My job is on the line, and I'll leave it there only so long. Understand?"

Turley nodded. "Is this really worth the risk you're taking? We'll will live to fight again another day, you know."

Turley saw the fiery glare in the man's eyes. "If it comes to that, we'll come back another time. I have a way of knowing when he's with her."

“I recall you saying something about that.”

“This could end up like a Boy Scout escapade, but if we can get their room number, without having my ass fired, we’ll both have what we need.” He stole a quick glance toward the hallway doors, then led Turley back to the lobby behind a thick row of plants. He peered between the leaves and saw Behlen and Lynn leave their booth. “Okay, he’s paying the tab. I’m going up to the fifth floor. Let me know what you see from here.” He turned and disappeared into the crowd. He had a way of doing that very quickly. Must have been his Army training, Turley thought.

Turley stood behind the plants as doubts loomed like thunderclouds. “Damn fool!” he muttered. Still, if this wild-ass scheme worked it would solve a few problems both he and a good friend of his were facing.

He took a position in a corner of the large lobby, behind another palm, as Behlen came out of the tap room, arm in arm with his lady, walked over to an elevator and pressed a button. Not bad, he thought looking at her. They stepped into the elevator alone and the door shut behind them. It would be easier and far less of a risk just to page Jamison and say they went up in the elevator in a big group. You don’t know which floor he’s going to, so let’s forget this crazy notion and go home. I have council business to tend to!

He watched the floor lights blink in succession, then they stopped. He grabbed his pager. “They used the west elevators and stopped on five.” Did it mean they got off the elevator there or did it stop for someone else? That would be for Jamison to deal with. Someone pressed the button and the elevator began descending, each floor light blinking in succession till it stopped at the lobby level and the doors opened. No one came out.

The fifth floor it was.

Richard Jamison slowly opened the stairway door at the end of a long hallway on the east side of the fifth floor. The elevators were located on the east and west sides, about midway down the corridors. He knew Behlen and companion used the elevator on the west wide, or so he was told, but all the same, he eased open the door and peeked carefully down the empty hall, just in case Turley had gotten his directions wrong. Something from his Army training: cross check everything.

He listened for the sound of voices, then heard a noise. He narrowed the door opening to a slit and peered through. A young woman pushed a housekeeping cart around the far corner, making her way down the east side, stopping at an unoccupied room near the elevator bank. She entered the room and he stepped out of the stairwell, looking and listening, then started walking up the hallway, looking as just normal as possible.

His only escape was to the elevators in the event Behlen showed up. But if Turley was right about them using the elevator on the west side, chances were their room was somewhere on the west half of this floor. One would think so, anyway.

He walked as casually as he could, for someone whose stomach was churning itself into tight, sweaty knots. He passed the elevators on his left. The cleaning cart was parked in front of a room across the hall.

Then his breath stopped. He heard Behlen's voice in the front hallway. He stopped and for a heart-pounding moment thought of ducking into the empty room. The specter of the cleaning lady screaming her lungs out wasn't pleasant. Behlen, being the cowboy that he is, probably would come charging down the hall to her rescue…No, wait! Think, for God's sake! He's here with another woman. The last thing he wants is attention. Leave it to some other brave cowboy.

He stopped and heard the soft click as the electronic key card released the lock, and again heard Behlen's voice. Well, either go to the end of the hallway and look around the corner or get the hell out now! Is this all really worth less than a year's salary?

His heart stopped again as he heard another noise, the whirring of a machine. How many times can the heart stop before it stays that way? He stood silently for a second, glancing anxiously down the hall. Then he closed his eyes and let out a sign of relief. A vending machine around the corner just made a batch of ice.

He stopped there, took a deep breath and peered around the corner just as Behlen stepped into his room overlooking Marquette Avenue. He'd have to get closer to read the number; the doorways were recessed about a foot into the entry.

A minute or more passed as he stood, half expecting the door to open again. He glanced behind him. It would look awkward if anyone saw him with his back to the wall, sneaking around in this ridiculous sleuth and quarry fashion. He kept a wary eye on the room where the cleaning lady was working.

He heard the whine as she started the vacuum cleaner. That should keep her busy for a few minutes. Christ, it was loud! Like a bagpipe in a jet engine. But it was useful background noise if he had to run like hell to the back stairway.

Slowly he turned the corner and walked toward the room, his ears tuned to any noise coming from behind the door. He had taken about five steps, glancing behind him, then froze. Another click from somewhere.

His heart jammed to a stop again as he saw the door open slightly. Shit! In a flash he spun around and dashed past the corner. Why was he leaving the room? For a moment of stark terror he slowed; the elevators were fifty feet down the hallway, the room across the hall was closer, but still occupied. He heard the thundering hum and whir of the vacuum. Which way was Behlen going, to the east or west hallway. Go for the elevator! Get the hell out and try another time. He turned back, then stopped himself. Think, for Christ's sake! You'd have to wait till the lift arrived and he'd be all over you before then.

He might be going for extra ice in the small room just around the corner.Behlen would have had ice sent to the room before their arrival, but he hadn't planned on him leaving the room again. One small item he hadn't factored into this nutty scheme. Their room was about sixty feet from the ice machine, a distance Behlen could cross in seconds with his long legs and rapid stride. There was no choice, other than being fired in the next five to ten seconds.

Jamison glanced quickly into the room being cleaned, then took a deep breath. His job and reputation hanging by an unraveling thread, he quietly stepped inside, turning to his left into the bathroom. His lungs seemed paralyzed. The lady was still vacuuming somewhere around the corner by the two beds. His spinning mind told him she'd do the linen first, then vacuum and clean the bathroom last. It seemed logical in his desperation, but if she worked it some other way he'd be facing his boss, former boss by then, the hotel security and the local police.

Here was this respectable guy, wearing an expensive suit, a bona fide member of the capitalist establishment, slinking around a hotel like some sick pervert! Meanwhile this cleaning lady, a small Oriental, would be weeping and trembling, pointing a shaky finger at him as tears rolled down her face, mumbling in her native language. Off he'd go, his career lying in ruins on the floor, his wife wondering what kind of whacko she'd married, if she stayed his wife.

He eased himself into the tub and shower unit. Jesus Christ! he agonized. If she walks into that room, and sees me standing in the tub…A brand new level of idiocity has just been reached!

Over the whine of the vacuum he heard the clunk and crash of ice tumbling into a container. His heart screeched to a stop as the lady steered the machine down the short hall, the sound rising as the beater brush flailed the carpet. He saw himself in the vanity mirror on the wall next to the beds so she couldn't see his image if she looked in that direction. The noise rose louder. He shuddered as the vacuum cleaner bumped against the bathroom door. He'd have to get out of there in the next few seconds. Goddammit, what a stupid waste! A ninety thousand a year job being flushed down the drain for this senseless caper! I'm a consultant to whom others bring their problems?

She switched off the cleaner and he held his breath. If she comes into the bathroom I'll have to keep her quiet somehow, including the use of force, whatever the consequences. He turned that prospect over in his mind for a second. The charges would then escalate to assault, bringing on a whole new set of problems. The next day all this would be in the paper for his colleagues, customers and friends, or former friends, to read about.

She turned and walked toward the beds.

He paused for a moment, then heard her begin stripping the bed linen. Time to move. Now! He stepped gently out of the bathtub and peered around the corner seeing the sheets piling up against the wall. She'd be occupied with that for another minute or so. He stopped breathing again, rose on the balls of his feet, turned toward the door, and in a quick step was back in the hallway. If Behlen had lingered near the vending machines he would be unemployed and blackballed in three seconds.

The hallway was clear.

Time to fish or cut bait. Either you pass by that damn room and accomplish what you risked everything to do, or run like hell the other way toward the back staircase and forget the whole insane business! I have a life to lead; get on with it. Forget you ever heard of Forrest Turley.

So he turned to the right, walked slowly toward the corner and looked down the hallway. He saw the back half of Behlen just as he walked through the doorway. For a second he debated, then heard the elevator stop and someone stepped out into the hall. Move, dammit! He rounded the corner and walked as normally as he could past the room whose door had just opened and closed. His breath was coming in surges and he felt as if his heart would rip its way through his bones and fall onto the floor, throbbing away, all on its own. The new arrival was only a few feet behind him so he kept on, glancing only slightly as he passed the room.

Five-fourteen.

When the elevator doors closed behind him, he let out the deepest sigh of his life and gently thumped his head against the elevator wall, overcome by a sense of relief greater than he'd ever known before.

He met Turley where he left him, gripped his arm, and abruptly led him down a long hallway and out into the street. They walked quickly for a block before Jamison spoke. "The next time you get a wild-assed idea like this don't get me involved, okay?"

"What?" Turley said. "You were the one who called me. Did you get yourself fired?"

Jamison steered Turley into an alley and looked down at him, his face still flushed. "Okay, Mr. council member…For the record, we never saw each other. I don't know you; you don't know me…We'll never meet again…You got that?" Turley nodded.

"...Five-fourteen..."

"Five-fourteen."

Jamison disappeared. Turley stood there alone for a moment, stunned. Pure, absolute insanity! But by God, it might have worked.

Turley rode the MTC bus to his home and dialed the phone number of a good friend who was working very hard these days to keep a poor church in the business of faith.

Chapter Twenty-four

Like every other aspect of their life together, Vince and Ann had different ways of handling finances. Being the more computer literate, Ann paid their monthly bills on the Internet and he struggled with that during the past five years. Seeing the difficulty he was having, along with his distrust of the system, she took over the task. Though he took one of their computers with him, he paid his bills the old-fashioned way: checks in stamped envelopes. He wrote the last check, then looked at the balance: Six hundred and sixteen dollars and payday in three days. Hardly wealthy by today's standards, nor what he knew in his recent life. Back then the balance would have been another two thousand—until Ann read the weekly ads. But he was scaling back and found he now had money available for what little he desired and what fit into his new life.

In all, it wasn't a bad feeling, so long as one was willing to ratchet down a bit here and there. It was limiting, operating on a single and definitely smaller income, but he was feeling freer now than at any time in the past. It was his choice where it went, whether to buy or withhold buying, and he discovered he was happier when surrounded by less opulence and fewer obligations. What was infinitely satisfying was freedom from that constant quest for some new article, gadget, household item, whatever, something that just couldn't be lived without another day. "I have done without this for so long," she would declare, "there is just no reason why I can't..." For Ann, these crusades consumed endless, untold hours and generated huge amounts of frustration. She often began the quest not knowing what she was searching for, just something, some vague urge that grabbed hold of her, and she was often dissatisfied when it arrived. To him, this was an aimless and hopeless waste of time, energy and money. Buy and return; buy and return. Standing in the customer service line once again, after Ann had declared, "Oh, no, this is not at all what I thought it was!"

He looked at the picture in the catalog, then at the article. They looked exactly the same. "How could it be anything else?"

She would look at him, astounded. "Well...it just was! Can't you see that?"

One time, after the fourth return of something she absolutely had to have lest the world crumble, he told Ann what he thought of the whole business and maybe she ought to stop, wait and look long enough till she knew what she wanted. "You're looking for some phantom in a dark room, and you don't know even if it's what you want when you find it. You were happier before you got off on this wild chase!"

He was informed of her version of how this all works out. The air in the house turned chilly. More evening meals at Arby's, the pub down the street.

And so he was here. He had been in the old Victorian dwelling on Mackubin Street for two months and he was becoming attuned to the waves and rhythms of a neighborhood that reached deep into the city's history. He grew up on the city's east side, closer to downtown, and in those days it was a community of blue collar families, back when father held thee job, usually in one of the factories, while mother stayed home and kept house. The family of the forties and fifties, still popularized in the TV sitcoms, and for some, a refreshing change from the half-wit vulgarities the media now served up as modern families. That wasn't a bad way of living, he thought. You didn't race around from one shopping center to another, pissing away your money.

While looking for housing, he drove through his old neighborhood and seeing it for the first time on fifteen years or more, he felt saddened. He saw crumbling houses with boarded up windows. The home of his childhood, and those of his friends, had fallen into pathetic states of disrepair. Wherever he finally landed, it wouldn't be any place close to here. He did, however, make one definite decision: Builders' Market was in St. Paul and by God he would no longer be another marathon commuter. He was going to live near his work, and an older neighborhood would do just fine.

It was twelve miles from their home on Bruce Avenue to his new job, and much of that trip was on Interstate 94, dodging heavy-footed drivers and those ubiquitous orange construction barrels and cones where lanes appear and disappear with frightening abruptness. One evening before he moved, he was driving home and was angling into another lane lined with barrels and noticed he was alone, or about as alone as one ever gets on I-94. Ahead was a barrel a little out of line with the others. He glanced in to the rearview mirror, then steered to the right, catching it square on the car's front quarter. It was wrong, of course, the good, law-abiding citizen that he was. But Lord it sure felt good hearing the thump and watching the damn thing go cartwheeling off into the darkness! A fist raised in silent protest to the ills of urban living.

It did cost him a new headlight seal beam ($59.58—parts, labor and tax).

The single life offered a few other advantages. He could leave things laying wherever he wanted, without hearing a sharp recrimination. His robe hung on a hook in the bathroom; a pair of shoes left beside the bed; unopened mail on the kitchen table; sliding closet doors left open; a pillow thrown kittywompus on the couch.

Ann's dictum was that nothing, absolutely nothing, was ever to be out of its place. Closet doors must always be closed; clothing was always to be hung in the closets and not left on a doorknob; all kitchen items must be placed in the cabinets and never left on the counter. There were to be no exceptions! It was as if she expected photographers from Architectural Digest to arrive any moment. Home was a showpiece, always prepared for anyone who might view it, and you lived your life around that rule.

He worked afternoons and evenings so that left him free to wander about his new neighborhood during the mornings. There were many different routes to follow. To the south, along Summit Avenue, were the large, brooding mansions built during the gilded days of St. Paul's early years, home to James J. Hill and other lords of the industrial revolution. It seemed haunted by the memories of F. Scott Fitzgerald and John Dillinger. To the east, was the towering monolith of St. Paul's Cathedral squatting atop a hill overlooking the spires of downtown St. Paul and the Minnesota River valley beyond. To the west were many more dwellings of the same era, most of which had by now become subdivided into smaller rental units but at one time housed large families with their coterie of maids, cooks, valets, coachmen and countless others of the serving class.

As he began these walks he noticed other aspects of the inner city. He saw people gathered on the streets and in the small parks in the neighborhood. Children rode bicycles and tricycles up and down the sidewalks; skateboarders, joggers and walkers were a daily occurrence. He saw groups clustered at corners, chattering in their native languages, or else speaking that inner city jive he found equally perplexing. Such gatherings on Bruce Avenue would have prompted some overly anxious resident to insist the police put an end to that disorder. Of course, this would never happen in Bellwood; the owners were far too busy for idle chatting. Vince also noticed that people stood in yards and talked with others. There were a few houses where no one ever appeared, but around here these were the exception.

There was another part of this life he found appealing: they had retail stores nearby! You could actually shop here for more than just your basics, though that was about all he shopped for anyway. You could do this by walking or driving a very short distance at a sane rate of speed. Not like those outer suburbs with their malls and shopping centers scattered to hell and gone, each surrounded with a convoluted web of streets and multi-lane arteries where everyone felt compelled to drive the winding curves at the speed of light. There was a center to the community here, where people came together, not just another random scattering of retail, industry and housing.

Mackubin was a mixed neighborhood both racially and economically, and in other ways as well. He saw the affluent and also the others who obviously struggled every day to make their living. He saw Blacks, Latinos, Orientals, people from the many African nations and Caucasians who spoke with thick European accents. Gathering here and there in small groups seemed the norm, and one day he asked his next door neighbor about this, a woman who lived there for fifty years. "This was how they passed along news in their native country," she told him. "They didn't have radios or TVs there so they exchanged news on the streets, same as they do here." Now he knew.

One warm evening he was sitting on his front porch, as was his custom, observing the movement and flow of the people, sensing its rhythms, and he wondered if Ann might somehow learn to appreciate this area. There she was, alone in her two bedroom apartment in one of the suburbs, keyboarding her way through the final phase of her thesis. She hadn't found another position, though he knew she had at least a dozen interviews. Her search was narrowed to superintendents and curriculum directors and flatly refused to consider anything else. "No!" she once barked when he inquired about this. "I have been in administration and there I shall stay!" Period!!

Though he didn't know the education structure and culture as she did, he sensed the day was coming when she would have to ratchet down and settle for a teaching position. "You're starting the same process that led me through more than a dozen interviews," he told her, "then to a job I thought I had left far behind. You may have to do the same, and if you do, it might change the way you see a lot of things."

"I will not go back for any reason!" Would it change her views as it did his? Might she learn not to expect the world from someone when their world had just been taken away by those nameless, distant market forces?

Did he really want her back? Dammit, this question was like a recurring demon! What would she be like? He thought about that for a long time as the sun fell in the western sky. There were times he felt not merely alone, but as if a terrible vacuum had settled in on him, and the emptiness made his heart ache. He still felt anger toward her stiff and officious ways and her unwillingness to just kick back and enjoy the moment. But was he really aching for her, or merely for the better side of her to fill in the gaps each day? For a very long time he sat on his porch and thought about that.

About ten years ago he had gone to a local business to do an estimate for electrical work. The business was owned by a woman who appeared to be about his age and after fifteen minutes talking about electricity he sensed she was single. It was more in her manner toward him than the absence of a ring on her finger.

Another fifteen minutes and they weren't talking about electricity any more. It was one of those rare meetings of harmonic personalities. He knew what would happen if he stayed longer. So, fighting against his pleading urges, his emotions begging him to stay, he gave her the estimate and forced himself to walk through the door. He sent one of his electricians to do the job. Albert Belland did the coordination. In the intervening years he often thought about her and whether she ever thought about him, fruitless though it would be. He drove past the business once or twice but never saw her again. It was one of those unexplainable things: two ships pass in the night, signals sent and received. A tacit understanding without needing words. Then they passed, each bound by its separate course and purpose to another destination.

Chapter Twenty-five

It was ten minutes past the hour, but after years of experience Vince wasn't surprised. Ann had a lifelong habit of being fashionably late for everything, including their visit today at a small coffee shop near his home. He could have met her in a fashionable mall in suburbia, but he wanted her to see the neighborhood where he lived.

All the same, he picked one of the better bistros frequented by the area's more trendy residents. He also picked a booth in a far corner.

He hoped she hadn't become lost. If she did he'd have a nasty message on the answering machine about his bad directions. He glanced at the clock, then saw her come through the doorway, a tight expression on her face as she glanced about. The set lines of her mouth proclaimed her presence on foreign turf.

The conversation went along harmlessly for several minutes. She talked about her apartment, their house on Bruce Avenue, nothing sensitive. Then he asked her what was most on his mind. "My attorney tells me you have stopped the, ah, proceedings."

"There are just too many things happening all at once." That much was true. Ann had a singular way of handling life's affairs. Though possessed of a powerful mind with sharp focus, it was good for only one issue at a time. Enter a second matter and her mental processes often ground to a halt until one was removed. She was finalizing her thesis and still sending resumes and interviewing for positions. Add to that the recent sale of the house and her move and it was far more than she was willing to handle. "I haven't changed my mind."

"I see." As best he could tell, his feelings were equal parts disappointment and relief, and at the moment, he didn't know which of them ran deeper. One day he'd wake feeling remorse, the next day it was relief, on another day some other emotion took the lead. He wished she'd just get the damned thing done. He was relieved that she hadn't consented to counseling. She never revealed her emotions to a new person, but had she done so, he could just imagine the spectacle: she'd be verbalizing, her words tumbling, cascading out in brilliant array while he sat there like some kind of a dumb-ass. "Have you heard about that job with the state?"

He saw her downcast look as her shoulders slumped. "I was one of three finalists, like all the others." She slowly shook her head, her voice soft "Maybe it was…possibly they knew of the issues I had with the district…I don't know."

That was at least the fifth or sixth turndown in three months. "You seemed such a good fit for the job." A smile broke through in her face, the first he'd seen in many months. "Would you like something to eat?"

"No, thanks." She'd never been heavy, a little undersized, actually, but today her face seemed thinner than usual, even a bit gaunt. He wondered why he should be concerned about her diet. She often skipped meals, toiling away deep into the night, laboring over the final editing of four hundred pages of text.

"I can sympathize with what you're going through. It isn't easy and it'll blow away a lot of illusions you've held. You're a little behind me going through the very same process. I hope you can find another position like you had, but have you considered alternatives, temporary though they may be? There's an opening for a teacher in one of the middle schools nearby. You might want to consider taking what's available and continue your search for what you want."

She finished her coffee and set the cup on the table with a rather definite thump. "I am not ready to give up on my goals, nor will I compromise in the least. I will continue pursuing these until they are reached, however much time that may require. I am not in a doctoral program to qualify for an entry-level teaching position, here or anywhere else."

Vince nodded. "Let's take a short walk." Short because of her aversion to physical activity. "I'd like to show you where I live."

"Is it safe out there?"

"Yes. I walked the seven blocks down here."

He saw an incredulous look break across her face as she turned to him quickly. "You did? On foot? I'll drive to your home and we can walk from there."

Ten minutes later they were walking along Mackubin Street toward the mansions lining Summit Avenue. They walked two blocks in silence, then a small group of children scooted by on bicycles. He and Ann stepped aside as they rushed by and he saw that familiar scowl of disapproval cross her face. For all the years she spent around young people she never felt comfortable amid that noisy exuberance of youth. Across the street another group of children was noisily occupied with a game, shouting as they ran and tumbled on the lawn. "And you really like it here?"

"Yes. Now and then I still get that feeling of being hemmed in, with narrow lots and houses so close together, but that comes and goes. I know a few others who live nearby. I don't want to be a total stranger. That's awful lonely."

They continued on for another minute or two in silence, then Ann said, "This part of the city seems predominantly, ah, non-white. Is that correct?"

"About half white. It's a mixed neighborhood economically, culturally, and just about every other way. We have everything here: Blacks, Orientals, Latinos and others. Lots of young families with small children. Some of those living here are quite well off, others are very poor, all living within a few blocks of each other. It's amazing how the neighborhood changes in just two blocks." He hesitated for a moment, then said, "I would think you'd find this an interesting area, with your thesis about multi-cultured curriculums."

Ann was silent for a moment. "It's getting late. Let's go to your house."

A few minutes later they were in his small living room. "I will send you a check next week when I have the bank accounts reconciled," she said. Then she turned from him and for long moments gazed through the front window, her face silhouetted against the light. He thought he heard a faint sigh. "There is something you should know...I've gone back and forth so many times...it's very difficult but…" She turned to him again. "Vince…there is another man in my life. He has been there for some time. I'm not sure why I'm telling you this. I have no wish to hurt you. I just think you should know. He is not the cause of our break-up."

For several seconds Ann stood by the window, her shoulders slumped, as if a burden had been lifted from her. Vince sat in stunned silence while phantom-like emotions whirled about, competing for expression as he struggled to put his scrambled thoughts together. An affair. She had been seeing another man. "Who is he?"

Ann shook her head. "It's no one you would know. He's a businessman, an investor."

"And he lives in Bellwood."

She glanced quickly at him for a moment. "Yes. He's a widower."

Oh, that simplified it all! Just one cuckolded mate to worry about here. Not a whole stream of lovers to truly muddy up the water. He took a deep breath. "He's fairly wealthy, I take it?"

"Yes. Vince, he really has nothing to do with our problem—"

"Then what does have to do with our problem? Ann, I don't understand why you first started the divorce action, and now you bring it to a halt. If you want this guy, then why did you stop the proceedings?"

"This is the first time we have actually talked about things for a very long time, isn't it?"

"A strange way to get it started up again."

"We are what we are, and it wouldn't be right to deny this. You know the kind of home where I was raised." Her parents were both college professors, Ph.Ds. and tenure, numerous publications to their credit. They had little in the way of a social life. All efforts were bent toward academic achievement, research and publications. Under their influence she gathered few friends in her lifetime. Friendships, they told her, were not important. They interfered with serious study.

"I know about your parents, but we're not limited by what they taught us. We have the power to change. You never learned from them to relax, to just kick back and enjoy the moment and the company of those who might be a little different from you."

"No, but somewhere along our path, we acquired other values, other goals, and those have shaped our separate hopes and aspirations. You rose in your trade and I was so proud to see you building the business. I could see you as the sole owner of a large construction company. But once you reached a certain level you seemed content to remain there, seeking nothing further, and you associated with those whom I thought were below your level. Please don't be angry by my saying that; we've had too many bitter words about that and they all came to nothing. May I ask you something rather personal?"

He shrugged. "Sure." She wanted to discuss something personal?

She sat in a chair and leaned forward. "Have you ever felt drawn to another woman since we married? I don't mean a real involvement, but did you ever feel attracted toward someone else?"

He was quiet for several seconds. "I don't know how one could be in the workplace for thirty years and not feel that pull at one time or another. You'd have to be brain-dead." He told her about the woman he met while doing an estimate. "By the time I finished it we were both feeling the pull. We talked for a while, then I forced myself to leave." He told Ann what he feared would happen if went back there. "Something I might feel good about at the time, but not later. I never saw her again. Yes, I know how that goes. What attracted you to him? Was it his wealth? his house in Bellwood?"

She frowned slightly as she gazed momentarily through the window, then back to him. "I don't know. He has good qualities, but I don't think of him as ideal. I can't deal with so many things at once. All I want is to complete the Ph.D. program, find another position somewhere and settle between us. That's enough. As for him…" she shrugged with a dismissive wave of her hand.

"Do you love him?"

Again that Mona Lisa smile, and her voice came as a whisper. "Love him? In the same way I loved you earlier? No. That wouldn't be possible. Too many years have gone by to make the same investment I made with you."

He looked at her for long moments. In her offhand way she said he still occupied a special place in her life. One that could never be taken by another. Yet here they were—separated and headed toward the end. Or were they? Had they come right up to the brink and now she was pulling back, unwilling to cut the last tie between them? "Those evening school board meetings, they didn't go that long, did they?"

She looked down at the floor as her face tightened. He saw her grip the armrests as her knuckles turned white. "Some did, but others…no. Oh, Vince! There really isn't much more I can say about that. I deceived you. For that I am sorry. I don't feel good about having done that to you." She glanced at her watch, then rose from the chair and let out a deep breath. "I struggled for a long time with our relationship, as you did, too. What happened wasn't your fault. We are very different people, Vince, so let's leave it at that. Thanks for having me here. I'm glad I saw where you live. I see why you like it here."

Then she was gone.

For two minutes he just stood on the porch, his hands in his pockets, no blinding revelations, no cogent thoughts filling his mind. Then he turned and went to the kitchen, took a can of beer from the refrigerator, opened it and returned to the porch where he sat in the rocking chair. "Well, shit!" he muttered. He didn't know if he felt better or worse for her visit. All those evening meetings when he thought she was battling for the curriculum. Instead, she was having an affair.

A goddamn affair!

Some rich bastard with a nice big house, right where she wants to be! She found some kind of paradise on Earth? Or was it that good? She didn't seem bent on marrying the prick, even swung the conversation away from him. Or…was that what she wanted but maybe this guy was backpedaling?

School board meetings! What a goddamn lie! She probably did attend most of them, for a while, then dashed off to this suburban palace for a stimulating evening of fine wine and…and all the things that went with fine wine.

He sat on the porch for another hour as the sun sank lower, the old houses and tall elms casting long shadows across the narrow street, three empty beer cans laying on the porch. He had never managed that complex emotion of anger, but he felt it mounting, one click at a time. His buttoned-down, trussed up parents taught him nothing about emotions. They had but one tool for that problem: repression. Christ, it was no wonder Freud was so busy in Vienna! The very shrine of Victorian repression. “Son of a bitch!” he hissed. “And she still came back to sleep with me after every tumble she took with this guy?”

Calm down, for Christ’s sake! Take a look at what you have. A degree of freedom, such as it is, I’m a clerk, as Ann said. So what if the store forbids use of that term?

But whatever freedom or independence might be mine, I’m still surrounded by this damn, hollowed-out feeling of emptiness. Whatever our marriage was, it filled a gap, just as it did with Ann, all her great aspirations and wanderings aside.

Well, they all did that, he thought. Fill a gap. It might be filled mostly with shit, but it’s still filled. He grunted. “You aren’t making any sense!” He drank another beer, tossed the can on the floor with the others and sat there for several minutes. Suddenly his jaw began setting firm and hard.

He rose slowly, weaving his way back into the house and to the pantry. He usually preferred beer in cans but about two weeks ago he bought a six-pack of bottled beer. Responsible citizens recycle glass, so he kept the empty bottles on one of the shelves. He picked up a six-carton and stood there for several seconds, as if thinking about something, then stumbled back through the living room and out the front door.

Night had clamped its black hand on the towering houses and the looming trees lining the streets. There was no moon. The lamplight at the corners cast an almond glow to the intersections, leaving the streets in between in heavy darkness. He meandered down the dark street in a clumsy, lurching fashion, turned a corner and continued for another block, then turned left into an unlit alley. He came to a long brick wall halfway through the block and saw the dim outline of garbage cans arranged in a row beside the wall. He felt the rush in his ears as he always did the few times he drank this much. He looked around and saw no one, only a quiet hush as lights glowed behind locked doors and windows.

He removed one of the bottles, gripped it tightly, then reared back and hurled it with all his strength. It exploded with a shattering crash against the wall, tiny shards of glass showering down on top of the cans with a metallic drumming sound. He laughed. Great! These are the old-fashioned metal cans. They'll make a helluva racket! Then he withdrew the second bottle and flung it against the bricks, staggering a bit as he released it, nearly losing his balance. A third bottle blasted against the wall, a fourth, then a fifth. He laughed hoarsely, staggering again as the night spun crazily. A back light came on farther down the alley and he saw the silhouette of a man behind a door window, peering out into the black night. Vince spat on the ground, picked up the last bottle and threw it as hard as he could. It shattered like the others, breaking the quiet night. He roared with throaty, hysterical laughter, staggering as he regained his balance. Slowly the man in the house opened the door and looked out.

Vince stared at him for a moment, then spat on the ground again. "Hey, asshole!" he yelled, jumping and waving his arms crazily, "I'm over here, ya dumb shit! Can't you see? Jesus Christ, ya blind, or something?" Suddenly he gritted hs teeth, swung and viciously kicked one of the cans. It slammed into another with a loud metallic crash, the tops of both spiraling upward, then crashing down on the mutilated containers. He was screaming in laughter. "Here's one for your goddamn rich buddy, Ann!" A hard kick and another of the cans crumpled and careened into the brick wall, filling the air with shattering sounds.

He saw the man still looking, still not sure where the voice was coming from. Then the man saw him. "Get outa here before I call the police!" he shouted in righteous indignation.

Vince stared at him for a moment. "Go screw yourself!" he shouted loudly, his voice ricocheting off the brick and stone walls of the houses. The light went off, he thought he heard the man mutter something, then the door was slammed shut and he was once again alone in the pitch dark alley.

He stood there for several moments, the mutilated containers scattered around him. Well, it was done. Yep, another inappropriate outburst, as Ann would say. Another antisocial way to express your anger. "Well, what the hell!" he muttered, spitting and lurching around. Couldn't remember ever doing this before. Oh, shit…! Time to go before the police arrive. You don't need that. He staggered home, slinking clumsily among the hedges and dark alleys.

An hour later he sat alone on his front porch, slightly more sober than before, the world slowing its wild spin, his toes a bit sore from place-kicking the cans. "Well, so what?" he mumbled. "The damn cans deserved what they got."

It slowly dawned in his soggy mind that in some inexplicable way, his life was starting all over. As if he had just completed one very long cycle and was about to begin another. To every season there is a reason. The words to a song remembered from long ago. Back in a time that had come to its end, the good right along with the bad. What a twisted way to shed your old life and start another!

He shrugged. Yep, created a big disturbance for those folks living over there. Great big mess for someone to clean up tomorrow. No, it wasn't right, sure enough, but oh, Lord, it sure felt good!

Chapter Twenty-six

Dave Behlen arrived at his office at 6 am on a day that matched his dark mood: gray and drizzly cold. With great reluctance, he agreed to a meeting with this guy from the city council, Worley, Turnby, whatever the hell his name was. Time just wasted on government! Intolerable! He kept trying to turn him down but the man just could not be put off. Okay, he condescended, make it quick and dirty. More important things await me.

The meeting was set in a small restaurant out in Wayzeta, ten miles west of Minneapolis, where he'd not be recognized. He insisted on that. Not a single client or staff member was now, or had ever been, of minority status.

But the source of his black mood today was due only in part to this persistent councilman. It happened last evening. He was totally absorbed in two extremely important American League baseball games on his extensive sports cable network, one game on each wide screen.

He heard Melissa arrive and begin talking with her mother in the kitchen where those two usually gathered. He wasn't about to join them: two outs, runners on second and third, full count on the batter, bottom of the ninth inning, score tied. That manager gets his team out of this without a run scored or he deserves to be fired before leaving the ballpark. Same for the pitcher and the opposing team: they fail to score and win, somebody takes the walk. You either managed the right way, taken always to be his way, or management was fired and players traded. Dead serious business!

Then, just as the big pitch was about to be served, Melissa breezed into the den.

"I've picked up the last of my stuff," she told him just as the pitcher went into the wind-up.

"Fine," he answered, not moving his eyes from the screen. Peace would finally prevail. This pitch had better be a low slider, catching the outside corner of the plate. Not one the batter could hit, but by God, if that happens, he'd call the team's GM in the morning. He'd done that before. The pitcher went into his wind-up, reared back, here comes the pitch and—

"Dad, Raul Montero is moving in with me!"

The slider whistled over the plate, just catching the corner.

Two inches high.

A mighty swing, a loud crack and the ball arched majestically, rocketing over the infield. The left fielder went back, back, to the warning track, back, up against the wall where the ball soared high over his outstretched glove and disappeared into the seats. Thirty-five thousand fans went berserk.

So did David Behlen.

Whatever he saw, it wasn't the game-winning hit. He saw very bright colors, crimson the most prominent, colliding violently before his eyes. He didn't even hear the loud cheering as he slowly turned to where Melissa and Cheryl stood by the doorway, a stricken look on his face. "Say again?" came the words from his constricted throat.

Melissa crossed the room and stood in front of him. "A larger apartment opened in my building so I took it. Raul and I will live there," she proudly told him, her face beaming.

Not a word from the big recliner, just that glazed-over expression as the two screens suddenly lost his attention. "You remember Raul, don't you?"

"...Isn't he..." His intestines were weaving themselves into a tight knot.

"He is an attorney for the Housing Authority."

She saw a dark cloud pass over him and he pointed toward the west, in the direction of Nuevo Del Rio.

"Oh, yes, he's also working with Peter Hoffler and myself on the rail matter. You remember Peter, don't you?"

Though he didn't move, Melissa could sense something working beneath that stunned facade, some sort of denial mechanism.

"I've known about Raul and his work with the village for more than a year, though we first met about seven months ago."

Though usually quick with words, he was struggling mightily, morbid visions flashing across his mind. She was living with a Mexican! A Mexican! All his business associates, the ones he saw at the country club, at the restaurants where he lunched, all had big weddings for their sons and daughters. It was a great event among the business colleagues he ran with and they always invited each other. But their offsprings' spouses were all lawyers, business owners or rising stars in the corporate world. They were never…They never married…outside their own group! Oh, good God, this was unheard of! How would he ever…? Finally a small bit of his circuitry cleared, and a few words found their way through.

He caught a glimpse of the TV where someone was interviewing the slugging hero who wore that six-year, fifty million dollar grin. "You've only known him for a few months but you're ready to go off and marry this guy?" More horrid visions swept across his overloaded mind. He could just see the looks they'd give him downtown and hear the whispers making the rounds: Did you hear about Behlen's daughter?

"I only said we are going to live together." That did nothing to assuage the frightening prospects still spinning in his head. "Raul and I share a common mission, and in many ways you don't understand, I admire him; what he is, what he stands for. I've dated enough men who don't come up to his level."

He shook his head, battling a swirling vortex that was drowning him, pulling him deep, never to return. "Melissa…I can think of at least six good prospects, bright young businessmen I know downtown. I could recommend any one of them. I don't think you've looked very hard. You got involved with this guy and all tied up in this rail thing, and now you're going head over heels for him! It just doesn't make any sense, Melissa!"

"Dad, I'm twenty-two years old. I know my own mind! I told you before, I'm returning to college in two weeks, I plan to finish in three semesters, then enroll in law school." His daughter was going to be a lawyer! "Doesn't that make you proud? The way I know you are with Kevin?"

More appalling spectacles danced dervishly across his reeling mind. Kevin would be a corporate lawyer. Solid. Predictable. A good conservative. One he could brag about to his colleagues. But her…He could just imagine the clients she would be serving, God only knew what issues they might dredge up and who'd be their next victim. It was that rail thing today, but what would come next? His own colleagues wouldn't be safe.

"All right," he finally said, partially collecting himself. "I know what I said before, about the financial help, but you need to take another look at this. I don't think you've—"

"You don't think I've worked my way through this. That I'm mindlessly running off on some crazy tangent with this child-like infatuation for someone because he's of another race and takes on issues you view as worthless. They don't fit into your rigid, intolerant version of what the world is supposed to be, about who fits into that pattern and who doesn't fit!" She stopped and took a deep breath, standing right in front of him, her fists balled, hands on her hips, glaring down at him. Cheryl noticed he seemed to sink further into his chair.

"Melissa, the bottom line of all of this is—"

"Dave," Cheryl said as she crossed the room and stood in front of him and beside Melissa, "You promised Kevin and Melissa you'd pay their tuition if they enrolled in college. Kevin did and you paid the costs. Now our daughter has made the same decision. Are you going to treat her differently? If you do, I will write the checks from my own account, then transfer fiunds from yours!

"You and I were her age when we decided to marry and we hadn't dated others very much, so why are you demanding that she do what we weren't willing to do? You should have stayed home that afternoon Raul visited us. I've met him twice and think highly of him. Every now and then you ought to get out of that tight little mold you created!"

My God, he thought, she sounds just like my daughter!

Shortly after that, Melissa left with a check signed by him: a quivering line made by a trembling, fearful hand. She refused to accept help for living costs. "I still have that neat job at the coffee shop," she reminded him again. "You know, where I meet writers, poets and other thinkers?"

Dave Behlen spent a restless night and rose well before five am, grumbled something to Cheryl, showered, dressed and left for the office. He'd make short shrift of this guy, Turling, whatever, then get back to reality.

He was feeling no better at one pm when he walked into a small, pleasant cafe in Wayzata. Turley met him in the lobby and escorted him to a back booth. "I appreciate your taking valuable time to be with us," he said as they made their way to the booth.

"'Us'? Behlen asked, his eyebrows arching. "I thought we were meeting alone."

"Mr. Behlen, I apologize. An oversight on my part. Oh, you know how it is, people like you and me have so much on our minds."

They came to the booth, Behlen glancing anxiously around as a bulky black man rose to greet him. "Mr. Behlen, I'd like you to meet a good friend of mine: the Reverend Aaron Young, minister at Waters of Life Church, which is located in my ward. You may have heard about the church."

"No, I haven't." he said as he shook the older man's hand with the same fervor he felt writing that check last evening.

Turley and Young ordered coffee. Behlen preferred water. "Mr., ah, Turley, what's your bottom line here? I don't have a lot of time." He glanced quickly at his watch, then around the room again.

"Yes, you're right," Turley answered. "We need to get on with it, to the bottom line, as you say. About this petition you have been circulating. I assume you first checked with city hall?"

"What does this has to do with anything?"

"If I recall correctly, you had something like a thousand signatures. Is that about right?"

Behlen shrugged. "Probably. So what?"

"If you had checked with city hall you'd have known that since you were seeking to place a funding issue before the council, you needed about nineteen thousand signatures, twenty percent of the votes cast in the last mayoral election. You were asking the council, in effect, to spend many millions on a road, were you not?

Again, Behlen shrugged. "All right, we were short. Do I go to prison for that? Is this all you have to say? I don't have time to discuss bureaucratic rules. I have a business to run!"

"We know that at least two hundred of those on that list were dead. Dead people signing petitions? That makes it illegal, Mr. Behlen."

"And that is something I should be concerned with?" he demanded, his expression turning from stone-like indifference to twisted spite. "Discuss it with of my attorneys!" He slapped their business cards on the table, all three of them, then began to rise from the booth.

Turley slowly raised a hand as Behlen was sliding out of his seat. "A moment, please. Does the number five-fourteen mean anything to you?"

"Absolutely not!"

Turley looked straight at him and dropped his voice. "Room 514? Clarkson Hotel? Tuesday of last week? Tall, slender, honey-blond hair?" He looked up at Behlen, who had now came to a stop halfway out of the booth, still leaning on the table. Turley saw a shadow cross his face. "Please sit down, sir. This is more important than any clients you might have waiting for you."

"Are you two trying to—"

"Mr. Behlen," Aaron Young cut in, "Mr. Turley, lost his wife and only child four years ago. He misses them very much."

"And Reverend Young lost his wife to cancer twelve years ago and still misses her very much. That's unfortunate, don't you think so, Mr. Behlen?"

He nodded. "Of course," he sighed as his neck veins suddenly began pulsing.

Turley went on. "Yes, a family is so important, and more so as we all age. Mr. Behlen, you have son who is completing law school and a daughter who will soon be starting law school, is that right?"

"My son graduates next spring."

Young nodded. "Yes. And your daughter? You must be just as proud of her." Behlen's face went beet red and Young saw the vein in his neck throb and drum above his shirt collar. "I'm sure your son and daughter will both be a credit to the trade. Sit down, please."

He sat, then leaned forward, arching his long frame over the table, and glared at the two men. "Look, would you two just get to the point of this? I don't waste valuable time!"

Young slowly raised his hand. "Now hold on, Mr. Behlen. We are, as you're fond of saying, driving as fast as we can down to the bottom line, and we shall be there shortly. Have a little patience. We understand your father passed away some years ago, is that right?"

"He did. Where did you get all this—"

"Your mother lives alone in south Minneapolis?"

Dave Behlen sighed, glancing at his watch. "Yes, she does."

"And I assume you visit her often, take her to church, out for lunch? You know, he kind of support old folks really need from their families?"

Behlen exhaled slowly "I do, yes. Now, what is it—"

"But not often," Turley said. Behlen shrugged. "She must be a gracious old lady, living out her last few years alone. What a tragedy in our modern, crank-it-up, bottom line world, don't you think? But when she goes to church, alone, I'm sure you'd want her to worship in comfort, wouldn't you? You know, without those drafts and cold floors. Old folks are so sensitive to that."

"Indeed they are," Young added. "I have many elderly worshipers, every Sunday, and during the winter it can be very uncomfortable for them. I think it's sad how they must always simply make do, don't you, Mr. Behlen? Your father was a factory worker, so that means your mother relies mostly, if not totally, on Social Security. Is that correct?"

"I help her occasionally." Again he sighed, clasping and unclasping his hands. "Gentlemen, can we get down to whatever it is you're after? I do have clients waiting."

Turley nodded vigorously. "It all comes down to this, Mr. Behlen," he said, his voice suddenly low and hard. "If the word ever gets out about your affair with this lady, I believe her name is Lynn Alveson, it could result in divorce action against you. This would be extremely expensive, considering your annual income is deep into the six figures, approaching seven. You know how those lawyers would work it, don't you? Can't you just see it all, right now? Her's would go right for the sympathy of the court, and they'd get it, too!

"Oh, they'd point out the many hours she labored every day with her tiny little business, trying to develop it and get a foothold in that big market, struggling against a small cash flow, while you, her unfaithful husband, have this big, successful consulting firm downtown. Major bucks! And if the court still had any doubts all they'd have to do is look at your tax returns and there you'd be. And your lawyer'd just have to sit there, fabricating some kind of bullshit that wouldn't go nowhere. Nowhere at all! Add it all up, Mr. Behlen: at least two hundred thousand a year or more to your ex-wife for maintenance. Then you add the legal costs, the health and life insurance, then the retirement benefits you'll pay her when the time comes, and that's not all. No sir, they're not done with you yet! Ooooh, no! They'll throw in that business about the illegal petition. How you tried to deceive the city council, and there would go any character and credibility you still had.

"Then there's another whole chapter to this. In the process I'm sure your business would be audited. All those tax people you just hate? What do you think they'll find?

"Have you paid all of your taxes in full? Have Social Security, state and federal taxes been properly withheld from your associates? How about Unemployment and Workers' Compensation taxes? All paid in full every quarter? Are you sure you have all of your people in the right pay status? Have your associates been fully paid for all services rendered? You'd better check closely because audits can be devastating, Mr. Behlen. Absolutely devastating! They not only hit you with all those back taxes, but then they add on penalty and interest, and it can kill you. I want you to know that, sir. Penalty and interest alone can double the liability. Did you know this? It can absolutely wipe you out!" Turley shook his head sadly. So did Aaron Young.

"Let me tell you, Mr. Behlen, I've had way too many of my constituents come crying to me, saying 'Oh, Mr. Turley, what can you do? They're gonna get me for all them back taxes. Can't you do something?' And all I can do is sit there and say 'No, sir, there ain't nothin' I can do for you. Not one thing.' Oh, its terrible, I tell you! Just terrible!"

Now Behlen held up his hands, his face gleaming under the lights, hands shaking. "All right, I hear what you're saying. So what does it all come down to?"

Turley turned to Reverend Young who pulled several sheets of paper from his jacket pocket and very slowly straightened them on the table, pressing out every little crease, as Behlen watched him, the neck vein throbbing as sweat gleamed on his flushed features, his fingers drumming the table. "It comes down to this, sir. As I have said, my faithful flock is a rather poor lot. Incidentally, do you know someone by the name of Paul Kasson?"

Behlen shook his head. "No. Should I?"

"He's the pastor at your mother's church. You know, the place where you said you take her to for worship on Sundays? Reverend Kasson and I have come up with a solution to this awful dilemma you're now in. He and I have done a needs assessment and this is what needs to be done to solve all of these thorny little problems you now have. First, it turns out that both churches will need a new roof. You wouldn't tolerate your mother worshipping in the house of God with the roof leaking on her head. A disgrace! I'll bet that roof on your home is just as water tight as it could be. New shingles, flashing and roof decking only come to only eight thousand-nine hundred, and God Bless all those wonderful people in our two congregations, for they have volunteered to do the work. Isn't that wonderful, Mr. Behlen?"

Dave Behlen grimaced, his face shining, fingers still drumming the table. Just marvelous.

"Next, it turns out we both need new plumbing. Nothing fancy, you understand, only the basics: new faucets and supply lines, shut-off valves and a new water heater at my church. Certainly nothing like the elaborate fixtures you must have in that nice home you own. That comes to, ah, nine thousand four hundred and fifty-two dollars.

"Then we have some electrical work. Again we're only talking plain old basics here: all new wiring, switches and outlets, a few lighting fixtures." He looked down at the sheet. "Oh, yes, your mother's church needs a new electrical service panel. Those fuse boxes are too dangerous when they're that old. Not at all like what you must enjoy, Mr.Behlen. Now we have some volunteer help for that, too, but of course much of that must be done by a licensed electrician. You wouldn't want to put your mother at risk, would you., Mr. Behlen?"

"Of course not" came his squeaky response, the cords standing out in his neck.

"Certainly not! Anyway, it comes to nine thousand seven hundred and ten dollars. Now, fortunately, your mother's church has a good furnace, but Waters of Life, that's mine, desperately needs a new unit. You just can't take risks with those old boiler systems. Very dangerous! But for the grace of God, the place would have burned down by now. Certainly not a nice, safe heating system as you have, I'm sure. What a shame you expose your own dear mother to such a risk!

"Anyway, the total for that is twelve thousand six hundred and eighty dollars. Quite expensive, unfortunately, but that was the very best we could do. You can trust me on that. Next, we both have many badly fitting windows and the good people suffer from drafts all the time. You know how that goes: first those old walls lean this way and they lean that way. Pretty soon it's so damn far out of line and you can't get nothin' to work. Not at all like those energy-efficient crank-out windows you must have. So, that comes to twelve thousand seven hundred and twenty. And the good news for you, Mr. Behlen, is that we're almost at the end of this modest list of essentials. Yes, sir!"

My God, Turley thought. That poor man really is going to slide right down to the floor!

"Now, that's the worst of it," Young explained. "Just a couple other items then we're all done. Both buildings need paint badly. With all volunteer help, God bless them again, that only comes to eight hundred and fifty dollars for supplies.

"Well, there you are, Mr. Behlen. We got bids and of course selected the lowest one, so that, together with all the wonderful people who will volunteer, will save you a great deal of money. Oh, we were very conscious about the cost! Yes, we were!"

"This is extortion!" Behlen hissed between clenched teeth as his neck veins throbbed and bulged, his face now crimson. A bulb of sweat clung to his nose.

"Call it whatever you want, Mr. Behlen. But you do understand the alternative...?" He smacked his forehead. "Oh, no...I almost forgot. Well, that's what happens when you get old. There is actually one more item: we must replace the carpet in both places. It is just down to the threads. A shame that your mother should have to walk on that when she comes with you to worship the Lord. She could trip on the loose threads and take a bad fall. Oh, you know what happens then! I'm just amazed at what you make your mother put up with, while you live out in that million dollar castle of yours! Anyway, that comes to just fourteen thousand six hundred and seventy-five, with a lot of volunteer help. So our grand total comes to...let's see...aaaaah...sixty eight thousand nine hundred and eighty-seven dollars, including materials, labor and tax. Let's say sixty-nine thousand for good measure."

"And you think I should pay all of this?" he snapped, his veins still quivering beneath his flushed skin, that bulb of sweat clinging tenaciously to his nose.

Turley nodded. "Uh huh. And you should pay it right now. Oh, also, we think we need to secure this arrangement."

"Secure it?"

Aaron Young rubbed his chin, then raised a finger. "Let's just say the arrangement needs one final touch. Just so that all parties involved don't around sayin' nothin' to nobody about nothin'. Okay?

So let's just adjust the final amount...: sixty-nine thousand...five hundred and fourteen dollars. A nice round number we can easily remember!"

Long moments passed in silence, as Behlen glared at the two men. "You sons of bitches!" he hissed, little ticks quivering on his crimson face.

Young shrugged. "Maybe. What does that make you, Mr. Behlen.?"

"I could sue you both for this!" he muttered.

Turley nodded. "Sure. If you're willing to face the alternatives." Turley glared back at Behlen. "We want a check, sir, and we want it right now, or we spread the word, before you can even get to the cell phone out in your car." Turley held up his pager phone, a finger poised above a button. "Your home number is predialed. Shall I press it? You think about it, Mr.Behlen. What we're offering is five percent of what the alternative will cost you. Think of this as the five per cent solution."

More long, silent moments. He hadn't fallen on the floor yet, Turley observed, but the facial muscles were sure twitching furiously beneath the sweaty skin. "One more thing for you to consider," Young said. "Once you've made this investment in our neighborhood, you certainly wouldn't want to see all these improvements be wasted when Waters of Life is torn down. Lanes or no lanes, Mr. Behlen, my church will remain where it is! That is my final condition. If you disagree with any part of this, payment or no payment, we let loose the alternative."

Turley raised a finger. “One more item, from me. Call off your dogs, Mr. Behlen. Anyone follows me around again, or I have another call, your wife gets the news. I had a problem, sir, and I’ve taken care of it.”

Behlen sat silent, numb, as if he’d been set upon by thieves. His facial muscles were twitching, the neck vein throbbing like a drumbeat, his face only a shade less crimson. Then he slowly reached into his jacket pocket and withdrew a checkbook. “You may make that out to Waters of Life Church, please,” Turley said. “Reverend Young is our fiscal agent.”

A minute later their meeting was adjourned. Turley was the first out of the booth, then Young followed. Behlen was slower. Aaron Young leaned down toward him and spoke softly. “You know, Mr. Behlen, you may be one great big, cheap, unprincipled, swindling son of a bitch, but somewhere down deep, there’s a very decent man trying to break to the surface. You consider that.” Then he placed his thick hand on Behlen’s shoulder. “You really ought to get to know Reverend Kasson some time soon. You and your mother are also welcome at Waters of Life. You have a very good day, sir. God bless.”

Chapter Twenty-seven

It hadn't been the most productive month for Dave Behlen and he was still fuming over that humiliating confrontation with Aaron Young and Forrest Turley. He wasn't accustomed to life on the losing end of anything, certainly not when brought about by the likes of those two, and that just added to his seething frustration. He said little to his employees, met only with his senior staff and kept it focused strictly on business, then abruptly retreated to his office.

This morning he pulled up the payroll accounting records on his computer, which he now did himself after firing Brad. Scrolling down the various columns he calculated that by the end of the year he would have a shortfall of nearly sixty thousand dollars in social security matching, workers' compensation and unemployment insurance contributions. The government called those "contributions" rather than taxes; it had such a positive ring to it.

What if he really was slammed with audits after a year? he pondered. What would penalty and interest come to? He did some quick calculations, one of his strong talents, and shuddered when it showed a total of almost one hundred thousand dollars. It pained him to think that all those government auditors just might know their business.

He sat and thought about that dismal prospect for a while, then scanned his Rolodex for a number. Another accountant he knew; one who had pulled back a few of his colleagues from the brink of their own bad judgment. A strategy was in the making; one part of it would soon be in place.

He sat for several more minutes, drumming his long fingers on the desk, then dialed another number that rang a hundred feet down the hallway. "I just can't do it," he said to her, referring to a conference next month in Philadelphia. "Yes, I know what I said then but, well, things have gotten complicated and I need to sort it all out. There's a lot at stake here right now…Yes, I understand, but that was then, and this is now, and…I Don't know…I really don't know what's going to happen with…Yes, I'm sorry, too and…it has nothing to do with you…just a few other matters that, ah…" That conversation ended abruptly with a click. It had been such a good friendship..

"God damn those bastards!" he hissed. Sixty-nine thousand bucks! Then they have the balls to tack on another five hundred and fourteen! Just to keep it honest! "Swindling sons of bitches!" It was a miserable experience with those two, but now he'd dealt Lynn out of the equation for step two of his emerging plan.

Now what to do? "How did I get maneuvered into this?" he agonized. And it was done by those whom he judged below him in the hierarchy of human affairs! He totally trusted the workings of the free market, as well as who knew whom, who held control and directed the flow of money and power.

In the brokering of power, he reasoned, those who represented religion or the poor were irrelevant, were at the bottom, without clout, and that's how it's supposed to be. One doesn't mess with natural laws that determined an immutable layering.

So, do I sit down with Cheryl and tell her what's been happening? Just say 'Okay, this is the way it is, so let's forget about it?' I mean, by God, lay it out the way it was? The cold logic of this appealed to him—a straightforward drive, directly to the bottom line. He thought about that for a long time, then stood again and gazed out the window. No! Too many risks. That leaves too many options for her.

He shook his head. You don't cut yourself off at the knees, then negotiate. All she'd have to say is: "Leave!" How would he ever explain that to his colleagues downtown? He could be contrite, swear up and down it would never happen again, promise to spend more time at home and hope she bought into that. That made sense, but contrition wasn't his natural attribute. Think again.

Maybe it would be best to keep the mouth shut. Did she know about Lynn, or the others before her? Likely not. Cheryl wasn't shy about expressing her feelings, so he would have heard from her by this time. Okay, so the bottom line here is she doesn't know. Revealing it was a huge risk and then a settlement with alimony, maintenance, as Turley called it. Would they award her two hundred thousand a year as he said? His taxable income last year was more than eight hundred and fifty thousand and would rise by another seventy-five thousand this year. Good God! The court wouldn't hesitate to award her a quarter million! But she couldn't stay in

Bellwood with no more than that. Therefor, he gambled, she would want him to stay. He was already beginning to feel better about this whole matter.

But wait, stop! Think, for God's sake! I pushed her into Bellwood; not the other way around! I liked what it said about me. It meant less to her. Suddenly the risks ratcheted back upward. He stood by the window, staring at the glass and steel bromide across Marquette Avenue. Then he reached his decision. No…can't take the risk. Too much to lose. Okay, bottom line is this: keep the mouth shut. Spend more time at home but don't do it all at once. Phase into it. Cut a few hours off work here and there and add them to the home life, whatever that was. Cut and add a few more later. Nothing that would cause her to wonder about his changing habits.

That good feeling surged back. He had a strategy now and that always made him feel confident. The final piece was in place. He'd leave work early today.

But not too early.

Heading south on I-35W, devils of another kind began nipping at him. He was approaching the Lake Street interchange, hesitated, then swung into the right lane and down the exit ramp. At the bottom he turned left, crossed beneath the freeway and turned left again onto Third Street, a narrow route hidden from the freeway by a tall sound barrier. He drove a few blocks through a neighborhood that emanated mixed signals: poverty and despair together with the promise of renovation. He parked his car close to the church, then glanced warily around. He saw the new shingles and the metal flashings gleaming in the bright sunlight. Then he noticed the fresh paint. It looked like a new building.

He hesitated, then walked into the small chapel. All of the pews were stacked against a wall while three men crawled on hands and knees laying new carpet. In the dim light it looked to be dark red. An electrician passed him heading downstairs where wiring was being run into a new service panel. Two others were installing double-pane windows.

For several more moments he stood there, uncertain when on foreign turf, then walked slowly to the front, stopping before the curved railing of the altar. He gazed up at the lean, sinewy figure trussed up on the cross, His head bowed in death, a thin red line weaving down His face from the crown of thorns. Just a carpenter's helper, a laborer, wearing nothing but a simple loincloth. Nailed hand and foot to a piece of wood. A shabby way to treat someone with more followers than all the TV evangelists and sports heroes combined.

From somewhere nearby came the voice of Aaron Young. Behlen turned and stepped behind a pillar in the corner as Young and another man came up the basement stairway. Young was talking vigorously, his voice carrying a youthful enthusiasm. It seemed to Behlen that he stood light and straight, not that stooped, ponderous figure he met at the restaurant six weeks ago. Behlen turned quietly and eased his way out a newly installed side door and walked quickly back to his car, noticing the new windows as he left. Double crank-outs.

All in all, not bad.

A few minutes later he was back on the freeway heading south, along with a million others. Sixty-nine thousand, he fussed, plus the amount those bastards tacked on just for insurance. Goddamn swindlers! How did they do it? How did they know where I was and who I was with? Is someone keeping a watch on me? Who? Someone at the office? He had a couple disgruntled associates. If it was one of them, how did they get the information? Did one of them have a skill I don't know about? He'd do some checking around.

Twenty minutes later he arrived home and found, to his relief, Cheryl was not there. Melissa's old Mazda was in the driveway. Probably picking up more of her belongings. Moving day for her was not a well orchestrated affair. Cheryl had made him his favorite dinner: Chicken and rice with slivered almonds ready for the microwave. Have a brandy and soda first. Time to review the strategy. He mixed the ingredients, then settled comfortably in his favorite recliner.

Okay, first we assume she doesn't know about the affair since she hasn't said anything. Make it appear we've dropped the rail opposition. I'll let the two assholes know this. Then we'll get a banker to take the lead and push it through the House a little later. I know one, a VP in a big bank downtown, who can swing enough votes and send a good highway bill to the governor. And when that happens, why, I'll just tell the assholes I couldn't stop it. Awfully sorry. So what if I have to pony up a bit more for some church? I thought they'd go for at least a hundred grand.

He sat back in the big recliner, once again feeling the world was back in its proper orbit, just as Melissa came down the stairs. "A surprise seeing you here before ten o'clock," she said to him, a hint of mockery in her voice. "I'm picking up the last of my things. Raul and I are fixing up our apartment. We want you to visit us soon."

He nodded, feeling the jab of the knife blade, turning and twisting. She was standing directly in front of him. "Hey, Dad, drop the footrest."

"Huh?"

She reached down and kicked the wooden lever on the side of the chair and his feet dropped to the floor. "What are—"

In one quick, blurry move she reared back, wound up and slammed her fist into the side of his face with a resounding WHACK! The brandy and soda flew out of his hand, splashing on the floor behind him. His head spun in a painful, confused blur, brilliant lights and bright-colored balloons dancing in a throbbing kaleidoscope. Before he could react she grabbed his hair with one hand, thrust it backward and poised her knee ominously above his groin. "You worm! You goddamn slimy excuse for a man! And you think I don't know about you and your little lady friend?"

One hundred and fifteen pounds, all stretched out along a five-foot eight inch frame, but she held this two-hundred and twenty pound man immobilized, his scalp screaming in agony and his lower regions close to the same, or worse, should she shift her weight ever so slightly. "What, what are you—"

"Don't try lying your way out of this! Oh, you'd better believe the number five-fourteen will have many implications for you!" He stared up into her blazing eyes. "My mother, the woman you've been cheating on, will be here soon, then we'll all sit down and have a very long and serious talk about this family!"

"Melissa," he reached up and placed his hands on her hips, trying to push her away. Then she shifted, her knee came down and he shuddered, turned pale and suddenly began sweating profusely, his lungs seized in paralysis, unable to emit the barest sound.

"I don't know how this will all turn out. She just might throw your ass out of this house, then again she may not! Listen to me and you listen real good and hard. You're going to back away from this freeway issue and the people who live in that little village will stay there because you are going to get someone from the establishment, a real wing-tip, white collar, bedrock conservative, to testify before the House Transportation Committee. You're also going to leave Mr. Turley alone, I know all about his treatments, so call off your filthy dogs! Do you understand?"

"You just can't—"

Down came her knee, slamming into a nerve ganglia—unbearable agony for any male and he screamed, squirming to get out of the chair but she held him fast, tightening her grip on his hair. "You're not listening! I want the name of a banker! A good, conservative, pin-stripe member of the white status quo, because this person is going to say that the great white establishment now feels the state should look years ahead and invest only in the rail plan. It must be someone those folks in the legislature will listen to. Give me the name!"

"Melissa, I don't know…AAAAGGGHHH!!!" The nerve ganglia sprung to life sending screaming messages searing into the brain as he gasped and trembled in agony, sweat pouring down his reddened face.

"Give me a name! Now!" She pressed her knee just a bit harder.

He closed his eyes, still blinded by salty sweat, teeth grinding together, while names raced through his ragged mind. "Burling…Paul Burling—"

"Who is he?"

"…Vice president of investments…" He gave her the bank's name.

She glared down at him, his hair nearly ripped from his scalp, her knee eager to send him into agony again. "Call him, now! You will tell him what he has to do! And if you mess this up in the tiniest little way I will have Raul persuade the court to order more damn support payment to Mother than you ever dreamed possible, so don't piss me off! You do this right and maybe I can save your ass with Mother. I have more influence with her that you ever did. You make that call, now, and when you're done we'll just sit tight till she comes home.

Trust me, I have many friends in strange places. I know what you do, I know where you go and who you're with." She continued staring at him as he sat with his eyes wide with shock, face pale as a ghost, his lower parts still trembling in pain. "You've got ten minutes to salvage your future in this home. Get moving! You're no longer in charge here. I am."

Chapter Twenty-eight

Vince had lived in the old two-story classic on Mackubin Street for seven months and now the trees stood stark and bare, Halloween-like, against the glow of the downtown lights in the gathering gloom of a November evening. The fallen leaves, damp from a day of steady drizzle, lent a musk odor to the cool, humid air. It was still early in the month but the dwellers of the northern latitudes know they have another two weeks before the dark of night comes early and greets them at the doorstep after a day's work.

About a month ago Ann called him. Would he like to meet for lunch on Sunday? Certainly. One of the few Sundays he wasn't scheduled to work. She suggested his favorite place near Victoria Crossing. What? he wondered. She wants to come to my neighborhood?

Today she was even on time. They finished the main course as they discussed small matters. The waiter refilled their coffee cups and retreated "Vince, I can't blame you for the anger you felt when we separated…I would like to know how you're feeling now."

He stared at her for a moment. She wasn't accustomed to talking about feelings, his, hers, anyone's. He had to think about that before answering. Nothing to be gained by bringing up her affair, former affair, whichever. "We've had sharp differences. I mean, your ways with the house, social ambitions, the friends I kept." He knew what he meant by ambitions. He wasn't sure where Ann was going with this line of talk, but sensed that mentioning Bellwood could be incendiary. Nor did he want to refer to the immense relief he felt being free of her confronting, fretful ways and where he could enjoy a beer with his friends. "You were right, we grew and changed. We just didn't go in the same direction. The big wedge came when I lost the business and before you experienced the same thing."

She nodded quietly. "I couldn't grasp what was happening to you. I always assumed when this occurred we made a sideways shift and kept going as before. Like the old days: one factory shuts down so the workers go to another. I thought you didn't care what happened to our standard of living when you were hired at Builder's Market. I saw this as your failing and I'm sorry for that. Then it happened to me." Her voice dropped. "I am a sadder one, but wiser for what has happened to us."

He looked at her and saw a strange, paradoxical expression on her face, as if a smile was struggling to break to the surface. "It's a humbling experience, isn't it? One day you're on top of the world, you have it all, then one day that all-important job disappears. You start looking but soon realize you must go back to square one. Like you said, we've always assumed we should look sideways. Then the world tells you no, look downward. I was a contractor; now I sell to contractors."

"We never talked about how we feel," she said. "We're all brought up to believe women are supposed to be in touch with their emotions and know how to express what they're feeling. Maybe it was how I was raised, but I'm not very good at it. Vince, in my roundabout fashion, I'm asking if it would be okay if I spent a few evenings a week at your house. For now, I mean."

This had occurred to him during some of his lonely walks, but he never expected it to come from her. "I spend my evenings on the final draft of the thesis, so we wouldn't be in each other's way, even when you weren't working." He knew one of his friends, the one who had the bitter divorce, would have said "Hell, no!" and been done with it. Ann there in the evenings, when he'd also be there? Was this what he'd been missing for all but the first month? Just her presence? When they lived together she was much more than just there, always fussing, confronting him about his friends, his slothfulness, or whatever else was irritating her. He was free of that now. What if this meant a return to those times? "I don't like the commute in the evenings, Vince. It's dark by the time I get home." That had never stopped her before, all those evening meetings.

"I'm not very tidy, you know."

She smiled and shrugged.

"I leave things laying around, clothes hanging on the doorknobs."

She said that was all right.

"The kitchen countertops are usually cluttered and I'm terrible about leaving closet doors open."

To this she smiled. A bright sun rose over his horizon. "Sure," he told her.

A couple evenings a week soon turned into a couple nights a week, but he had two bedrooms so there were no awkward moments or other complications. They spent little and lived modestly—closer to the ground, as he described it.

Just before this, Ann had made a difficult decision. She had an interview for a curriculum director in Des Moines and another in Green Bay, five hundred miles away, the following morning. Both had gone very well, she told him, her eyelids heavy from the long drives. Within ten days she received two very complimentary letters, both telling her how they appreciated her interest and that they were sure she would locate an excellent position. But not in Des Moines or Green Bay.

That was when her iron will broke. She accepted a teaching position in a nearby middle school. By then she'd spent most of her severance pay and had only eleven weeks of unemployment insurance left. She scoffed when the unemployment insurance people told her the more one is specialized and the higher one is educated, the longer it takes to find a replacement job. Ridiculous! she thought. I hold a master's degree and nearly a doctorate! They were right. Another long-held assumption fell to the wayside. She agonized, wondering what the world was coming to, then accepted the job. Her annual income dropped forty-five thousand dollars.

On this evening they were there together, she in the study laboring over a phrase in her dissertation, he in the living room reading a novel. Finally he stood, placed the book on a side table and walked slowly to the open door and leaned against the jamb. "Toil, toil, toil. Will you ever be done with that monster?"

She looked up at him and smiled, not as thinly as before, and rubbed weary eyes. “I can’t find the right words to express this thought, but yes, the monster will soon be done.”

“It’s getting late. Why not stay for the night? We could go out for a late dinner.” She had clothing and a complete set of everything women need, both here at and her apartment.

“Let’s take a walk first. Just a short one.”

What? A walk? After dark? Here? She rarely left the house after sunset. Until the last year. They walked down Mackubin Street to Summit Avenue, then west to St. Alban’s Street. At a corner they came upon a small group of black men talking in a foreign tongue and she suddenly stiffened and gripped his hand, holding her breath as they passed the group. “What are they doing?” she asked him, once a safe distance from them.

“Chatting, passing on local gossip.”

“Why do they do it out here?”

“It’s just the local stuff, whatever’s going on. They do on the street corner what others do over the phone or by e-mail. The same as they did in their native country. Nothing to worry about.”

They walked on to St. Alban’s Street, then back the same way, her hand still holding tightly to his. How long had it been since they did this? Since he last felt the warmth of her hand. In those moments, on a dark street of a chilly November evening, he felt the years roll back to an earlier, more agreeable time. They stopped in at a small cafe nearby and ordered a light snack and coffee.

An hour later she was again at work in the study. Vince walked past the open door to the kitchen and returned a minute later and saw her staring out the window, above the closed half shutters. “You look deep in thought,” he said and took a step into the small room. She turned slowly to him, her hands resting on the keyboard wrist pad. “Worried about your dissertation, or something at school?”

She shook her head. “No, not really.”

“About things past and present?” It just came out, without his thinking about it.

She looked up at him and for a brief moment he thought he had stepped into another deep hole, the kind that would have brought a sharp rebuke not long ago. Something crossed over her face; a dark shadow. This was quickly replaced by another expression. It reminded him of a painting he saw somewhere; a man stood gazing at some unrecognizable form in the distance, wearing a strange, obscure expression. It might have been part sadness, it could have been longing, possibly hope, but other elements seemed mixed in as well. There was the smallest hint of another emotion: was it a sense of relief or a fragile happiness?

“It’s not easy for me to say things like this, but…I’m very sorry for the hurt I caused you with this…this man. I could have kept quiet and you would have never known about it. This man has everything. He is wealthy, but very much into his own world. Not like you.” He wondered if that was a compliment or just a comparison, but the soft way she ended her words told him if she was comparing, he was coming off quite well.

"This...was ongoing last May when you told me about it, but now...?"

"No," she answered, her voice almost inaudible. Then she hesitated, remembering how Carter reacted when she told him Vince moved out. He said little but there was the most subtle change in the tone of his voice, and in the altered body English. It was so subtle she missed it at the time; it only came to her hours later when she was lying in bed with Vince during a sleepless night. She twice left messages on his answering machine. She was available, she was telling him.

And he turned from her.

In her solitude she did what was rare for her: she turned inward, to examine all that she valued in life. "It has ended."

What was she looking at? he wondered. Someone who had failed her? One who could not keep her where she had been in life? Or was she looking at him as he was many years ago when she was completing college, a newly-minted graduate with a bachelor's degree in hand, while he had this fantastic job with an electrical contractor, at a wage she would not reach until ten or more years into teaching. He had been out in the world; and he knew much about its workings. In those early days she valued that experience. She had little of it herself.

But as the years rolled onward and she rose in the education hierarchy, first-hand knowledge seemed less important than what one gained in classroom study. She looked at him again and there was something softer now, not that hard, judgmental glare he saw when telling her he had accepted the job at Builders' Market.

Was she seeing him for what he was? he wondered—the same man with just a different role, a new title, a different set of duties and living on a more humble level? That was what his heart was telling him. So much to understand: she was here, with him; then she was back at the apartment, alone, as he was. She had been with another man and concealed it from him. He didn't want to know any more about it. It was done. She was here, with him again, and that drove away the empty loneliness.

This woman sitting in his small study was what he remembered from long ago. The one who looked up to him, who spoke to him in a soft and tender voice. Then it came over him: a powerful urge, an overpowering longing for the woman he had known in that better time, when they shared a life much as they were doing now when she was with him.

Something that had long laid dormant began stirring. It swirled and grew stronger, a river bottom churned by a turbulent current, propelling him into the room, to her chair. He held out his hand and she took it in hers. That same warm, soft feeling he remembered during their walk, when she had reached for him in a moment of fear and clung to him. He saw something in her eyes, a clarity and sparkle. She rose slowly and stood before him as he looked into her hazel eyes, running his fingers through her dark brown hair. She lay her head gently against his chest and he gripped her shoulders, holding her close as the clock tolled the passing of time. She moved and his hands slid down her side, over the flare of her hips and down to her thighs. He felt her leg muscles tighten as she rose on the balls of her feet and she looked up to him, then closed her eyes. Their lips brushed, side to side, warm, soft, inviting.

Then they came together, soft flesh of her desire blending with his own, and he wrapped his arms around her waist feeling the throbbing welling up from deep within his soul. His heartbeat rose to a thunder; he felt her breath surge as her chest rose and fell rhythmically with his own. He slid his hands upward, to the small of her slender back, up again to her shoulders. She wore no bra. She kissed fervently, her tongue sliding into his mouth as she throbbed and he felt his lower region swell as his pulse raced wildly.

Long moments passed and it seemed as if his heart would tear itself loose and leap joyously out of him. Her arms were around his neck and she gripped with a strength he hadn't known her to possess. The pure sense of her power heaved within him as he slid his hands over her hips that now undulated with his in their throbbing rhythm, then down behind her thighs. He gripped her and pulled upward, and she responded, pulling hard on his shoulders until she was straddling his waist, her tongue still filling his mouth. He bore her weight with little effort, remembered from a time long ago, and carried her across the hall to the bedroom.

She slid to her feet, her hands quickly working at his clothes, as he did with hers, till bare flesh mingled tight and warm with bare flesh. Moments passed, she dropped to her knees and he shuddered as the warmth and wetness of her mouth closed in on him. Distant memories charging back into his whirling vortex, unfocused consciousness, to times remembered when passions ran unreigned, tamed only later by a world their innocent minds hadn't known to exist.

She rose again and swept the quilts aside, pulling him down beside her as he felt that ineffable joy of willingness, then he was beneath her as she swept her chest across his face, over his lips, as time ran by unnoticed, uncaring. With that strange power of hers she rolled and pulled him on top of her, working magic with her hands and all her other gifts she gave him, as he gave to her, in joyous, unrestrained return.

In the murky swirl of desire, time slid back, years not well spent peeled away, as if some wonderful, fantastic machine hurled them back to an era dimly remembered, but now sharply recalled as their desire swirled and pumped, from man to woman; from woman to man. The evening passed, then the night passed in a swirling ecstasy of shared passions loosened, then freed from the encrusted restraints imposed so long ago, for purposes so obscure, so meaningless.

For an hour or two before the sun rose she lay sleeping, her head on his shoulder, as he took in the joy of her warmth at his side. His arm was around her, resting on her back as he felt the rhythmic rise and fall of her breathing. He inhaled the full scent of her hair that brushed against his chin. This was what he missed in the lonely hours of his solitude. It was less the flaring desire of flesh long denied its pleasure than the belief that the intimacy fueling great desires, missing for so many years, was again within his reach, and within hers. They had passed through a full cycle and come back to the place where they started together. For this joyous night they had gone home together, to a time far better than what came to them as years passed and time wove a coarse fabric into the warp and flow of their lives.

Chapter Twenty-nine

The stars sparkled in the crisp mid-winter night and the half moon cast a silvery almond glow to the small buildings lining the dark street. Five people sat around an ancient oval table in a small wooden building that served as Nuevo Del Rio's community center.

On the table was a copy of the St. Paul Pioneer Press. Someone scissored out an article, had it enlarged, framed, and hung on the wall. It contained a photo of the Governor surrounded by a gaggle of reporters and functionaries as he signed a bill passed by the Legislature an hour earlier. That bill authorized one hundred and fifty million state dollars needed to draw down the matching federal funds, together with one hundred and ten million to be chipped in between Hennepin County, the City of Minneapolis and a smaller share from the outlying areas. In all, just over four hundred million dollars was allotted for construction of a rail line from the new Franklyn Avenue station, angling southwest to Interstate 35W, then south along the right of way ending two miles to the north of this room.

It was the most contentious piece of legislation in recent times and it meandered repeatedly through the procedural maze of House and Senate amendments. From there it traveled to the joint conference committee where the differences were hammered out, sent back to each house for another vote, more amendments, more praises and dire criticisms, then another run through the joint committee.

It sent both houses into tumultuous, bitter debate late into the night hours, fraying weary nerves, not a few members asking themselves why, in the name of the good Lord, they ever let the voters put them here. Both chambers resounded with cries of righteous indignation, claiming this was the ultimate, the very apotheosis of fiscal irresponsibility! A giant step toward socialism! Worse, this was communism; or whatever other 'ism entered their fevered minds. Ramming a collectivist Russian-type plan down the throats of the poor taxpayers! some were claiming.

Those of other persuasions rose to praise its supporters for their far-reaching vision; for the courage to pass judgment spanning great distances of time placing Minnesota at the cutting edge, daring to point to a future of multi-modal transportation, reducing the congestion and disruption brought by total dependence on autos and the roadways.

Rolando Torres leaned forward, anger still glowing in his bright eyes. "And I tell you again, we haven't won this thing! They are still out there," he pointed east toward Bellwood, "gathering money, lawyers and political influence. They can bring this to a screeching halt. You remember that! With more support from this group, my demonstration at the Bellwood gate would have been successful in drawing the public's attention to this problem months ago!"

Peter suppressed a groan as Torres cast a fiery look at the group, skipping over Melissa, who glared at him. Torres was not quick at reading facial expressions but he definitely saw her "take me on again" expression.

Peter turned toward Torres. “Rolando, ease up. The Governor signed the bill two days ago.”

“Nothing but a piece of paper and just as worthless! Remember that!”

“He signed it, the funds will be appropriated. Yes, there’s still room for delaying tactics, maybe an injunction or an appeal. But you do realize that the one who was leading the opposition abandoned his position a couple months ago? You know of whom I’m talking?”

Torres grunted. “He’ll be back! Are we now to believe that for all these many months he led strong, vigorous opposition, then one day he completely changes his mind and walks away from it? Just like that?”

“Not usually, but I have it on good authority that he relinquished all opposition to the plan.”

Torres tilted his head and glared back at Peter. “And we should believe that? As if he’s saying, ‘Yesterday I hated that plan but gosh, today I think it’s really good.’ What happened to bring about this miracle?”

Peter pondered for a moment, recalling a recent conversation with Melissa and others at Waters of Life Church, then shrugged slightly. “He, ah, reexamined his options, thoroughly considered his alternatives, and though he will not support the plan, he has ended his opposition. People do change their minds, you know. Under the right circumstances.”

Torres turned to Melissa, taking the hard edge off his voice. “You don’t know what brought about this supposed change in attitude, right in the middle of the pitched battle? Don't you find this just a bit unusual?"

Melissa leaned forward, without that challenging look he saw earlier. Even so, he tilted back from her. "You may recall last September Raul and I took an apartment in St. Paul, so I haven't lived with him for five glorious months. But yes, he's out of the loop."

Torres shook his head and grunted. "Suddenly, someone from the banking establishment, white shirt, wingtip shoes, solid conservative, the whole bit, turns up at the Legislature and says rail is the preferred way to go from the standpoint of the established financial community? We're to believe your father did nothing to stop this man from testifying?"

Melissa shrugged. "He had options, Rolando, and chose as he did. What else can I say?"

Cardenas held up a callused hand. "There is no need to quarrel. We must be happy. We will keep our homes and that is good."

Peter thumped the table. 'I agree. Now, Manuel, it is time. You must tell us the great secret about this table. I have waited many months, years, to hear this from you."

The old man smiled. Soon, Peter. Soon."

"But—"

"Have patience, my son." He often referred to Peter that way as he had a son the same age. "All things in their own good time. Raul, tell us the business about the access road."

"Last week we came to agreement with Mr. Behlen on a plan for a frontage road paralleling the freeway. But rather than running it right through the village, it will begin a mile north of here and angle southeast, directly into Bellwood."

"There will be a row of trees along this side of the access road," Melissa added. 'The Bellwood people insisted on this."

Torres snorted. "All the better so we don't have to look at those bastards driving their fifty thousand dollar cars to their six hundred thousand dollar homes."

"What do you mean 'we'?" Melissa snapped, her face once again glowering at him.

Peter raised a hand. "Melissa! Enough! Rolando, lighten up, will you? When you strip away all of those symbols of wealth, they're people pretty much like the rest of us. They have their priorities and they fight for them, just as we have our priorities and fight for those. If you invested the time, money and effort of eight years of medical studies, internship and residency, or spent seven years in law school, or took a great financial risk and worked many years to build a successful business so you could spend forty thousand dollars on a car and a half million for a home, would you put the priorities of others who had not done this ahead of your own? No, they're not attuned to our interests, but we're not attuned to theirs, either."

Torres grunted and glanced at his watch. "I must go." Cardenas nodded quietly. "I leave you with one thought." He pointed to Melissa. "Don't believe for a moment that he has left and gone away. He may have stepped out for now, but he'll be back, and when he does, he'll have a whole train of lawyers and politicians behind him.

You watch him very closely." Then he rose, walked abruptly out the door and into the cold night.

It was quiet around the table for a full half-minute while Cardenas fetched the wine bottle, four glasses and three cigars. "Oh, Lord!" Peter sighed. "I know he means well but he reminds me of the man who keeps hitting his head with a hammer because it feels so good when he stops." Then he looked at Cardenas. "Now, Manuel, please, it's time you told us about this table."

Cardenas nodded. "Yes, it is the time. But first, we must have our wine." He filled the four glasses and lit his cigar, sending clouds of smoke curling to the ceiling. Another long drive home with a buzz in my ears, Peter thought, as he ignited his own cigar. "Peter, look under the table, at the pedestal."

Peter pushed his chair back and grunted as he twisted himself down and beneath the table, one hand gripping the top lest he fall to the floor. "Ah…the light's not very good down here but…it looks very old from what I can see." With another grunt he hauled himself upright, face flushed with the effort, and looked at Cardenas.

"'Did you see the top, the metalwork?"

"You didn't tell me to—"

"Well, look again." Another cloud of smoke wafted upward. Melissa gulped down her wine and motioned for a refill, unaffected by the haze building around them.

With another grunt Peter torqued himself down and peered into the shadowy light. 'Oh, I see, some very fancy scrollwork! Wow, you don't see that kind of workmanship any more! Very good quality." Again he heaved himself up and looked at Cardenas. "so, what is it?"

"Did you see the top part? Where it fastens to the table?"

"You didn't tell me to look there."

"Then look there." With a heavier sigh he swung himself back down and under. "You're out of shape, Peter. You must get rid of that stomach. You didn't have that last year."

"Yes, thank you, Manuel, I'll do that," came the voice from beneath the table. "It, ah, appears to be some sort of…I don't know…a metal rectangle…looks to be bolted to the bottom of the table."

Cardenas nodded. 'Yes, it's a metal rectangle bolted to the bottom. But what do you suppose it was once, many years ago?"

"I don't have a clue, Senor Cardenas," he answered, still dangling under the table.

"You remember how old this building is? You can come up now if you want to."

Peter struggled up again and looked at Cardenas, his face still flushed. "You said it was, what, more than fifty years old?"

'Sixty-eight."

"I see. Sixty-eight. Hmmm…Was this a school?"

Cardenas grinned. 'My people didn't have schools then."

Peter nodded. "Right…Ah…was some famous treaty signed here?"

Cardenas laughed. "Your people broke them all."

Peter held out his hands and shook his head.

"In those days this was a funeral parlor."

Peter went noticeably pale, even for an indoors person.

"I see…and that…that pedestal was, ah, it was the tray where…" He nodded and gestured with his hands. "Where they…were embalmed?"

"Many of my people, the old ones, were made ready here to meet their Lord. But you must not worry; it was scrubbed very well. The ladies used much soap. Then it was fastened to this tabletop. It works very well, don't you think?"

"Oh, yes, it's very sturdy…Yeah…it works real well." He had visions of stiff corpses laid out on the tray, their blood pumped out, something else pumped in, all to keep the remains fresh for a few more days.

"Peter, Raul has helped us with an application for some federal money. What was it, Raul?"

"Rural community development."

'Yes. This old building is a fire hazard, you know. But for the grace of God it would've burned down years ago. We were given money to build a new community center. There will be new furniture. Even a computer for our people to use."

"Melissa will do the training," Raul said.

"This is wonderful!" Peter exclaimed, a broad smile starting to replace the shocked look.

"Yes," Cardenas said," we are very happy about this. Now, Peter, my people want you to give you something; a small gift from the village for all the help you have given us. It must be something that is very important to us, or it is not a true gift. That is the way of my people. We want you to have this table for your office. I will have the men move it."

Peter's jaw dropped, his eyes wide. "Senor Cardenas, this table has been a part of your community for many years. You and your people meet around this table, discuss many things, make many decisions. It is so much a part of your history, are you sure you want it taken from here?"

"We will have a new one soon. You see, it can leave here, but if it stays with a friend of our people, then it is with us as well. Embalming washes away their sins, so on this table my people were given new blood for a new life. But the ancient wisdom remains with us, and for all who come later. We offer this to you, our friend, and may its great wisdom stay with you and guide you. That is the tradition of our people."

The macabre images dancing in maniac fashion a minute ago disappeared in a flash. This was rare for one who did not live among them. "Senor Cardenas…I am grateful…It will be an honor to have your gift in my office."

An hour later Peter walked through the doorway of the house he once shared with Mary and his daughter. Emmy saw him and came charging, leaping as he caught her and lifted her up. She was sixteen months old, babbled constantly in her own dialect, and much to Peter's joy, began going to him when he visited. He wondered what his absence meant to a mind that young, but somehow she still connected him to Mother, and that made it safe to go airborne into his lap.

They played for a few minutes as Mary watched, then Emmy slid off his lap, grabbed a toy and lumbered off to play by herself. “I’ve made strong coffee, French Roast,” Mary said. “I can smell Manuel’s wine and cigars across the room.”

He smiled. “There’s no graceful way out of it. I know that has been a burden for you.”

“That’s a good place to start,” she said as she placed steaming cups on the coffee table. They sat on the sofa, two feet of space between them. For a half hour they talked about the safe things: their finances, monthly bills, Emmy, the nosy neighbor, his new practice.

“When Emmy arrived, my world collapsed down to her, our home and the burden of law school. All thoughts of a career marriage fell away. You kept the same hours and routine with Advocate Services, and in the village. I remember chiding you about having a child in the home, but it was as if nothing changed for you. After a few proddings you stayed with Emmy during the evenings when I was studying or attending classes, and I appreciated that as well as bringing Emmy with you to your new office. She made a big hit with your staff. Peter, has this experience, the separation, been what you thought it would be?”

He was quiet for a moment. ‘I still have no idea what it was all supposed to be. You asked me to leave so you’d have more time and space to yourself. I didn’t have a plan of my own. It was one day at a time. I brought home a lot of work and that filled the evenings. I’d go to my old coffee shop now and then, but my friends were always busy with their own careers and families. It was like looking into the past…it felt very empty.

"Raul needed help, so I resumed some involvement at the village. Cardenas doesn't know I negotiated most of the arrangements with Dave Behlen concerning the frontage road. Raul is bright but he has problems dealing with those in-your-face people like Behlen, despite the advantage we had over him. All of that came to about sixteen or seventeen hours a day—enough for anybody. Can you believe it? I've become a private businessman! The very sort I used to rail about in my former life. So, I had no illusions or great aspirations. Then or now."

"I'm glad you're involved with the village again."

"You are?"

"Because it's what you need. The reasons I gave you for separating were vague, even selfish."

"I don't feel anger any more—"

"Your voice betrays what you're feeling. You've merely channeled it off into your work."

Peter mulled this for several seconds, then rose from the couch and walked to the tall window. "Don't they have a term for that in psychology…sublimation? Transference? Something like that…Okay, I was angry."

"You still are. Just understand that it's there."

"So that's what fueled those long work weeks. I wasn't able to help you when you were thrashing around for some kind of identity, whatever it was you were searching for at the time. That was before you decided to study law. Maybe if we'd talked more about it then, we might not be where we are today. We both need to reexamine where it's all going for us. There's Emmy to consider. We don't need the money that comes from working that much. We've always lived on less. That table was not a going away gift. It was given with the understanding that I would continue working out there. I can lean on Raul for some of that since he has no family commitments. Well, dealing with Melissa Behlen every day would be enough for any man."

"For a long time I was following a star, and that star was you. Somehow I thought you would lead me where I wanted to go. I never thought to look at alternatives. So much for hitching your wagon to someone else's star."

"Five or six years ago you started looking for something you couldn't define. You were dissatisfied with everything, but you didn't know why. It affected our relationship. The communication fell off; the sex life went into the tank and soon after that we were just two people with the same address. It was rolling smoothly downhill before either of us noticed what was happening. There's a residue of anger in both of us. You're right. Let's just accept it at that and go from here."

"Would You please come over here and sit down? You remind me of my father when he'd start pontificating about something." He sat on the sofa, now a foot away from her. "When we separated I was going to rise to a new level; scale heights unknown to me. I had visions of earning a doctorate in sociology, taking a teaching position at a prestigious college. I would write scholarly publications so my colleagues and students could learn from me. I thought of associating with some philanthropic organization and doing great things, solving all sorts of urban ills. You were my ideal. But instead of rising to those heights I spent the entire time maintaining the status quo here with Emmy. One day I walked by the stack of books, looked at one, then opened it and began reading. What happened?"

"That may have been all you really wanted. Something propelled you through a very difficult course of study and led to what seemed like a dead end. Then one day you dived into it again. Was it the same purpose you always had, only that it became stalled, then one day you got it back on track?"

"And all sociology notions went out the window."

"Something that looked good as it passed by—much like your friend who wanted to be a writer but didn't want to work at writing. There was a reason somewhere that finally brought you back to where you had been."

"The more I study the more I'm convinced that there is a niche for me and it will be in social law. I'm not the misfit I imagined earlier."

"You need a place to start and I have something for you to think about. We're gaining new clients and we need someone to research and direct the two paralegals and the legal assistant I hired last month, a gentleman for whom I once overturned an unemployment claim denial, then later helped with a divorce settlement. You could spend part of the time in the office assisting them, then be at home with

Emmy researching the Internet. You could download any file you need. That would make you an in-house lawyer, which is legal without the license. Don't worry about the bar exam. As Senor Cardenas always says to me, everything in its own good time."

They sat for a few minutes, mostly watching Emmy on the floor with her toys, going from one to another as the attention span of most toddlers requires, the foot of space having disappeared A stiff dose of French Roast drove away the odor of Cardenas's wine and cigars. "Peter, it's time we used some better judgment about us and where we're going."

"They say that time and distance help to sort out matters. Maybe so, but it was here all the time. I have a wonderful idea. Let's sit back and watch some no-brainer TV program. The networks give us so much to choose from. Let's just be together."

Chapter Thirty

The winter snow lingered longer than usual but now it was late April. The Canadian air masses were driven far to the north by the warm Gulf currents and there was a lightness in the air brought on by the gentle winds of spring. Neighbors were busy raking leaves and dead grass flattened for months beneath the crush of winter. Everywhere people were moving about, freed from the restrictions of snow and ice. Bicyclists pedaled up and down the streets, skateboarders glided about and joggers sprinted vigorously. The long slumber of winter gave way to the livelier pace of spring and summer.

Vince Martinson entered the brick building at Victoria Crossing, walked down a short hallway and entered the law offices of Hoffler and Nordmeyer, Inc. He spoke briefly to the receptionist, Lisa, a women close to his age, then went to his office. He could feel her eyes follow him. It was a daily occurrence. Her husband left her a year ago and for whatever reason, she began confiding in him. It all had a familiar ring: one of those empty nest syndrome crises. No kids to worry about any more; time to make the big break, so off he went.

He related a small part of his own experiences one day when he took her to lunch, but he was too involved in his own issues to step any closer. She told him about her husband's long string of affairs. He was a dentist and one day must have found someone with just the right teeth and off he went. He sensed she was vulnerable but he had no desire to complicate his life any more than events had already done for him.

Ann had been staying with him two to three nights each week, though they still kept their separate rooms. Lisa knew that she and Vince were separated. She did not know Ann stayed in his house.

That matter aside, he was actually enjoying his new job as legal assistant to Mary and the attorneys of Peter's law office. His previous experience reading electrical codes and working with city and county governments had proven valuable, for it helped him through the maze of legal terms and processes he was learning. It required a lot of legwork and driving to obtain the endless supplies of documents and records from the city and county clerk offices. He was on a first-name basis with most of their office staff, a habit he learned years ago and one that served him well. Show a little courtesy and respect for them and they'll bust their butt for you. Be arrogant and demanding and see how long it can take to get those records you want. Sorry, sir, our copier isn't working right now. Check back later. Much later. He quickly learned about the hostility, or maybe it was more like fear, often shown when someone from an attorney's office comes calling. He had doors slammed in his face and was told more than once to haul his ass off the property, right now, unless he wanted someone to haul it off on his behalf. His time in the electrical business thickened his hide.

It was still a new business and Peter hadn't made any commitments concerning profit-sharing, but his regular rate of pay was better than what he received at Builders' Market. He didn't miss all that evening work he did there, though now he often took statements during the early evening hours when witnesses were available. He missed the interest and support Tim Horvack, their HR director, had always shown toward him, as well as being able to answer customer questions and assisting them in solving their building problems, though on occasion those people could become just as much a pain in the rear as they could be in this trade.

Peter recently negotiated a contract with the Metropolitan Council for legal services relating to other Twin City light rail projects that were in the early planning stage and he wanted Vince to play a part of that process. A very long term process if the Hiawatha Corridor and the I-35W lines were any indication. Vince studied the rail issue closely and soon became a widely known source of information. His opinions were being sought by attorneys in other cities, some several hundred miles away. "I'm starting a two-year paralegal program this fall," he told Ann. "It will move me a notch higher in the legal food chain." She seemed a lot happier with this than the Builders' Square job. "I have a very good teacher: Peter's wife."

"I'm proud for you, Vince," Ann told him. Something in her tone said this was genuine.

All the forces that had been at play with Mary now seemed to converge where Peter and his partner were leading the firm. "Something had passed by," she told Peter, "briefly craved, then forgotten without regret." Was it worth the ordeal of retaking the bar exam, along with another three hundred dollar fee? At a later date, maybe.

Peter was not afraid to step to the cutting edge of current thinking. He would avoid growing to where he had dozens of associates all locked in mortal combat for the few partner slots that may become available. Five associates at any time would be enough. "Competition is healthy," he told his staff, "but at Hoffler and Nordmeyer collaboration would prevail." He had three female staff with young children and he was arranging space down the hall for day care. The table from Nuevo Del Rio now dominated their conference room. "This table is just beautiful!" one of the women said to him. "It's an antique, isn't it?"

"Yes. It's sixty-eight years old."

"I can just imagine all the many times people have gathered around it. All the many uses it must have seen."

"Oh yes, it's, ah, had many uses."

This was how Peter ran his new business: seeking ways to enable his staff to do their work and keep a handle on their family life. He wasn't bound by the long-standing practices of most of his colleagues. "You have an unlicensed attorney supervising paralegals?" someone from a large firm asked him.

"Indeed I do. She's a very good trainer."

"But I heard she only puts in twenty hours a week," he said, accustomed to the eighty hour grind.

"She works another ten hours a week researching and e-mailing the staff. Accommodate a bit and it's amazing what can be done." He knew the man was plagued with high turnover.

The answer came in a gruff snort. There was just no end to all these wild stories circulating about Peter. "You're paying tuition for someone to go to college?"

"He's in paralegal training and has a real talent for this work."

"But he might leave you. Then what?"

"He won't leave. Invest in your people. Show them you're supporting their professional development and they'll stay with you. You might want to try it yourself."

Another snort. "I hear a bunch of Mexicans were at your place a while back. That true?" He would have avoided that scene at any cost.

"They brought me a beautiful gift; something very important to me as well as to then. Hand-crafted generations ago." A grunt of disbelief and the man turned to colleagues of more like mind. Could be a close friend of Dave Behlen, Peter thought.

On an afternoon late in April Vince arrived home. He took off his suit jacket and hung it on a doorknob. Ann had been staying with him for the past week due to some evening teacher conferences. They kept the same arrangements as they had earlier: she had one bedroom, he had another. They had not touched since that evening last November.

He wondered what she thought in those night hours alone in his house.

Two months ago she completed all requirements for her Ph.D. She didn't want any celebration though he eventually prevailed on her to have dinner at one of the finer restaurants in the area. "You work your ass off for three years researching, studying, writing, editing, rewriting, reediting, then when the prize is finally awarded you treat it like it was an everyday incident. Let's at least go out for dinner…Dr. Martinson." He knew her failure to land a superintendent's job, or, at the very least, that of curriculum director, disappointed her and blunted her sense of achievement. She interviewed unsuccessfully for two superintendent positions in the past four months in the outstate part of Minnesota and for an opening as curriculum director in a St. Paul suburb. "The Holy Grail would be easier to find," she once lamented to him after receiving another rejection letter. God, it was quiet in the house!

He walked into the kitchen, opened the refrigerator door, withdrew a bottle of beer and popped it open, then saw the envelope on the table. His heart began surging as he opened it and pulled out the note. It was written in her usual cryptic style.

Vince:

It would be best for both of us to discontinue the relationship we have had for the past five months. I have moved my belongings to my apartment. Next week I will be in Ohio for an interview, then another near Pittsburgh. I want to thank you for allowing me in your home and for use of your computer. I have removed all my material from the hard drive. You are, and have always been, a good and worthy man and I hope you will find a way of feeling the same toward me. The pathways of our lives have diverged and, I believe, will never converge again. I wish the very best for you.

As Always,

Ann

He stood stock still for a full minute, feeling nothing but a dull, pervasive void. The note slipped through his hands and fluttered to the floor. He stood where he was, then slowly turned and walked to the den. Just a chair and his computer sitting mute on a table, the dull green screen staring blankly, as lifeless as he felt at the moment. He turned and went into her bedroom, but all that was Ann was gone. He opened the closet doors, saw nothing, then closed them again. He shuffled back to the kitchen, his feet dragging, picked up the note and read it again.

"Vince…As always…Ann."

Twenty-four years, then one day she asked him to leave. She turned to another man. Then she came to him. Now she left him. He walked through the front room and stood on the porch. A car passed slowly; someone rode by on a bicycle. Things he always noted before. He saw nothing now. Then he went back inside, threw on a jacket and left the house, the beer forgotten on the table.

He walked down Mackubin Street and turned right on Summit Avenue. He'd gone this way many times, recently with Ann, always enjoying the variety of people, the children playing nearby, the street traffic and the general rhythm of a neighborhood that was now his. On this evening he saw nothing, felt nothing. He walked like a zombie, as if in a deep trance, oblivious to the noises and sights around him, stumbling on a sidewalk heaved up by roots of an old tree. His senses were gone, just a vast, pervasive numbness. He walked several more blocks in this fashion, hands in his pockets, gazing at the sidewalk a few feet ahead of him. He came to an intersection, not noticing the name of the cross street, turned absently and walked another block.

He passed a restaurant. It was the one where he had taken Ann after she received her degree. He walked slowly by, glancing through the windows. What were those people celebrating? he wondered. Some great achievement or just another day of health and well being? He walked on absently. He couldn't shake the memory of that night in November when she made love with him. It was so spontaneous, so unrehearsed, and for that reason, so wonderful. For just those few moments of passing time, he felt bonded to her again and to a world they shared in a time when life seemed so clear, so purposeful. Before the waves of change swept them into a swirling cauldron that seemed to twist and spin their lives for the coming years. When the world intruded upon two young and hopeful people who shared a love that was now only a distant memory.

What a goddamn fool, he thought. From that magic moment in November when he shared his flesh with hers he'd strapped on rose-colored glasses and saw her as she was during those early days of ecstasy and discovery. That was what he wanted when she shared his house: a return to a time of wonder and excitement, when each moment would bring him another pleasure just as it had with her.

Didn't he hear her message? She said she would go anywhere if offered the right job. Now it might be Ohio, maybe Pittsburgh. Whatever myths he was harboring should have been blown away when he heard her say those words, for she had told this to him several months earlier. How powerful works the mechanism of denial. Anyway, he thought as he wandered down Summit Avenue, you're a free man, now, for whatever that's worth. Unencumbered by the burden of a mate who became incompatible for whatever reason. Yes, he would be lonely as hell without her, or without that person he thought he had living part time in his house. That was who he missed. The woman who partnered with him on that ineffable evening in November. It was less the coming together of flesh in heated desire; it was far more the sharing of deep craving, of reaching back to a time when it all seemed so clear, so certain; a feeling he somehow knew that in her soul she held in common with him when their past was made present in the precious hours they had together.

There will be another, he told himself. You're past fifty but there's a lot of life still out there. Some place. Someone whom you'll want someday and who will make you forget Ann. Some day I will walk this same route and see what I can't see today. I will look up again and see people; I will sense the flow and throb of life as it is lived each and every moment. But today I will wrap heavy layers around me and for brief moments it will warm me in its protection. It will turn away the cold wind and all that is harsh, all that I wish to be gone and to haunt me no more.

Strange how we have to invent these fantasies; cling to those hopes, ideals and all those myths that we build, then use to surround ourselves. All the beliefs we internalize about ourselves and about the world and how it all comes together. Barriers we erect to ward off the storms and tempests of living every day. But without the security of these beliefs and aspirations, hopes, myths and desires, the layers of walls and the fences we build, perhaps we would all go stark raving mad.

—The end—

About the Author

Bruce Netland is a survivor of a decade of urban living, watching the roadways steadily clog with growing traffic levels. He has studied other modes of transportation and presents this story as a challenge to our current thinking about how people move about in our crowded cities. He is now a Workforce Center system manager and a resident of Duluth, Minnesota, where drivers are challenged more by the city's hills than its only freeway.